The Route That Takes You Home

The Route That Takes You Home

***

by Melanie Lageschulte

The Route That Takes You Home

by Melanie Lageschulte
Fremont Creek Press

Kindle: 978-1-952066-23-8
Paperback: 978-1-952066-24-5
Hardcover: 978-1-952066-25-2
Large print paperback: 978-1-952066-26-9

Cover photo: 1000 Words/Shutterstock
Author photo: © Bob Nandell

Also by Melanie Lageschulte

MAILBOX MYSTERIES SERIES

The Route That Takes You Home
The Path to Golden Days (2023)
The Lane That Leads to Christmas (2023)

GROWING SEASON SERIES

Growing Season
Harvest Season
The Peaceful Season
Waiting Season
Songbird Season
The Bright Season
Turning Season
The Blessed Season
Daffodil Season
Firefly Season

SHORT FICTION

A Tin Train Christmas

* 1 *

Kate slowed the old Buick as she approached the next rural crossroads, then eased her mail car to the side of the gravel road. She flipped on the hazard lights, even though there was no other vehicle in sight.

As the dust settled around the car, covered its beige paint in another layer of powdered gravel, Kate unhooked her seatbelt, took a deep breath, and took in the view.

In late July, if the weather cooperated like it had so far this summer, rural Iowa was always awash in shades of green: thriving acres of corn and beans, lush pastures, thick canopies of leaves on the volunteer trees along the creek banks. It was a lovely landscape, capped today by a serene blue sky, and staring at it for a few moments helped clear Kate's mind.

Her Chicago friends would say there was nothing to see. But Kate had grown up here, and she knew better.

The Campbells, back in the last mile, were still working on their house, and a fresh coat of gray paint had appeared on its front since she'd come by Saturday. A red-winged blackbird swooped from one side of the gravel to the other, and a sign indicating the next curve in the road offered the perfect hunting perch for a sharp-eyed hawk.

That wasn't all. There were several new residents just up the road, in the pasture on the right. A herd of sheep had moved in over the weekend, the kind that were cream with black legs and faces. Kate tried to recall their breed, but came up short. Perhaps a decade away from Eagle River had erased some of the finer points of country life from her mind.

No, she realized, it had been longer than that. Closer to fifteen now. Her first stop had been the University of Wisconsin in Madison, where she'd met Ben during senior year. When he got a job as an inspector for the federal workplace safety agency's Chicago office, Kate followed him there and started her career with the postal service. Life with Ben had been wonderful, all Kate had ever hoped for. Until everything changed.

Kate took her eyes off the pastoral landscape and stared at her bare left hand, resting there on the steering wheel. They'd separated four months ago. But sometimes, she still felt a second of shock when she noticed her rings were missing. After four years, she couldn't quite shake the habit. Where had she left them this time? On the kitchen counter, or the nightstand?

And then, she'd remember.

The engagement ring, which was heavier and had sharper edges, narrowly missed Ben's face the night he admitted to an affair with a co-worker. After the shouting and the crying ended, and Kate and Ben resigned themselves to the fact their marriage had, too, he'd insisted she keep both rings. They'd fetched a fair price at the jewelers, and part of the proceeds covered what she'd paid the movers to bring what was left of her life back to Eagle River.

The rest went toward Kate's acquisition of Bertha, the old Buick, which she'd snagged from the Eagle River carrier whose retirement gave Kate the chance to come home. Bertha was cantankerous but tough, a proven partner in all kinds of weather, and her dashboard clock never lied.

It told Kate she'd been sitting at this rural crossroads for two minutes already. She had to move on.

"The mail must always go through." Kate gripped the steering wheel and took another deep breath. "Neither rain, nor snow nor sleet, nor dark of night; nor mosquitoes or tornadoes, or bad hair days ..."

In that case, Kate was a champion. Every work day, her strawberry-blonde waves were pulled into a low ponytail, which left an easy resting spot for her navy ball cap. Sure, she spent her rural-route shifts basking in Bertha's robust air-conditioning, but every lean out the window, every dismount to drop a box on a farmhouse's porch, was one more chance to get a sunburned scalp.

Kate twisted to reach into her mail case, which sat to her left, and double-checked the deliveries for her next six stops. Everything in a postal-service vehicle was backward compared to the usual way of things, and Kate had decided it was a fitting metaphor for where her life was these days.

She'd been on the Eagle River force for almost two months but, as the most-recent recruit, she didn't have a permanent route. Her role was clean-up duty. Vacations, sick days, rotating days off, Kate stepped in and filled the gap.

This area northwest of Eagle River was Mae's regular route. But with the senior carrier on her usual extended summer break, Kate was starting to really get a feel for its roads and residents. She was five days in on this eight-day stretch and, at last, things were finally feeling familiar. She was getting better at guessing which last name would be on the next mailbox. How far it was to the next creek bridge, what the next bend in the road would look like.

But while her work shifts took her all over Eagle River's streets and down the country roads that surrounded it, Kate always ended up in the same place: the town's post office, a cozy brick building on one corner of Main Street. And it was a place that had always felt like home.

Grandpa Burberry had worked there for years before he'd taken the postmaster job in Prosper, the next town over. He was retired now, but Kate had fond memories of hanging out with him after school at the Eagle River office: leaning against the counter, side by side, as Grandpa helped his neighbors and caught up on the gossip; or sticking a newly gifted dime into the bubble-gum machine by the front windows.

Getting their mail was still an important connection to the rest of the world for so many people, whether they picked it up at the post office or had it delivered to their front doors or the ends of their driveways. And despite the long hours, fickle weather and sometimes-challenging personalities she'd encountered over the years, Kate couldn't imagine doing anything else.

With her stacks for the approaching farms now in order, Kate turned off Bertha's hazard lights and flipped on the blinker. She still had the road to herself, but it didn't matter. Safety regulations were the heart and soul of the postal service, and it would be just her luck some farmer would come up behind her, see her "operating a vehicle in a reckless manner," and call in her license plate.

The Robertsons' farm was the next stop. A handful of marketing circulars, a utility bill, and an important-looking notice from the Hartland County assessor's office in Swanton. The Smiths down by the next corner had a copy of the twice-weekly county newspaper and two colored envelopes addressed to "Tamara." A similar card had been in yesterday's pile, which Kate took to mean Tamara's birthday was coming up soon.

Of course, not all the deliveries brought glad tidings. A jury summons, sympathy cards. Severe-looking envelopes from the IRS, final notices from collection agencies.

Kate saw it all, a silent witness to people's private lives. But she'd learned long ago not to judge her customers by what she dropped in their mailboxes, or tossed through their front-door slots, on any given day. Life was far-too complicated for that.

Kate soon passed over a tributary of Deer Creek, drove up a slight hill, then started down the gentle slope to the next farm. If only she knew how to pronounce this name. The "Milton" part was easy enough; it conjured a mental picture of an elderly farmer, the kind who still wore overalls. But "Benniger" gave her pause. Maybe the last name sounded just like it was spelled. But then, Kate had learned long ago that not everything was what it seemed.

There were just two envelopes today, nothing out of the ordinary. The farm was the same, Kate decided as she slowed for the rusted mailbox at the end of the driveway. White house, red barn, their paint not quite ready to peel. But the lawn looked emerald-green healthy, even from this distance, and a bed of showy perennials nodded in the sun on the south side of the house.

What Kate saw in the front pasture, however, quickly caught her attention. Several cows milled about, but it was the woman crouched on the ground that made Kate tap her brakes sooner than usual. In front of the other woman was another cow, down on its side.

When she saw Bertha slow her speed, the woman jumped to her feet and ran down to the road. "Hey!" she shouted from across the fence. "You have a minute? I need help."

Kate's pulse quickened in that old, familiar way as she leaned out the window. Because of their daily interactions with residents from so many walks of life, mail carriers were trained to respond to all kinds of emergencies. However, an incident in a cow pasture would be a new one for Kate.

"What can I do? Are you OK?"

"I am. But this girl's about to deliver, and quick." The woman smiled and pushed some wayward blond hairs back under the brim of her wide straw hat. Her polo shirt had a logo on it, but it was too far away to read. Kate noticed the splotches of blood on the woman's arms and her jeans.

"I just need an extra set of hands. How about yours?"

Kate glanced at the cow, which let out a bellow of distress. It had been years since she'd helped pull a calf, but she could still do it. Couldn't she?

Two of the postal service's most-important rules were (1) stay on schedule and (2) never leave the mail unattended. But no one else was around to help. The farmyard was empty, other than for what had to be this woman's dust-covered truck.

Kate had kept busy since she'd moved back to Eagle River but, to be honest, it had been some time since she'd felt especially useful. Or did anything that deviated from her regular routine. On most days, that brought her comfort. But on a hot, humid afternoon like this one? Maybe, just maybe, it made her a little restless.

She could spare ten minutes. If she locked Bertha, the mail would stay secure.

"I have some old gloves in the trunk," Kate called out the window before she turned up the lane. "Let me pull in, and I'll be right there."

* * *

The gravel widened into a circle between the house and the barn, wrapped itself around a small structure that probably covered the farm's well. There was a walk-through pasture gate near the truck, and Kate pulled in next to it.

She popped Bertha's trunk and rooted through its sizeable stash of season-appropriate gear: gloves of various weights and textures, old towels, a small shovel, insect repellant, a first-aid kit, rubber galoshes and an umbrella, extra hats, toilet paper, trash bags, and sanitizing wipes. If the mail must always go through, one had to be prepared for just about anything.

Kate selected a wide-brimmed canvas hat and a pair of farm gloves with a vinyl coating on their palms. With Bertha locked down and the keys secured in the zippered pocket of her shorts, Kate decided she was ready for whatever waited on the other side of that gate.

Just as she was about to lift its latch, she realized she wasn't alone.

What had to be the biggest barn cat within two counties had spotted his latest visitor, and now ambled toward Kate with a gleam of distrust in his golden eyes. He was a handsome boy, with thick black fur and a white chest and paws, but Kate sensed he wasn't fond of trespassers. She ignored his growl and frown, and hurried off into the pasture.

"I'm so glad you stopped!" The other woman gave a quick wave of greeting. "I'm Karen Porter, by the way. Prosper Veterinary Services."

Kate let out a gasp of surprise. "You're Karen! Bev Stewart told me all about you." Bev, a retired teacher, was one of the part-timers at the Eagle River post office. Come to think of it, she and her husband only lived a few miles from this farm. "I'm Kate Duncan."

"What a small world! Bev told me about you. We're in the Prosper library's book club." Karen started to extend her hand in greeting, but thought better of it and wiped it on her pants.

She must do an awful lot of laundry, Kate thought as she joined Karen next to the laboring cow. *And I thought my work clothes got dirty.*

"Bev said you and I should have lunch or something, that you're wanting to meet more people since you've moved back. And you should meet our friend Melinda, she works at Prosper Hardware." Karen gave the mother-to-be a reassuring pat. "Well, enough socializing for now, let's get this lady set straight."

The cow let out another moan. "It's OK, honey." Karen tried to soothe her. "We're going to get you through this. I called for backup," she explained to Kate, "but I don't think she wants to wait."

"I'm a bit rusty at this." Kate adjusted her hat against the bright sun. "My parents farm, but it's been a while since I've been on calf-delivery duty."

She heard a hissing noise behind her, and turned to find the big cat crouched in the grass. He must have slipped through the fence and snuck up behind them.

"What's gotten into that guy?" Karen wondered. "He's quite the guard dog."

"I've already been growled at, up by the gate. But he doesn't seem to mind you. Do you come here often?"

"Nope." Karen positioned herself behind the cow, and Kate crawled after her. "Maybe once, if at all? I was just driving by today, on my way from another call, when I spotted this girl in distress. I knocked on the door, but no one seems to be home. I couldn't go on by, leave her like this."

Kate was now sweating and a bit flustered, but found herself smiling. She was glad she'd stopped to lend a hand.

The cat was still staring at them, but at least he'd moved back a bit. There he sat, with his ears pinned back, watching the proceedings. At least he was mindful of the cow's distress. The rest of the herd had merely tossed their visitors a few curious glances, then wandered off.

Karen pulled a pair of long rubber gloves from her tackle box. "This will be easy. Well, for you. And me, too, since you're here. But this girl? Maybe not so much."

She motioned for Kate to get shoulder-to-shoulder with her. "I'm going in. When it's time, all I need you to do is help pull."

"Got it." Kate nodded, then blinked. "How should I hold it, though? What will happen?"

"That's the big question right now. I don't know how this little one's going to come at us. Just grab on to whatever you see and pull as hard as you can."

The cow wasn't pleased with Karen's efforts, but Karen gently shushed her and kept working. "Oh, here's the issue.

Pretty common, really." She looked up and over the cow's flank. "Good job, Mama! Let's go a little more, huh?"

Kate waited, nearly holding her breath. When Karen gave her a nod, she reached over and held fast.

"Hold steady, if you can." Karen's face was flushed with effort. "Yes, like that! Move back a little if you have to. I think we're about there."

The cow gave one more loud bellow, and the calf was on the move. Between the mother's contractions and Karen's efforts, the newborn came at Kate with more speed than she'd expected. She fell back on her heels just as the afterbirth spilled all over her shorts and shirt.

This will take some explaining when I get back, Kate thought. And then: *Oh, what a thrill it is to be here when this calf comes into the world!*

"There we go!" Karen shouted. She gave the calf a quick examination, then nodded. "I think Mama can take it from here." She grinned at Kate. "I'm so glad you came along when you did. Perfect timing, in fact. I'd only been here a few minutes when I saw your car."

Another truck had just turned up the lane. Karen rolled her eyes and laughed. "There's my assistant, if you can call him that. You're much easier to work with than he is."

The *toot-toot* of the truck's horn caused the cat to growl again, then run back to the gate. An older man carefully stepped down from the cab, then reached back inside for a tackle box. He had to be closer to eighty than sixty.

"Who is that?" Kate raised her eyebrows.

Karen snorted. "Thomas McFadden, doctor of veterinary medicine." She nodded vigorously as Kate's eyes widened in surprise. "Yeah, he's still licensed. It's a long story, but I'm sure he'd love to tell you every bit of it. Thank goodness you have mail to deliver so you can make your escape."

Karen's business partner, John "Doc" Ogden, was almost back to his usual self after being sidelined for several weeks due to an on-the-job injury. Thomas, Prosper's retired veterinarian, insisted on helping out until Doc was fully mended. Desperate for another body, Karen and Doc hadn't been able to say no.

Thomas turned out to be a godsend, as he could still handle office visits and simple on-farm tasks like vaccinations. The only problem? His opinions on female veterinarians skewed to the negative.

"Did I miss the party?" Thomas seemed genuinely disappointed when he ambled up to Kate and Karen, the cat at his heels. "Pulled many a calf in my time. Why, I'll never forget this one, in the summer of 1974, I was ..."

"Thomas," Karen interrupted. "This is Kate Duncan, Eagle River mail carrier and volunteer vet tech. She beat you to it, I'm afraid."

Kate swallowed her laughter and waved.

"Well, now." Thomas pushed his white hair out of his face. It was surprising how much of it he had left. "You mean to tell me, you two girls handled this all on your own?"

Kate pointed at her soiled shirt, which was probably beyond saving. "I believe so." She exchanged a smug smile with Karen. "Well, speaking of that mail, I'd better get going. I guess I'll have quite the report to file when I get back to the post office."

Thomas gave her a shrewd look. "Kate Duncan, huh? Oh, you're Wayne Burberry's granddaughter." He raised his chin. "I was the veterinarian in these parts for several decades, and one of my sons still lives just a few miles from here. I know every family around, that's for sure."

Karen's voice was overly bright as she got to her feet. "Well, I guess if you know everyone, do you happen to know where these people are?" She gestured toward the house. "I knocked, but no one came to the door. Seems pretty quiet."

Kate pulled off her gloves. "I thought the same." The three of them started back across the pasture, the cat out in front.

"It's like they're away, or something. Not just gone for the day."

Kate had only been back in Eagle River for two months, but she'd become adept at evaluating the scene as soon as she drove into a farmyard.

The popularity of online shopping meant rural carriers were getting more up-close-and-personal with their customers, as they spent a great deal of time dropping packages on porches along with popping mailboxes.

Kate couldn't have described it, but when no one had been around for days, a place carried a certain kind of presence. Whatever it was, she felt it here at Milton Benniger's farm.

Just before they reached the gate, Thomas stopped in his tracks. "Kate's right." He scanned the yard, then frowned. "This place feels ... deserted, somehow."

He studied the cat, who'd returned to what was apparently his guard post by the barn's main door. "You're getting plenty to eat, mister. Fat as a toad, so someone must be feeding you. But look." Thomas pointed toward the front of the house. "See there? The grass is all dead, like there's usually a vehicle parked by the front porch. It rained hard last night, and two nights before that. But there are no ruts in the dirt, nothing at all."

"They must be on vacation, then." Karen dumped her gloves into a plastic tote in her truck's bed. "I'll ask Doc what he wants to do. We can just mail out a bill."

Thomas guffawed. "Milton Benniger, on vacation?" Thomas pronounced the surname as if the "g" was silent. "He's an old bachelor farmer. Well, I don't know if he's really that old." The quick correction told Kate that Milton must be close to Thomas's age. "But anyway, he's not one to jet off to Hawaii. Charles City's about as far as he gets."

He surveyed the yard again. The air shimmered with heat, the oppressive silence broken only by the occasional chirp of a bird. He shook his head, then started for the barn. "I don't like how this feels."

"What are you doing?" Karen marched after him, Kate right behind. "We don't have permission to ..."

"Nonsense! It's just the barn. I don't know what we're looking for, but I'm not ready to leave yet." Thomas slid the door's iron latch to the side, then glanced over his shoulder at the house. "We may go there next. I can't put my finger on it, but something's just not right."

* 2 *

Kate wondered what they might find in the barn. But it was very clean, especially by barn standards, and the cows had feed in their troughs and an automatic waterer. And that, with the pasture and the little creek that ran through it, was certainly adequate for this time of year.

Two small pans of water, and a large metal bowl half-full of kibble, proved the black cat and any potential feline friends (or enemies) were also being fed.

The black cat had either decided he could trust these visitors, or was simply tired of guard duty. By the time Karen, Kate and Thomas finished their barn tour, he'd fallen asleep on a stack of straw bales next to a sunny window.

Nothing seemed out of place. Kate was glad, and was also grateful to be in the barn's cool shade for a few minutes. "Well, this is good news. The animals are fine." She started for the door. "I really should get going. My afternoon break, if I want to mark it that way on my log sheet, has come and gone, and then some."

"Thank you, again, for stopping. Sorry to keep you hanging around." Karen cut her eyes toward Thomas as the trio crossed the yard.

Then she laughed. "Let me know if I need to write you a note or something, prove where you were."

"My clothes should be enough." The bloody mucus had started to dry on Kate's shirt, but the heat of the day only intensified its sharp smell. The aroma made her uneasy, and she tried to focus her thoughts on something else. "I'm just glad I could help. And we definitely should have lunch sometime, like Bev suggested."

She fished her car keys out of her pocket, and was about to unlock Bertha. But suddenly, Kate felt there was something else she had to do before she moved on. For a moment, she wasn't sure what it was.

"What is it?" Karen studied her closely. "Did you hear something?"

Thomas was back to his truck. But he, too, seemed hesitant to leave. Kate saw him scanning the yard one last time, his brow furrowed with concentration.

And then, Kate remembered. She turned toward the house and, before she even realized what she was doing, broke into a jog. Karen and Thomas hurried after her.

"I just need to check if ... oh, no, there it is!"

A tiny, open porch hugged one side of the house. And there, right where Kate had left it, was the parcel she'd dropped off four days ago. One side of the cardboard was a bit wrinkled, as if it had been sideswiped by wind-driven rain and then dried out in the hot July air.

Thomas rubbed his chin. "When did you deliver this?"

"Thursday." Kate's voice trembled. "No one came to the front door, and I wasn't sure I should leave it on that porch, where it might be visible from the lane. Besides, everyone around here usually comes in through the back way, right into the mudroom or kitchen. I knew someone would find it ..."

"As soon as they came home," Karen finished the thought. "I would have done exactly the same thing. Milton must be gone. That's the only way I can explain it."

It had taken Kate a little time to adjust to the country ways of parcel delivery. Rural carriers were allowed to drop off packages without handing them to a resident, unless special circumstances required a signature. But they were expected to place the parcel out of the weather if possible, such as on a covered porch or, for smaller items, tuck them between the storm door and the house door.

The system worked well, as parcel theft was rare in rural areas. There were some funny stories of animals, domesticated or otherwise, ripping their way into pet-food delivery cartons. But otherwise, the code of the country was in effect: If it isn't yours, leave it be.

"What about the mailbox?" Karen wanted to know. "Was it empty when you opened it today?"

"No, there were a few pieces inside, and he got two more." Most people picked up their mail every day, but not always. Kate closed her eyes and tried to remember. Were the other items already there when she came by Saturday, or did she add them then? She couldn't be sure. "But it's not overflowing, nothing that would raise a red flag."

There were about a hundred stops on this rural route, and Kate was only filling in. No one would expect her to remember every stop from every day, including herself. But now, when something here didn't seem right, she wished she could.

"If he went on vacation ..." Karen raised a hand against Thomas' impending counterattack. "I know, I know, that's not like him. But if he did, you think he would've stopped delivery."

"Or at least had a neighbor pick it up." Thomas waded through a bed of phlox and peeked in a window. "This looks to be the living room." An ominous sound came from his throat. "Clean as a whistle, looks like."

"Is that so strange?" Karen made a face.

"For an old bachelor, I'd say so." Thomas pressed his face to the glass. "Hey, I think there's a window open on the other side there."

Thomas had to go look, and Kate followed. The sash was indeed half open, but the screen was still intact. Sometime in the past few days, rain had blown in and soaked a spot on the hardwood floor of the old farmhouse's dining room.

Kate shook her head. "If he's so neat and tidy, I can't believe he'd be careless enough to leave a window cracked like that."

Karen had wandered out to the garden. Her face was filled with worry when she returned. "Tomatoes everywhere, a great crop. But most of them are rotting on the vine, like no one's been here, or at least, has been able to pick them. Same for the peppers, and the beans. I'd say only wild animals have been in there for a few days."

Thomas went over to the garage and tried the side door. It was unlocked, but there was no truck inside. The machine shed was the same.

They reconvened on the side porch, where the parcel still waited for someone to retrieve it. Kate stared at the box again, and took one more look around Milton's yard. Surely he was just away for a few days. But something about this entire situation made a chill crawl down her spine.

All she knew was that when she dropped this box off on Thursday, the farm felt different than it did now. Which was abandoned and, quite possibly, hiding something.

Thomas carefully lowered himself to the porch's painted wood floor. Kate thought he wanted to read the return label on the box. But instead, he lifted the door mat and swiped his free hand underneath.

"What are you doing?" Karen gasped. "I'd be more worried if his truck was here, but it's not. You can't just ..."

"What if he's in there, down on the floor, needing help?" Thomas barked back. "You know there's a spare key out here, somewhere. Why, I've let myself into people's houses many times before, and not just for emergencies. Of course, folks never used to lock up like they do now."

"Is this an emergency?" Kate's heartbeat began to pound in her ears. "Because if it is, or if it might be, I'm not allowed to leave. Not until the authorities show up."

Thomas straightened up and stared at Karen. Neither gave an inch. Kate could feel the tension in the air, as well as the vast divide that separated these two. Veteran, newcomer. Male, female. Old, young. And then, Karen reached into her back pocket and pulled out her phone.

"I don't know what's going on here, but we have to find out. And no one is going to do any breaking and entering, no matter how well-intentioned." She glared at Thomas. "Why don't you go sit in your truck and blast the AC until someone shows up? It's over ninety in the shade. You're about to keel over in this heat."

"I'm not." But Thomas' lined forehead carried a sheen of sweat. "OK, fine." He shuffled away.

Karen rolled her eyes as she dialed the sheriff's non-emergency line. One of the deputies was in that part of the county, and would be sent in their direction. In the meantime, the dispatcher said, everyone at Milton's farm was to stay put. And not touch anything.

"Thomas left his paw prints all over that barn door." Karen shook her head. "And that window, and this floor mat. I just hope Milton's OK, but I don't think he'll be pleased to find his flowers have been stomped on."

"We were in the barn, too. I guess if they think there's anything suspicious going on, we'll have to get our fingerprints dusted." It was Kate's turn to make a call. "Someone will need to come get my case and do the rest of my route."

"I'm so sorry about all this." Karen tried for a smile. "I just needed help pulling that calf. Who knew this would turn into such an eventful afternoon? But I have to admit, Thomas is right about one thing. If something's wrong, if Milton's in some sort of trouble, we can't just walk away."

One of the deputies "being in the area" could mean anything from a few miles away to a several-minute drive. Hartland County was predominantly rural, meaning the sheriff's crew was always spread thin. And this farm, in the far northeast corner, was nearly twenty miles from the county seat of Swanton.

Eagle River, which had about twelve-hundred residents, had its own small police force. But the really tiny towns, like Prosper, instead relied on the sheriff's department for all their law-enforcement needs.

So it wasn't much of a surprise when Bev's mail truck rumbled up Milton's lane before the sheriff's deputy arrived. Bev had been the postmaster's first call, since she was off today and only lived three miles away.

"Well, hello ladies." Bev smoothed her short white hair as she stepped down from her truck. Her relaxed manner and easy smile soothed Kate's jangled nerves. "There's quite the breeze picking up, we might get us another storm tonight. Kate, I see you've met Karen. I've been wanting to introduce you two, and here you are!"

Bev glanced toward Thomas' truck. "I see you've met someone else, as well." She turned to Karen. "What kind of mood is he in today?"

"Well, beyond his total and complete shock that two women pulled a calf without him, he's got it in his head that something's happened to Milton." Karen's smile vanished. "But I'm starting to wonder that, myself."

Bev studied the side of the house, as if it might offer any clues, then shook her head.

"I don't really know him; he usually keeps to himself. He's in his early eighties, I think, lived here all his life. One older sister, she moved out West soon after she married, but she passed away a few years ago."

Bev shrugged. "That's all I know. Most ordinary person you could ever meet. But I don't mean that as anything against him," she added quickly. "He's quiet, sure, but I've never heard a bad word said about him."

Then Bev gave Kate a kind smile. "Honey, those clothes! It's beastly hot out here. You have anything you can change into?"

Dressing in a barn would be one more unusual footnote to this crazy day, but Kate didn't have any spares in Bertha's trunk. One more thing she should add to her stash.

"I should have thought ahead," Bev said as they started toward Kate's mail car. "I could have loaned you something. Afterbirth is its own special kind of nasty. Before I go, remind me to text you my super-duper laundry concoction. Being a farm wife for thirty years, you figure out what works, and stick with it. But those may be beyond hope."

"I have large trash bags and towels, I think that'll be enough to get me back to town. I'm just glad you were at home and able to help out."

Bev held the door of her truck as Kate set the mail case inside. "Oh, it's no trouble. It's not every day we have a, well, whatever is going on here." She gave Kate an understanding look. "How are you holding up? This is pretty stressful."

Kate nodded, and blinked back sudden tears. "Yeah. But we have someone coming to take over." Then she laughed. "You know, the right public employee for this sort of thing."

"Call me tonight, if you need to." Bev patted Kate on the shoulder. "Just do your breathing and stay in the moment. The deputy will take care of everything, don't worry. You ladies are doing the right thing." She smiled. "And that includes keeping Thomas out of the way."

A few minutes after Bev drove off with the mail, Kate spotted a deputy's cruiser coming down the road. Its emergency lights weren't flashing, and that helped ease Kate's racing thoughts.

She kept reminding herself that because Milton's truck was gone, he surely was, too. This was all a random misunderstanding, but it had been the right move to alert the authorities rather than just cross your fingers and drive away.

Even so, Kate couldn't shake her unease. It wasn't likely, but what if Milton was inside the house, injured or worse? What if he'd wandered off somewhere? It was also possible he'd left home, but then had a medical issue, or his truck broke down on the side of the road. Between the recent storms, and the heat ...

The food and water in the barn could have been left out this morning or two days ago, there was no way to know. Milton was elderly, and lived alone. She didn't know him, but the thought of any harm coming to this old man made Kate's stomach churn.

And that mailbox. If only she could remember what had been in it, and when.

The deputy gave a brief wave when he pulled up by the house, and Karen returned the greeting. "Oh, it's Steve Collins. He drives through Prosper a few times a day, makes sure no one's getting too out of control."

Steve was probably around forty, Kate guessed, and had a thoughtful way about him. He asked Karen, Kate and Thomas a few questions, then disappeared around the corner of the house for a moment. Kate could hear him on his phone, likely talking to the sheriff.

Deputy Collins doubted Milton was inside, but said there was enough justification for him to enter the farmhouse by whatever means necessary.

"Are you going to kick the door in?" Thomas could hardly contain his excitement.

"Not if I can help it."

When the deputy started poking around on the porch, Thomas said nothing but raised his eyebrows at Karen and Kate. *See? What did I tell you?*

The key wasn't under the mat, or beneath the stack of empty chore buckets by the door. But it was hidden inside a fake rock in the adjacent flowerbed, and Deputy Collins soon disappeared inside the house.

As Karen and Thomas debated whether he would get scolded for nosing around, Kate broke into a sweat. And it wasn't just from the heat.

Across the farmyard, she saw the black cat slip through the pasture fence and retake his sentry position by the barn door. With his huge white feet planted square in the dirt, his yellow eyes darted from the strangers by the house to the squad car and back again, a look of hostile suspicion on his furry face.

Kate tried her best to feel the opposite.

Steve is staying calm, she reminded herself. *He doesn't seem too worried. We just have to be certain everything is fine, and then we can leave. There's no ambulance, no shouting, no blood ...*

But there was. All over her shirt and her shorts and, despite her best efforts with an old towel, still on her bare arms. The smell was overpowering now, and the dry afterbirth was rough and tight on her skin. Kate put a hand over her nose, tried for another deep breath, and fought the urge to run.

Deputy Collins popped back out on the porch and gave the group a satisfied nod. "The good news is, Milton's not in there. I even checked the basement and the attic." He scanned the farmyard and shook his head. "But the bad news is, he's not here to tell us what's going on, either."

He reached into his pocket for a notebook. "Tell you what. I'll take statements from each of you, check all the outbuildings and the windbreak, then I'll see what the sheriff wants to do next. Maybe a neighbor's been in touch with him. We'll sort it out. Anyway, please tell me anything that comes to mind, no matter how small of a detail it might seem."

Thomas was eager to go first, and recited a long-winded description of everything he'd witnessed in the past hour.

While she waited, Kate tried to focus on the beautiful flower beds that bordered Milton's farmhouse, enjoy the riot of high-summer colors and the perennials' lovely fragrances.

It took encouragement from both Karen and the deputy to get Thomas to leave once he was done. Karen was on her phone, talking to Doc, so Kate was next.

Just relax, it's almost over. You're not in any danger. It's important to stay calm and tell the deputy everything you know.

"Let's talk over here, by the front porch." Steve gestured around the corner, and Kate followed. He ran through several questions and scenarios, and Kate was glad she was able to focus and share as much detail as she did.

"Must have been quite the change, moving back here." The deputy's manner was easy and friendly as he checked his notes. He glanced at her stinky clothes, and grinned. "Eagle River's about as far from the big city as you can get."

"Yeah, but I'm settling in. Things are quieter, for sure. The simple life, isn't that what they call it?" She tried for a laugh, and almost made it.

Steve's expression turned serious. He studied her for a moment, then finally spoke.

"I know your grandpa," he said gently. "And Kate, I know that you ... I heard about what happened, back in Chicago, when you were on duty."

Her bottom lip began to tremble, and it was only a moment until her hands did, too. She blinked back tears and looked away.

"Today can't be easy for you." Steve measured his words carefully. "You know, my wife's a nurse in Mason City. We may be rural around here, but we look after each other. There are several excellent folks you could talk with, if you need to."

"I'll be OK. I've gone through that part." It all tumbled out at once. "My doctor in Chicago, she gave me a referral back here, before I left. Just in case."

"Glad to hear it." Steve exhaled and nodded. "You make that call if you need to. Don't wait, don't let it build up inside you. I know, from experience, that's not the way you want to handle things."

Kate's next round of tears was mixed with relief and gratitude. "Thanks for saying something. I don't know how many people know and, well, it's not something that comes up in random conversation."

"True. But it's normal, and healthy, to talk about it you need to." He glanced toward the west, where heavy clouds had begun to pile up on the horizon. The sun was still shining, but the air had turned syrupy with humidity.

"Looks like it could blow up some wild weather tonight." Steve checked his phone. "I better get Karen's statement and lock this place down. I think the only open window's the one in the dining room, but I'll check them all again before I go."

Kate thought of something. "What about that box? Might it be evidence?"

"Hard to say. I certainly hope it doesn't come to that. I'll take it inside for now. How about I clear that mailbox, too, before I go? I'll leave everything there in the kitchen."

"Oh, I could ..."

Steve gave her a kind nod. "You've done more than enough for today. Time to stand down." He smiled. "I have some old towels and wipes in my cruiser. And a trash bag or two, if you need them for your seat."

Kate was able to laugh. "I've got that covered, but thanks. Guess I need to keep a change of clothes in my car, though, too."

"It's always best to be prepared out here. You never know what's going to happen, huh?"

"Do you carry dog treats? I find they are quite handy."

"Oh, absolutely."

Kate promised Karen they'd find a day to have lunch, then waved to Karen and Steve as she started back to her mail car.

Steve was right; it was time for her to let go, leave everything in his capable hands. Kate pulled the trash bags and towels from Bertha's trunk and made sure the driver's seat was fully covered before she climbed inside and turned the key.

But as soon as she was settled, with Bertha's engine purring away and the air conditioner gently cooling her sweat-sticky face, Kate couldn't push the memories away any longer.

She was halfway through her usual route, that dreary day in January. The snow wasn't too deep and most people had their sidewalks shoveled clear, but there was still some ice on the paths that required her full attention.

If she had been more mindful of her surroundings, more aware, would things have turned out differently?

She'd never know. And sometimes, when she stared at the ceiling in the middle of the night, that was the worst of what still haunted her.

The young man, he really wasn't more than a boy, seemed to appear out of nowhere. The police later said his tracks came out from behind a nearby brownstone, but Kate hadn't seen him until it was too late. And she barely got a glimpse of the revolver in his hand before she felt its icy metal jammed against her temple.

You have money, I know you do! he'd shouted at her. *Hand it over! Give me your bag. Now!*

It was true, Kate had cash on her that day. She always did, as she sold customers a few stamps from time to time. But she carried less than twenty dollars, just enough bills and coins to make change.

A mail carrier never left their quarry unattended. Kate clutched her tote bag close to her parka, and refused to give it up. She could see people running toward her, neighbors yelling at the boy to leave her alone, to drop the gun. As terrified as she was, Kate could almost smell his fear.

His hands started to shake; she felt the end of the gun slide away from her face. At the last second, he shouted a string of profanities and struck her upside the head with the revolver. He started to run but slipped on the ice, someone told Kate later, and three men tackled him and held him down until the police arrived.

The ground rose up to meet her, and then her cheek went numb. Her head throbbed under her thick knit cap, then she saw her blood sliding out into the snow. She couldn't find the words to call for help, or even scream.

Then there were people crowded around her, she could see their feet and hear them calling to her, telling her help was on the way. She was turned over, saw the gray sky instead of the bloody snow, and then someone was holding her in their arms. The faces in the circle looked a little familiar, her customers, her friends, but everything was spinning and she couldn't be sure.

Then came the flashing lights, blue and red and white; a police officer holding her hand. Sirens wailing, a medic asking for her name and Kate feeling an odd thrill when she got it right, gave him the answer the neighbors told him he wanted.

There was talk about stitches and worries about a concussion. She had to go to the hospital, just to be sure. "You're going to be OK," someone said as they helped her sit up. "Everything's going to be fine."

But it wasn't. Not that day, not for a long time. And even now, sometimes, not at all.

* * *

How long had she been sitting here? Kate looked down at her bare, stained hands, at how white her knuckles were as she gripped Bertha's steering wheel tight. She glanced in the rearview mirror and stared at the pale scar on her right temple. It had faded, just like everyone said it would. It was rather small, really, and it was easy to hide if she fixed her hair just right.

She took a deep breath and looked over her shoulder. Karen and Steve were still there, next to Steve's cruiser, chatting about something. They smiled and waved again, and Kate gathered her courage and waved back.

Bev had taken the rest of the mail, but Kate still had to fill out what was going to be a rather-interesting report when she got back to the post office.

She pulled on her sunglasses with trembling hands, slipped Bertha into gear, and started down the lane.

* 3 *

It was about five miles from Milton's farm into Eagle River, and Kate had steadied her nerves a bit by the time she reached the post office.

As she'd marked the miles of gravel and pulled out onto the county blacktop, Kate tried to focus on today's happenings rather than the past.

Deputy Collins didn't seem too concerned about Milton, and maybe she needed to do the same. After all, his truck was gone, and he wasn't in the house. While the deputy would give all the other buildings a look, just to be sure, Thomas had already conducted a simple sweep of the place and found nothing suspicious.

Surely Milton was just away for a time; a neighbor likely knew where he was, and when he'd be home. After all, someone was looking after the cows, and that bossy cat ...

Kate had to smile at the feline's oversized personality. Thomas was sure Milton didn't have a dog these days, so that big tom had obviously appointed himself the farm's chief of security. And other than his suspiciousness of strangers, he seemed content enough.

Was Kate really so sure something had happened to this old man, or was it just the memories of her own traumatic experience that had her on edge?

As she waited at Eagle River's lone stoplight, Kate had to admit her emotional reaction to the afternoon's events at Milton's farm was mostly about the latter.

"Until we know more, until something comes up that tells us there's a problem, I need to put it out of my mind." She took a left when the light turned green, crossed the river bridge, and took a right toward the post office's back lot. "I just need to file my reports, get home, and get out of these nasty clothes."

If the post office's brick exterior was simple and unassuming, its interior was even more so. There was a staff entrance in the back wall, along with two small, multi-paned windows. Inside the tiny entry, which was often littered with wet and muddy boots, another insulated exterior door kept the wide-open back room relatively comfortable. Or at least, as much as the ancient furnace and air conditioner could manage.

This big space had a large wooden cabinet with cubbyholes along one wall, as well as two long metal-topped counters for sorting mail.

More nooks and crannies made up the bases of these tables, and the whole space always carried a faint, sawdust-like scent from the high volume of paper and cardboard that came in and out every day except Sunday. Lockers for the carriers were along another wall, by the hallway to the storage room and restrooms.

There was also a break room, notable for nothing except that its dented refrigerator still hummed along after three decades of service, and a postage-stamp-sized office intended for the boss of the shop.

But just like Grandpa Burberry, Roberta Schupp preferred the postmaster's metal desk and lone file cabinet sit out in the open. Her post sat just beyond the metal tables, only a few feet from a scuffed wooden door that opened into the public lobby and its counter.

None of the other carriers were around at this hour, as they weren't yet finished with their routes. But Kate decided she was glad about that. While she was feeling better, it might be good to not rehash her wild afternoon until tomorrow morning.

She changed her clothes, stuffed the gross ones into a trash bag, and pulled a metal-legged stool up to one of the mail-sorting counters to fill out her paperwork. Roberta kept meaning to take all the carriers' forms paperless, but that would mean buying several laptops for them to share, and the money just wasn't there.

Roberta was up at the counter. As the only staff member stationed at the building, she rarely had time to linger at her desk. Kate watched through the wooden door's small window for a time when her boss was no longer waiting on a customer, then entered the front of the shop.

"I take it the calf's doing well, and Mama, too." Roberta's brown eyes sparkled over the rim of her low-slung reading glasses after she reviewed Kate's report. She had lived on a farm all her life.

"Good lord, I don't know how they do it. Cows, sheep, any of them. Personally, I was out cold when I delivered both of my kids."

Roberta's son and daughter were headstrong teenagers these days, and she always said their antics kept her in fine form for managing a crew of mail carriers. As for Milton's whereabouts, Roberta wasn't too concerned.

"I don't know him, myself." She thought for a moment. "But it seems to me if he's that private, then he's not going to put out a press release when he leaves town for a day or two. Karen did the right thing, though, calling the sheriff. Better to be safe than sorry."

The substantial weight of the oak counter felt good under Kate's barely clean arms. The adrenaline had drained away, and she was suddenly exhausted. "I'm just glad it's over.

Thanks for calling Bev to pick up my case. I was already so far off schedule, and …"

"That's what I'm here for. Effective management, clear objectives and time-sensitive delivery." Roberta rolled her eyes, but then she smiled.

"Honey, I think you should get some sort of award, or something. Run-ins with critters are part of the job at a shop like ours, but I don't think anyone has ever assisted in that kind of delivery. Don't bother to hang around to help me out, it's been rather slow. Just go home and rest." She leaned in and whispered. "I'll punch you out later."

Roberta's compassion further put Kate's mind at ease. But then, Kate should have expected as much, as her new boss was known for her roll-with-it attitude and sharp sense of humor.

She was Eagle River's first female postmaster, a position that might have caused someone else to toe the government line as closely as possible, worry that out-of-the-box thinking might muddy the path for anyone who might come along later.

But not Roberta. Kate's boss let her big heart and sharp mind guide her decisions as much as she could.

Country life meant Eagle River's carriers met up with a mix of weather woes and colorful characters, sometimes on a daily basis. And according to Roberta, some handbook drafted by the big boys out in Washington, D.C., wasn't the most-reliable reference for how to handle every situation that came her way.

"Thanks for understanding," Kate told her boss. "I'm really drained."

"I can imagine." Roberta's face was kind. "Of all my folks to end up in that situation." She shook her head. "Do you think you can come in tomorrow, do it all over again? Mae's not back until Friday."

"Absolutely. I'll be here. I'll just take it easy tonight."

"Oh, one more thing," Roberta said just before Kate turned away.

"Leave your messy clothes there by the back door. I'll take them home, toss them in the burn barrel. If you put them in the dumpster behind your building, they'll just draw all kinds of critters. Roland will throw a fit."

Kate only lived four blocks away, but she was glad her personal vehicle was in the back lot. In this heat, and given how tired she was, the walk home seemed like too much. Bertha lived full time at the post office, as Kate's apartment farther down Main Street only came with one parking space. Some of the carriers thought that was too stingy, but Kate just laughed. A free parking spot? After living in Chicago for ten years, she was thrilled.

While she'd changed her clothes, Kate couldn't say the same for her tennis shoes. When she came in the back door of her building, which housed Sherwood's Furniture on the ground floor, Kate took her sneakers off and stuffed them in a plastic bag. Roland Sherwood was fussy about keeping the tenants' stairs dry and clean, both for safety reasons and because, well, Roland liked things the way he liked them.

The vintage building had high ceilings and no elevator, which meant the tenants' trek up from the first floor could be a daunting one, especially when groceries or laundry were involved. Kate held tight to the handrail as she climbed. A few more minutes, and she could hop in the shower and scrub this day away.

There were only three units in the building, and the faint chatter from a television told her one of her neighbors was already home. The sound of her key in the lock brought Charlie to the other side of the door. Kate could hear her Himalayan mix's meows of greeting even before she jiggled the scuffed metal knob and pushed the door open.

"Hey, there." Charlie circled her feet and rubbed against her bare legs, not caring in the least that she smelled of strange places. His fur mom was a mail carrier, he'd grown accustomed to these mysteries long ago. Kate dropped her things inside the door, and reached down to pick him up.

"I've missed you," she whispered into his plush fur, and was rewarded with a round of purrs. "And I'm so glad to be home."

When Kate stepped out of the shower, renewed and refreshed, she had two messages on her phone. One was from her parents, asking if she wanted to come out to the farm for supper. The other was from Ben.

Their Chicago bungalow had been on the market for only three days when it sold. The process had gone so smoothly, and so fast, it made Kate's head spin.

But there was a new wrinkle, a small one that was just newsworthy enough for Ben to call. And for her to feel like she needed to ring him back. The buyer's loan paperwork was taking longer than expected, given the hot real estate market, and the closing had been pushed back a week.

Kate knew it didn't matter, not really. Her marriage, which she'd valued far more than that house, was over the night Ben confessed to his affair. But as she thought about the weeks that followed her on-the-job attack, Kate knew their life together had unraveled long before then.

Meeting in college, they'd tied all their future plans to each other. Then came the move to Chicago, six years of living together before they got married.

Neither of them cared too much about a piece of paper, and they were very happy with how things were. So much so that when they decided to tie the knot, more because they wanted to start a family than anything else, Kate decided to keep her last name.

It had been a smart decision, but she hadn't known that at the time.

When the children didn't arrive as hoped, Ben and Kate managed their disappointment and carried on. More years flew by. Ben thrived in his work; Kate did, too. But there was an emptiness in their lives that even Charlie, who'd touched Kate's arm with one fluffy paw when she'd entered his room at the animal shelter, couldn't really fill.

Charlie watched her now from the closed toilet seat, and his blue eyes tracked her comb as Kate untangled her hair. Given his lush coat, it was a blessing that Charlie loved to be brushed. Several times a day.

"I've had a crazy afternoon," she told him. "You'll get your turn soon. I promise."

If Kate hadn't been attacked that gloomy January day, how different might her life be now? Ben had rushed to the hospital, of course, and held her hand through the rough days and nights that followed. Her head healed quickly, and she was grateful. But the night sweats and nightmares were in no hurry to leave her alone.

After a week off, she'd returned to her route. Her customers had been overjoyed to see her, cheered her on as, day after day, she tried to walk away from the trauma. But every time she hiked up that same street and past that same building, it was just too much.

Her supervisor switched her to another neighborhood, which helped, and it seemed like her life was settling back into its old, comforting patterns. But then, Ben started coming home later and later. Weekend runs into the office went from rare to routine. And when he'd finally told her the truth, her heart was shattered. But maybe, she hadn't been all that surprised.

Ben moved out, and Kate stayed. And then, a few weeks later, Grandpa Burberry called to say his old buddy Ken was finally retiring from the Eagle River shop. Did she want to come home? He'd make a few calls, she'd put in for a transfer, Ken would sell Bertha to Kate for cheap ...

Kate sighed as she stared at her phone. Part of her wanted to listen to Ben's message again, just to hear his voice. Another part of her wanted to toss the phone on her bed and burst into tears.

It was a very nice bed, by the way. Literally showroom new, thanks to Roland's Memorial Day weekend sale. Everything else in this apartment she'd brought home with her from Chicago, a mismatched jumble of possessions that had the worn-in comfort she craved these days.

Roland had reminded her several times that he offered free delivery within twenty miles of his store. Which meant that, because she lived just up the stairs, he'd also knock off ten percent for anything she wanted to buy. Haul-away was included, you know. It was a nice service for customers, sure, but it also supplied the popular second-hand section in the back of his store.

Maybe, when she found a house of her own, she'd take Roland up on his offer. But for now, this one-bedroom apartment with its month-to-month lease suited her just fine.

Even so, as she walked Eagle River's tree-lined streets and drove through the surrounding countryside, Kate sometimes dreamed about what, and where, her next home might be. She probably didn't want an acreage. Her parents still lived on their farm, just west of town. Between visiting them and working for the post office, she spent plenty of time in wide-open spaces. A snug little house on a quiet street in Eagle River might be more her style.

That's what Kate needed right now, too: peace and quiet. She'd text Mom back, say some leftovers were more her speed tonight. As for Ben, well, any rain was now supposed to hold off until after sunset. Maybe she could get a walk in after dinner, clear her head before she returned his call.

Kate took one more look in the tiny medicine cabinet's silvered mirror, and set her comb aside. Once she made sure the tub's drain was completely clear (the pipes had to be as old as the building itself), she and Charlie headed for the kitchen.

The apartment was railroad style, with the rooms lined up the length of the building. Her bedroom looked over the back lot, then a long hallway linked the bathroom and tiny kitchen to the combined dining and living space in the front. That was Kate's favorite room, as it had three tall windows that gazed out over Main Street.

Her neighbors had different layouts, with one unit clustered toward the front and the other to the back, but Kate loved the feel of her place. It reminded her of the first apartment she and Ben had rented in Chicago. With fewer cockroaches, thank goodness.

The sale of the Chicago bungalow would go through, there was no doubt about that. She'd be glad when it was done, but the transaction made her sad, too. Their former home was her last tangible tie to Ben. Charlie had always been more her cat than his, and they both had secure pensions as public employees. With no custody issues to fight over, their divorce proceedings would soon dwindle down to paperwork signatures and legal fees.

She'd get her half of the house's sale, and be able to move on with her life. Kate was free, or soon would be. If only she felt more excited about it.

"Wallowing in the past does us no good, right?" She dished out Charlie's wet food and set it next to his always-available bowl of kibble. He was a picky eater, and only the best would do. Kate expected she'd have to order his top-shelf grub from an online store, as she couldn't imagine anyone around Eagle River carried what he liked. "And I get to come home to you, so it's not like I'm alone."

Charlie might be a regal cat, but he was also loveable. With Kate crouched on the worn linoleum next to him, he ignored his dinner long enough to give her hand a gentle head butt. His purrs soothed her, just as they always had.

"Royalty eats first," she told him as he finally tucked into his meal. "But the staff's going to find herself something, too."

Kate loved to cook, although it was a challenge in a kitchen this small. There were extra enchiladas from last night, and she chopped up a salad to go with them.

Once the enchiladas had their spin in her compact microwave, she took her plate to the square, bar-height table tucked in the corner of the living room.

While she ate, she made a clear-eyed evaluation of her apartment. The walls were white, nothing more. A cheap, short-pile brown carpet covered what Roland said were sturdy hardwood floors, but they were in rough shape and he didn't have the cash to have them refinished.

Kate had done what she could, like hanging floral curtains and spreading a vibrant area rug in the living room. A few pictures adorned the blank walls, and a textured throw was tossed on one end of the couch to give Charlie a special napping spot and bring more color into the space.

But there was only so much one could do with an apartment. Maybe it was just as well, as she'd had little time and energy to feather this nest.

Besides, she'd never planned to stay for too long. It was temporary, somewhere to be other than her parents' farm while she settled in at the post office and tried to figure out where she really wanted to live.

And as the evening's sunbeams slipped through the high windows and spread their glow across the rug, Kate had to admit this wasn't the place. Not for much longer.

Other than Kate, there was no dishwasher. As soon as she'd tided up and settled on the couch, Charlie was right there next to her. Once his evening brushing was completed, he hustled to the front of the room and jumped up on his carpeted perch.

"What's going on out there tonight?" Kate joined him at the window even though she was pretty certain what she'd find: a scene that hadn't changed one bit since she came home.

This block of Main Street was all retail on the ground level; or at least, it was for the storefronts that were occupied. Most shops, including the furniture store, were open Thursday evenings, but shuttered by six every other night of the week.

Her hometown's business district wasn't as robust as it used to be, but the buildings along Main Street still showcased their vintage charm. Most of the structures were brick, as were a good number of the town's older homes. The storefronts had been constructed with tall windows and ornate cornices, and the town's active historical society worked hard to ensure they stayed that way.

Eagle River was incorporated in the early 1860s, thirty years before many other towns in the area, and its streets were filled with history. Situated on a major river, it grew into a commercial hub long before railroads came through the county.

Early settlers had hoped their community would be chosen as the county seat, but being in the far-northeast corner tipped the odds out of their favor. That honor went to Swanton, which now boasted over ten thousand residents. As that was eight times what Eagle River had, it was safe to say that Swanton had won.

But Eagle River's residents were proud that they still had their own high school, which shared a new campus with the middle grades on the southwest side of town. Elementary students attended classes at the old building, a few blocks east of the business district.

Main Street, which was part of a state highway, was bookended by agriculture-based companies that had been prominent in town for decades: an auction barn on the north side, and a farmer's cooperative on the south edge of town. In between were two banks, a pharmacy, a coffee shop called

The Daily Grind, and a sit-down restaurant. And two drinking establishments: one that was a bright, cheerful sports bar; and one that was the opposite. Eagle River also offered a convenience store, the usual insurance offices and trade-industry storefronts, and an auto mechanic.

Kate was exhausted tonight, but she was restless, too. She went for a run every morning, alternating between Eagle River's still-sleepy side streets and a paved trail along the river that used to be a railroad line. But after such a crazy day, she needed to get moving again if she was to have any hope of sleeping well tonight.

She could wander down to The Daily Grind, but decided she'd had enough social interaction for one day. But even if she went, it wasn't likely she'd run into many people she knew. All her close friends from high school had long ago moved away, just like she had, and Kate hadn't found the time yet to make new friends.

Well, except for Bev. And now, she hoped, Karen Porter. Maybe things were looking up, just a bit.

"I think it's time for a walk," she told Charlie as she reached for her workout shoes. "A change of scenery might do me good. I know you'll keep an eye on things while I'm out."

The furniture store's front stairwell landed in a tiny lobby that only housed a door to the street and three in-the-wall mailboxes. Kate turned north on the sidewalk, and aimed for the stoplight.

A truck rolling down Main tooted its horn, and Kate returned the driver's quick wave with an automatic smile. She had no idea who was behind the wheel, hadn't had time to look before the vehicle went past.

But she'd grown accustomed to people recognizing her from when she walked a route in town. It was also very likely the driver was being friendly, for no reason at all.

Kate soon was at Eagle River's busiest intersection, where the state and county highways came to a crossroads just south of the bridge. She lingered on the corner, lost in her thoughts, and waited for the light to change.

How much of one's life is consumed by waiting? she wondered. *Waiting for something to happen. For something to end, for something else to start.*

Two cars went through the green light for the state highway. Kate's signal, which would take her west, told her to stay right where she was.

But on this quiet, humid summer night, no one else seemed to be about. She stepped off the curb, crossed Main Street, and was soon in a residential area.

Kate didn't know what she was looking for, really. She had started monitoring the local housing market online but it didn't take long, as there wasn't much available. In a town as small as Eagle River, that meant her options were very limited.

All she could do was stroll through the neighborhoods, try to get a feel for what part of town she liked best, then watch and wait for something to arrive.

In short, she was looking for a sign. And not necessarily one stuck in someone's yard. But something, anything, that said her new home might be close at hand.

* 4 *

Kate didn't find any new houses for sale. But then, she hadn't expected she would. It was her post-walk conversation with Ben that kept her mind in gear long after she went to bed. Because for the first time in a long time, they didn't talk about their failed marriage. Instead, they talked about Milton. And Ben had so many questions Kate couldn't answer.

A storm front rolled in just before ten and, as Kate listened to the rain drumming on the roof of her building, she couldn't stop reviewing their conversation. Charlie had scooted to his safe space under the bed at the first growl of thunder, which left Kate alone with her swirling thoughts.

She had meant to only tell Ben about the calf, how she'd put her farm-girl skills to use for the first time in a long time. But their chat had quickly turned to the rest of her afternoon.

"That's just what I'd expect you to do." The pride in Ben's voice had been unmistakable. "Jump in and help; no matter who, or what, needs it. You were in the right place at the right time, and you did the right thing. Good for you!"

His comments had brought tears to Kate's eyes. They used to talk like that, share all the details of their days, laugh over the smallest things. But there wasn't much chance to reflect on how times had changed, as Ben quickly zeroed on Milton's possible disappearance.

He wasn't a law-enforcement officer, but years of investigating workplace safety incidents had honed his observational and critical-thinking skills. And the more Kate reviewed the situation with him, the more she suspected something wasn't quite right.

Her unease hadn't been completely based on her past trauma, she could see that now. But she couldn't say for sure what made her feel this way.

Was it about how much mail had been in the box? Maybe, maybe not. Right now, it was only a hunch. For Milton's sake, she hoped she was wrong.

"Go with your gut," Ben told her before they hung up. "If there isn't big news about this guy, one way or another, within a few days, most people will probably forget about it. But stick with it. Sounds like he doesn't have much family around, if at all. Someone needs to stay in his corner."

Kate checked her phone before she headed to the post office the next morning. There wasn't one mention of Milton on any of the local media's sites. But a sheriff's deputy appearing on your front porch would be breaking news for most people's friends and family, so word about the situation had surely spread by now.

Her best bet to find out more was to get to work. Because the Eagle River post office, for better or worse, proved to be a robust source for local gossip. The stuff wasn't always true, of course, but that's what made it so interesting.

The crew was a mix of older and younger residents; some were lifetime locals, some transplants. But all of them, between their professional and personal lives, were well-connected in the community. Maybe someone had already uncovered something that would put Kate's mind at ease.

Jack O'Brien, one of the senior carriers, didn't know anything concrete about Milton's whereabouts. But that didn't stop him from offering his favorite theory from Roberta's chair.

"Milton Benniger is no more in danger than I am," Jack pronounced with a definitive nod, his feet kicked up on the boss' desk. "Why, I bet he's just gone for a day or two. I don't get what all the fuss is about."

Then he spotted Kate. "Hey, there's the veterinarian! What's on the case list for today? Some sick chickens, maybe?"

She shrugged and smiled as the rest of the team erupted in claps and cheers. "Who knows? No two days are the same in this business." Then she pointed at Jack. "I see you took the throne early today. Milton may be safe and sound, and I hope he is. But we won't be able to say the same for you when Roberta shows up."

That brought groans of admiration from the group. Jack was full of bluster, and Kate had been a little intimidated by him when she started at this shop. He had seniority, and she was the newbie. But Kate knew she was really settling in here if she could trade jabs with someone like Jack.

"Well, it's the comfiest chair we have." Jack's feet hit the floor when the back door squeaked again. "Hey, Roberta!" He was suddenly all smiles. "Nice morning, huh?"

"It'd be nicer if you'd vacate my premises." Roberta dropped her purse on her desk. "My office, first, if I can call it that; and then this shop, next. I'd say it's time you started to sort, then get on the road."

"Sure thing." Jack hustled to his feet. "I tidied up a bit, dusted your desk off for you."

"No, you didn't."

"Well, I kept your chair warm, then."

Roberta rolled her eyes. "It's going to be ninety today. I don't think there's any risk of hypothermia. But thanks."

Kate was in the break room, filling her thermos with coffee, when she felt a gentle hand on her shoulder. "The Swanton newspaper called me this morning, first thing," Roberta said in a low voice. "Sharon's gotten wind of things, obviously, as the deputy had to file an incident report. First, I thought she was after a cute story about the calf's delivery, but she's focused on Milton. She wanted your cell number, but I didn't give it to her."

"Thanks." Kate sighed with relief. "I don't really ... I don't want to get into all of that."

After what happened in Chicago, she'd been pestered for days by reporters wanting her story. But Kate had only wanted peace and quiet, and the chance to heal.

"I don't think the sheriff's talking, anyway, and it's his call." Roberta returned Jared Larsen's greeting, then turned back to Kate.

"I got the impression she took a run at Karen and old Doc McFadden, and didn't get anywhere with them. An editor's job is to be nosy, I know, but she kept asking me pointed questions, the kind that told me she doesn't know anything beyond whatever limited information was in the report."

Then Roberta looked Kate in the eye. "I think I'll have Allison take that route today. I could really use you on foot in town, since Aaron is still on vacation."

"Thank you, so much." No more needed to be said. "I'll get my stuff together, and head out."

The last of the carriers soon arrived, and they gathered around the long metal counters and settled into their pre-route tasks. Bev was next to Kate, sorting the parcels and boxes for the day's routes.

"All this online shopping is a blessing and a curse," Bev said as she checked another address against the route lists. "We have to cart more stuff around, but it's also a way to get to know our customers better, going up on their porches and knocking on doors. Of course, when the holidays arrive, you're loaded down like Santa's sleigh!"

"That's exactly how it feels." Kate smiled. "It's one of my favorite times of year, despite the extra work. Thanks again for everything, Bev. Not just for coming out yesterday to pinch-hit, but for taking me under your wing. You've really helped me settle in, and I appreciate it."

"No problem! I've only been on the force for about six months now. When you arrived, I was no longer the new kid. At my age, it's been fun to do something different. I'd like to think teaching all those years helped prepare me for this job."

Allison Carmichael, who was one of the younger carriers, called down the row toward Kate. "I only heard bits and pieces about this special delivery. Why don't you give us all the details?"

Kate did, to more cheers and laughs from her co-workers. And that's when the stories started. In a place this rural, territorial dogs weren't the carriers' only challenges.

Jared was once chased back to his mail car by a hotheaded rooster. Marge Koenig proudly noted she'd helped round up on-the-lam pigs four times in her twenty-five years as an Eagle River carrier, and she'd be disappointed if it never happened again.

Randy VanBuren now walked a town route, but had once faced off with a territorial buck blocking a country road. He'd had to chase the menacing deer out of the way, using only a blanket he had in the trunk as a deterrent.

"I could have been gored by those antlers," he insisted, although Kate wasn't sure her co-worker had been seriously in danger. In hindsight, it was the story that mattered. "But you do what you gotta do, because the mail always goes through."

Randy toasted his colleagues and took a big swig of his coffee, and the rest of the group roared with laughter. Kate joined in as she picked up one pile of sorted mail and put it in the case at her feet.

With the animal situation thoroughly discussed, at least for now, talk turned back to Milton. Allison knew one of Milton's closest neighbors, and that family hadn't seen the old man for a few weeks. But then, they rarely did. Deputy Collins didn't seem too worried yesterday when he knocked on their door, but still.

"This just doesn't sit right with me." Allison frowned. "I think he's what my grandma would call a 'recluse.' Doesn't travel, keeps to himself. Sure, maybe he's just gone. But why would he just take off, for no reason? I just hope he's not lost or needing help."

Jack shaped a stack of mail with a *thud* on the metal counter. "Like I said, I think he's fine. Even so, I can't believe the sheriff hasn't called up volunteers to walk the fields, just to be sure. Between the storms we've had in the past week, and the heat? Why, it could be as dangerous to be stuck outside somewhere right now as it is in the middle of winter."

Bev slid a stack of parcels down the table toward Jared. "If there's no reason to be concerned, I wish they would come out and say it."

"Could they be keeping it quiet for some reason?" Marge wondered.

"Maybe he ran off with his girlfriend," Randy suggested. "Maybe they eloped."

The mail room's bustle ground to a halt.

"What do you know about that?" Jack quickly forgot his insistence that people mind their own business.

"I don't know anything." Randy sighed. "I'm kidding, OK? I've never even met Milton."

As the gossip swirled around them, Bev nudged Kate with an elbow. "You look tired. Whatever happens, I don't want you to worry about this. There wasn't anything more you could do. I mean, there was that calf, being born just when Karen came down the road. It made her stop. And then she flagged you down. If none of that had happened, no one might yet know that Milton's gone." Then she corrected herself. "I mean, if he is."

Kate hadn't thought about it that way before. "You're right. That's quite the coincidence."

"Not a coincidence, honey. That's fate."

"I just wish I knew more." Kate now had her last pile of mail in order. "It was a relief that he wasn't in the house, that the deputy didn't find him in distress, or worse. But that mailbox! I wish I could remember what was in it, and when."

Roberta clapped her hands to get her crew's attention. "OK, everyone! Let's get out there and get it done. And no matter how tempting it might be, I don't want any of you throwing gas on the fire about what's happened to Milton Benniger."

"If anything has," Jack interjected. "See? This is what's going to be the problem."

"As you all know, discretion is an important part of our job," Roberta reminded her team. "In a situation like this, I'd say that extends to doing our best to keep people from panicking."

Murmurs of agreement echoed around the room.

"With that said, please keep your eyes and ears open today. Those of you in town, take note of any interesting tidbits that might come your way. If it seems credible, or even if it doesn't, encourage those folks to call the authorities. And those out in the country, take note of anything new you come across, anything suspicious."

"Eyes and ears." Jack looked at each of his coworkers in turn. "This post office covers over eighty square miles. There aren't that many of us, but we still number a few more than the sheriff's department. We're public employees, too; we have to do our part."

Marge picked up her mail case. "Someone must know where he is. If the animals are being looked after, and it sounds like they are, maybe there's an explanation. I hope we hear one today. But in the meantime, let's stay alert."

"I hope Marge is right," Kate said to Bev as she loaded her mail bag with deliveries for the first third of her route. Eagle River was so small, she could walk back to the post office to replenish her load. "I think I'll feel better when we know what's really going on."

Bev seemed lost in her own thoughts for a moment, and Kate noticed. "You're worried about him, too, aren't you?"

"Clyde and I can't stop talking about it. We've been at our place thirty years now, just a few miles from Milton, but he's like a stranger. That's not right; he's alone out there, and at his age. We all want to pat ourselves on the back for being neighborly. But sometimes, I think we're all too wrapped up in our own lives to make a real effort. That needs to change."

Then Bev nodded, as if she'd come to some sort of a decision.

"Don't mention this to anyone," she whispered to Kate. "But I might be able to find out more. If I do, you can't tell anyone what I tell you, much less how I got my information. But it's worth a try. I think it'll help us both sleep better tonight."

Kate was relieved, and said so. But then, she gave her friend a quizzical look.

"Bev Stewart, what exactly are you up to?"

"Can't say for sure." Bev winked. "Not yet, anyway. I'm off at two, then I have some errands to run in Swanton. But if I dig anything up, I'll give you a call after supper."

* 5 *

The Hartland County courthouse anchored one corner of the Swanton town square, its three stories of Romanesque architecture capped by a clock tower. The building was beautiful yet imposing, which was exactly the intent when it was built in the 1890s. Its goal was to serve as a landmark on the rolling prairie, a visible reminder that law and justice were firmly entrenched in this region.

And even in the late hours of a sweltering Tuesday afternoon, the place still buzzed with visitors. So much so that Bev had to park half a block away, and felt a bit lightheaded by the time she reached the courthouse's wide front steps.

"Should have worn my straw hat," she muttered as she tried to smooth her hair. "It's too hot to be out here without something on my head." A blast of cool air greeted her as she entered the two-story lobby. There was a short wait for the security checkpoint, then Bev sent her purse through the sensor and stepped through the metal detector.

"Why hello, Bev. What brings you in today?"

She'd expected to run into someone she knew, and had worked out her story on the drive over. Most official business for Hartland County residents was conducted at this facility. And, after living her entire life in the area, Bev knew a lot of people.

"Hey there, John." She gave the man from her church a warm, quick smile. "I'm getting the registration renewed on the truck. It's that time of year again!"

Before he could respond, Bev sailed on. If only this was such a routine errand. But her destination was another department in this building, one she would prefer no one she knew saw her enter. After all, word traveled fast in this county, and gossip flew at the speed of light.

Bev wedged herself into a nearly full elevator. Her stomach dropped as the car lifted up.

I'll only stay a few minutes, she reminded herself as she checked the directory for her destination. *Just a quick visit. Besides, I need to get groceries before I leave town, and it's almost four already.*

A man coming out of the sheriff's office gave Bev a quick nod as he held the door. She'd expected to find a near-empty waiting room on a summer afternoon, maybe an attorney or two waiting their turn. But the place was crowded and, based on how they all stared at Bev, nearly everyone seemed downtrodden or angry, or both.

The deputies' offices and garages were housed on the far corner of the courthouse's property, and she'd expect that place to be full of hustle and bustle. Not here. But Bev had never visited the sheriff's office before. And now, she wished she hadn't.

But then, Bev squared her shoulders and returned the cold stare of a rough-faced woman slouched in the chair closest to the door. Bev had spent decades in a classroom, managed every kind of behavior and personality imaginable. And she paid her taxes, just like everyone else. She had a right to be here.

"Can I help you?" The sharp-eyed receptionist called to Bev from behind the counter, which was fronted with a wall of what was surely bulletproof glass. Bev raised her chin and marched to the window.

"Bev Stewart," she announced in a calm, clear voice. "I'm here to see the sheriff."

This was met with a raised eyebrow. "Are you now. Is he expecting you?"

"What are you on the hook for, Grandma?" A disheveled young man on the right leaned in. "Because we've all got our grievances with the big guy. You'll have to wait."

He looked vaguely familiar, but Bev couldn't quite place him. A past student, maybe? Well, he was about to get a lesson about respecting his elders.

"I'm not here for that." Her sharp tone made the young man sit up straight. "In fact, my business is certainly none of yours."

She turned back to the receptionist, who now wore a small smile of solidarity. "I talked to the sheriff about an hour ago. He said to just come by."

"Take a seat." The woman jerked her chin at the waiting room. "If you can find one that's tolerable. He's wrapping up a call, but I'll let him know you're here."

"Thank you." Bev found an empty chair in one corner, and clutched her purse close to her chest. While she waited, she made sure her button-down blouse wasn't too wrinkled from the humidity. She was glad she'd swiped on a bit of lipstick before she got out of the car.

Maybe this was a bad idea. But Kate was concerned about Milton, and she'd been through enough in the past how-many months. And the more Bev thought about her neighbor, she couldn't shake the feeling that things weren't quite what they seemed. Surely a few words with the sheriff could put them both at ease.

Still, it had taken all her considerable courage to make that call. Sheriff Jeff Preston had a good reputation, even if the disgruntled folks around her now might disagree. It was the reason he'd moved into this post years ago, and been reelected by comfortable margins ever since.

If she offered Sheriff Preston kindness and respect, and explained her errand, surely he'd tell her what she wanted ... no, what she *needed* ... to know. Or at least, not kick her out of his office.

The receptionist was on the phone, and now she motioned at Bev. Then she pointed at the closed door next to her window. "Go on back."

This was met with groans and eye rolls from the others, but Bev got to her feet and started for the door. Before she could reach for its knob, a buzzer noise made her blink. Of course, the interior entrance was locked. The receptionist obviously took no guff from anyone, but even she couldn't control the peanut gallery that was this waiting room.

Bev let herself through, then went down a short hallway. This door, at least, was open.

Sheriff Preston, who was in his late fifties but still had a surprising amount of brown woven through his close-cut hair, glanced up from the papers in his hand and gave Bev a wide smile.

But after she returned it warmly, he looked away and cleared his throat. And when his blue eyes met hers again, there was a slight wariness in his expression.

"Hello, Bev." He pointed at the two chairs in front of his desk. "Take your pick. You sounded so concerned when you called. I'll try to give you some peace of mind, if I can."

"Thank you, sheriff." Bev's breezy tone faltered on that last word. Goodness, why was she so nervous? Wasn't it the sheriff's job to make sure his constituents were informed and their minds at ease?

"I'll try not to take up too much of your time." She kept her purse in her lap, as it didn't seem right to dump it on the floor. And clutching it gave her hands something to do.

"You know why I'm here. I just hoped you might be able to share, well, whatever it is you're able to share. I understand there are rules about these things, but ..."

"You bet there are." The sheriff's wide grin was back, and his chuckle eased Bev's nerves a bit. "Let's do this: You ask me whatever you want to ask, and I'll answer if I can."

"It's pretty simple, really. I want to know what's going on with Milton Benniger's disappearance."

When the sheriff didn't respond, she changed her request into a question.

"Or shall I refer to it as the incident with Milton? I don't know what to call it. Not a word has been released by your office about what happened yesterday. I'm hoping that means everything's fine, that you know where he is."

More silence. Sheriff Preston seemed to be considering his options, preparing to choose his next words carefully. Why?

A chill ran down Bev's spine. If this was all a simple misunderstanding, then the sheriff had nothing to hide. "If there's nothing to worry about, then I'd hope you'd just say so. People are worried. Not just about Milton, but perhaps for themselves. If there's any threat to the community, I assume you'd let us know."

He crossed his arms. "Your assumption is correct. We'd put something out if we thought there was any chance of harm to anyone else."

"Anyone else?" Bev wouldn't let it drop. "So you're saying Milton might be in danger. Or, he *was*." She closed her eyes for a second. "Oh, dear ..."

Sheriff Preston leaned over his desk. His expression was grim, but his eyes were kind. "I can't say much, not at this stage. We have an ongoing investigation on our hands, which means we can't release anything that might jeopardize it."

"I understand. It's just that Milton is my neighbor, and I'm worried about him. I'm also worried about Kate Duncan, our newest carrier."

Sheriff Preston nodded. "I know she was out there yesterday. Deputy Collins took her statement."

Bev shared how the incident had rattled Kate, as well as what happened to her on the job in Chicago. The worry lines on the sheriff's forehead deepened; Bev knew he understood how work-related trauma could follow someone home.

The package that was still on the porch was bad enough, she explained, but Kate was taking it hard that she couldn't recall what was in Milton's mailbox, and when.

"We carriers feel responsible for our customers. For some people, especially folks like Milton, we might be the only person in regular contact with them. Even if it's from a driveway-length distance." Bev took a deep breath and tried for another smile.

"I know you're in a tough position here. But are you sure there isn't something you can tell me? Give us both some peace of mind while you sort this out?"

Sheriff Preston sat back in his chair and stared at the wall above Bev's head for a moment, then gave her a lopsided grin.

"Oh, I see. This is about leverage, is it? Old friends, and all. You thought that ..."

"Old friends?" Bev burst out laughing. "As I recall, we'd been dating for almost two years when I caught you under the bleachers with Debbie Miller."

"Debbie Miller!" Jeff's draw dropped. "Oh, come on. She offered me a drink. It was homecoming, you know. Basketball practice didn't start for a month yet, but I couldn't risk getting caught."

"Yeah, sure." Bev rolled her eyes. "In that case, you should have been drinking from the bottle. She didn't have to pass you a shot like *that*."

"As I told you, again and again*: She* kissed *me*. What was I supposed to do? Run away?"

"Well, none of the other boys ever did. I guess you wondered what all the excitement was about."

"It wasn't great. And it wasn't worth losing you over, that's for sure. I still can't believe, after all these years, that's the whole reason you broke up with me." He sighed. "I was planning to propose to you in the spring, right before graduation. You know that."

Bev had to look away for a moment, so she studied the trees outside the office's wall of windows. "It wasn't meant to be. We've had a good life, both of us. Just not in the way we expected when we were seventeen."

"It's funny how things work out." Jeff smiled as he glanced at the two photos on his desk. One was of him and his wife, the other was of their three now-grown children. "Bev, I'd like to tell you more, really I would."

He thought it over, then leaned over the desk again. "OK, maybe there are a few things I can share."

When Bev gasped with excitement, he held up a hand. "But you have to swear, you won't tell anyone other than Kate. This might ease her mind, and yours, too. Although it hasn't put mine to rest. At least, not yet."

"I'm all ears."

"As of right now, I don't know where Milton is. But I also don't know if that's a problem, or not."

Deputy Collins found nothing else of note at Milton's farm. Once the house was secure, he stopped by the four closest neighboring farms and simply said there'd been a welfare inquiry about Milton. Had anyone seen him lately?

At three places, no one had any idea about Milton's whereabouts. But the fourth stop netted him something of interest.

Jasper Tindall said Milton stopped by a few weeks ago, and asked if Jasper would do chores when he went on vacation. Jasper had been surprised, as Milton always stuck close to home, but agreed to give his neighbor a hand.

There was just the small herd of cows, and a few cats. Milton expected to be gone for a couple weeks; if Jasper looked after the animals, and checked the mailbox every few days, that was good enough. Two of his cows were about to give birth, Milton said, and he would be able to relax if a good neighbor could help him out.

"That's it?" Bev threw up her hands. "Well, that makes perfect sense. That must be why you haven't released anything to the public. There's nothing to say. It's summer, and people like to get away for a few days. End of story."

Jeff picked up a pen and flipped it back and forth between his fingers. "Not necessarily. And now, this is the part you must promise not to spread around."

She nodded.

"Milton also handed Jasper three thousand dollars in cash, said he'd give a day's notice about when he'd leave, and made Jasper promise not to tell anyone he was gone. And then, he came back to Jasper's last Tuesday. Said he was leaving in the morning. And that was it."

Bev's jaw dropped. "You pay well for good help, but that seems like an awful lot of money for someone to just drop by once or twice a day. And the secrecy!"

She frowned. "Where was Milton off to, Japan? How long did he say he was going to be gone?"

"He didn't say where, or for exactly how long. Or at least, that's what Jasper says. As of today, if Jasper's being straight with us, Milton's been gone for six days already. Wherever he went, if he is indeed on vacation, he took that old truck of his. Because it's not at the farm, and we've put out a bulletin to surrounding counties. No one's seen it anywhere."

Bev shrugged. "Well, it's a free country. I guess he can do as he pleases."

"Milton drives a 1981 Ford. Dented tailgate, rusted fenders, just what you'd expect. I wouldn't take that old beater any farther than Mason City."

Jeff said Milton didn't have a cell phone, as far as anyone knew, but he was going to request the farm's landline records from the phone company. He wasn't sure there was enough probable cause for that, not yet, but it was worth a try. And from what Kate had told the deputy, and the stack of mail accumulating on the Tindalls' kitchen counter, Milton hadn't halted delivery of the Swanton newspaper, either.

Jeff could call the newspaper office to confirm that, of course. But the truth was, he was trying to avoid talking to Sharon about this for as long as he could.

It was a tough situation, and Jeff was trying his best to find his way through it. People were starting to talk, but he didn't want to alarm anyone more than necessary. And he didn't have any evidence, right now, to prove anything one way or the other.

Unusual? Yes. Suspicious? Hard to say.

Bev took this all in for a moment. "So the official word is, Milton's skipped town of his own choice."

"Yep."

"But it sounds like, just between you and me, you're not sure that's what really happened."

"Yep."

"So, what happens now?"

"Not sure. We'll keep watch on his place. Deputy Collins lives in Prosper, he's closest." Jeff tapped the pen on his desk. "This is off the record, too, but we already have a few volunteers walking the fields and woods around Milton's home, just in case. We'll make runs at some of the other neighbors, and anyone else who knew Milton well. But that doesn't seem to be very many people."

The sheriff raised an eyebrow. "And keep tabs on Jasper."

Bev gasped. "Do you think ..."

"It's too soon to tell. I hope not, but we have to follow any and all leads."

Jasper and Carrie Tindall seemed like good, kind folks. Bev couldn't imagine Jasper harming anyone, for any reason. But Jeff was right: Jasper's story was suspiciously light on details. Except for the wad of cash that (allegedly) changed hands.

"I know you'll do what's right," she told Jeff. "Roberta's reminded all of us that we're the eyes and ears of our community. All the carriers are to pass on anything unusual they hear, anything that might be helpful."

Jeff smiled. "Glad to hear it. We're a small department, being so rural. We need all the help we can get."

"That's exactly what Jack O'Brien said."

Jeff chuckled. "Yeah, I bet he did. He's going to want to be deputized before this is all over. But seriously, I'd appreciate any details the carriers pick up when they're on their rounds. Or off, for that matter." He smiled again; a grin that, all these years later, still made Bev's heart flutter. Just a little.

Stop it, she told herself. *You're an old married woman. Happily married, too.*

"Well, if we hear anything, should we just call your office?"

"We're trying to keep a lid on it for as long as we can. How about this: You get something, just call me direct, OK? I'll sort things out."

"Deal."

Bev held out her hand, and Jeff shook it. Then gave it a little squeeze. "It's good to see you again," he said softly. "It's been a while."

"It has." Bev let go and reached for her purse. She was halfway to the door when she remembered something.

"Oh, I was going to ask you: Is it true the first grandbaby is on the way?"

The proud grandpa-to-be rubbed his hands together. "I can confirm that. Yes, Jessica's due in December. It's going to be a whole new world for us. I can hardly wait."

"I'm so excited for you." And she meant it. "Tell Sandra I said hello. And thanks, so much. Kate and I will keep this information to ourselves. You have my word."

* 6 *

Kate was stunned by Bev's news. The tidbits about Milton were troubling and fascinating, but that's not what really got her attention.

"I had no idea you had an inside track with one of the most influential people in this county! And it sounds like he misses your friendship. I mean, not that you'd ..."

"Absolutely not." Bev laughed, but then she gave a wistful sigh. "I was madly in love with him, back in the day. But it was the crazy teenage kind, the kind that doesn't usually last. Even if I hadn't caught him with another girl, I don't think we would have stayed together."

Bev was determined to be a teacher, would attend Northern Iowa the next fall. Jeff wanted to go into law enforcement, always had. His great-grandpa was Eagle River's police chief, long ago, and that kind of civil service seemed to run in his family.

Jeff planned to go to Des Moines for his two-year degree, then attend the state academy and, finally, move to wherever was necessary to secure his first job. His goal was to make it back to Hartland County, but there'd been no guarantee how fast he could make that happen.

"When you're eighteen and in a place like Eagle River, Des Moines seems a million miles away," Bev said. "Anyway, we run into each other, now and then. Even so, I hadn't seen him in a year. I wasn't sure if he'd even meet with me."

"Of course he would. You have a history. A good one, even if it didn't last." Kate lifted the kitchen sink's drain and let the suds gurgle away. "I just can't get over what he told you about Milton and Jasper. I can't imagine asking for that kind of favor without telling someone exactly how long I'd be gone, where I'm going."

She shook her head in wonder. "And that pile of cash! Maybe I need to start a pet-sitting service as a side hustle. It makes you think it was for more than doing chores. But what?"

"It's so strange." Bev's voice was full of concern. "Milton might be a little eccentric, but I've never heard of him being, um, what's the term? In cognitive decline? But he's in his early eighties, I guess anything's possible."

There seemed to be three potential scenarios at play. The worst of them was that someone had harmed the old man, intentionally or not. In that case, the arrow right now pointed at Jasper. What he told Deputy Collins wasn't only strange, it could be an attempt to conceal his own behavior. Concocting a story about Milton suddenly leaving, with no definitive details, would be one way to distract the authorities and buy some time.

But Bev found that one hard to believe. What possible motive would Jasper have for hurting his neighbor? And if he really wanted to concoct a story, she hoped he would have the sense to make it more believable. Of course, stranger things had happened. And criminals weren't always the sharpest crayons in the box.

It was more likely that Milton left home by his own choice. No one could say why, but the reason might not be worth all this concern. Maybe he'd simply come back next week and explain his whereabouts. But even in that case, it was possible something had gone wrong with Milton's plan.

His truck broke down, or he had a medical emergency. Or if it hadn't yet, it still could.

While Sheriff Preston didn't have enough evidence so far to justify the time and expense of a massive manhunt, his department had put out word with surrounding agencies and hadn't received one tip. If Milton had flagged down help, or been taken to a hospital, he surely would have been located by now.

The third option was far-fetched, but at this point, Bev and Kate didn't have another possible explanation. What if Milton had left of his own free will, but for whatever reason, never planned to come back? There were stories, from time to time, of people who wanted to start their lives over somewhere else. They planned it out, socked money away ... and then one day, they were simply gone.

It didn't seem likely someone Milton's age would craft such an escape, and what could possibly be his reason for doing so? And with no close family, there wasn't anyone to "run away from." If he had a hankering to pack up and head for the Caribbean, well, that was his choice.

Bev said Milton's farm fields were sold off long ago, he just had the acreage to look after. If he wanted to move, wouldn't he just sell his livestock and put his place on the market? Why all the secrecy?

"None of this adds up." Kate weighed the options as she wiped down the ceramic-tile counter. There was a chip on one square near the refrigerator, and it always needed an extra scrub. "At this point, I don't know what to think."

"And here I thought talking to Jeff would put our concerns to rest. I feel like we have more questions than before. And I wanted answers."

"Me, too. Maybe I shouldn't, but I feel some sort of responsibility toward Milton. Maybe it's just because I've been out to his place, helped with that calf." Kate shrugged. "I'm glad the sheriff cleared up the bit about the mailbox, that

Jasper's been checking it every few days. But it sounds like Milton doesn't have many people in his life, and it's not right for anyone to be forgotten. Maybe he'll show up, I hope he does. But if he doesn't ..."

"You know how I feel about this," Bev said. "He's been just down the road, all these years, but I hardly know him. He always seemed like a loner. But now I'm thinking, what if that wasn't by choice? Was he unhappy, needed help? I hate the thought of anyone being isolated in that way."

Kate looked at Charlie, who glared at her from the rug in front of the refrigerator. It was time for his evening brushing, and he knew it.

"I guess we just keep our eyes and ears open, like Roberta said, and see what happens. You know, Ben always said jumping to conclusions is the worst thing you can do when working a case. It can lead you down the wrong road, one that can take weeks to backtrack."

"Is this what we're going to do? Play detective?" Bev laughed, then turned quiet. "Maybe we already are. But is it the right thing to do?"

"I think it's the only thing we can do." Kate draped the damp dishtowel over the oven door's handle. "And I feel like I have to do something to help."

Then she smiled. "Besides, Jeff's counting on us. If we want to get any more dirt out of the sheriff, we need to do our part and see what we can dig up."

With Charlie brushed and settled next to her on the couch, Kate picked up the remote and absentmindedly flipped channels. Nothing caught her eye, much less took her mind off Milton's whereabouts.

The money. The neighbor. The story that doesn't quite add up ...

Ben had been so curious about Milton last night, so full of questions. She was tempted to reach out, give him the update, get his reaction.

But, no. She wouldn't. Not even a text. It was still hard to face, sometimes, but the part of her life that included him was over. Even so, another bit of advice drifted into her mind, something Ben always believed: *To solve the problem, you have to know the players.*

If Milton was a bit of a recluse, he probably wasn't prominent online. But the only way to know was to look. Bev said his family went way back in this area, had been some of the first settlers along the Eagle River. Kate loved history and genealogy, and knew how easily so many of those doors opened through a computer screen.

She reached for her laptop. With her fingers poised over the keypad, she considered her options. And then, she started to search.

* * *

The next day was Kate's day off, which gave her time to check two things off her to-do list: Accept Grandpa Wayne's invitation to join him and his friends for breakfast, and attempt to find out more about Milton Benniger.

Luckily, she could do both at once. Grandpa's breakfast buddies were a who's-who of Eagle River; or at least, they liked to think they were. They gathered at Peabody's, the restaurant on the north side of town, for hot coffee, hearty meals and fresh gossip at least twice a month.

And after a few hours of online searching the night before, Kate needed some new sources. As she suspected, Milton didn't have any social media accounts. All she found were the usual, obvious things, such as county-assessor records for his farm.

The Benniger family did have deep roots around Eagle River but, while the historical lore was certainly fascinating, none of it gave Kate any insight into Milton himself.

While the Bennigers were a prosperous farming family during Eagle River's early days, most of their descendants apparently chose other professions. As time went on, many of them moved away. One of Milton's great-grandfathers had been in charge of the Farmers Savings Bank in Eagle River in the early 1900s, but the rest of the clan apparently hadn't done anything noteworthy enough to earn a mention in the county historical information she found online.

Peabody's was on the other end of Main Street, over the river and up near the auction barn. The trip was eight blocks at most, but it was a hot, humid morning and Kate decided she didn't want to walk.

The parking lot was about half full, typical for early on a Wednesday, and she was met by the mouth-watering aroma of bacon, fried eggs and piping-hot pancakes as soon as she opened the restaurant's front door. Young families and groups of old friends gathered around the laminate-top tables. The place was noisy with conversation, so much so that the old-school country music favored by Eloise and Henry Peabody was kept to the background.

Wayne Burberry's blue eyes lit up when he spotted his granddaughter, and he rose from his chair to wave Kate over to his table. She didn't know why he bothered, as her grandpa wasn't easy to miss in a crowd.

He was tall and, even though he was in his late seventies, still broad-shouldered. His once-blond hair had long ago turned silver, but he was secretly proud of how much of it was still on his head. Grandma Ida wasn't crazy about the mustache, but Grandpa Wayne was determined to keep it, and she'd long ago given up the fight.

"Pull up a chair, my girl." Three more of the regulars were in attendance, and they'd pushed two tables together in anticipation of Kate's arrival. "Now, you have to tell us how things are going down at the post office."

"Geez, Wayne." Max Sherwood rolled his eyes. "Let her get settled, first. Besides, it's not like you never hear what's up. I know Randy keeps you informed."

"Apologies, Mr. Mayor." There was a sarcastic note in Wayne's voice that made the group laugh. Max was no longer Eagle River's leading citizen. He'd stepped down two years ago, when his fourth term ran out. But while he considered himself retired from the furniture store, he couldn't resist popping in on occasion to lend his son a hand. Or, from what Roland told Kate, hand out professional advice that wasn't always welcome.

A petite, white-haired woman approached with a platter in each hand. "Here's the first of it. Max: your eggs, sunny-side up. And Harvey, they just about smoked your toast."

"Just the way I like it." Harvey Watson accepted his plate with a nod of thanks and reached for the carousel of jam packets.

"Hey, Joan." Kate smiled at the older woman. "I didn't know you were working today."

"I'm not. But two of the staff are out, so they're short-handed."

Wayne shook his head. "Everyone's on vacation, seems like. But Joan, you're only on the schedule for Saturdays and Tuesdays. You shouldn't be busing tables today."

Joan Murray was a retired nurse, and the medical profession was prominent in her family. Her husband was retired from private practice in Charles City, and their son was a doctor in Cedar Falls.

"You know I like to keep busy, and I wouldn't be able to enjoy my breakfast if you guys were whining about not having yours." Joan patted Kate on the shoulder. "Good to see you, honey. Since I'm already up, let me put in your order. What's it going to be?"

Kate's mouth watered as she glanced at the breakfast menu. Grease and carbs were the main attractions, and she was suddenly starving. Her morning run wouldn't make up for this caloric overload, but she didn't care. She requested two pancakes, two scrambled eggs, and a sausage patty.

"You get hash browns and toast," Joan reminded her.

"Eloise never skimps on the butter," Wayne told his granddaughter. "And the pancakes are plate-sized."

"Oh, that's right." Kate reconsidered. "OK, just one pancake. And only the hash browns, please, with the eggs and sausage. And coffee."

Joan pointed at the pot in the middle of the table. "Hot and black is all we have."

"Perfect. It's the same at the post office. I'm used to it."

Joan went back to the kitchen, and the men went back to their gossip. As she considered the best way to bring up Milton without showing all her cards, Kate half-listened to some tale Harvey shared about the goings-on in Prosper. Apparently, there was a raging debate about what color to paint the community's water tower.

"What are they going to do?" Max's concern made Kate want to laugh out loud. Really?

"We've lived there for over fifteen years," said Grandpa Wayne. "I don't see what's wrong with the color it is now. Some sort of white. Good enough for me."

Harvey and his wife farmed between Prosper and Eagle River for decades, not far from where Kate grew up, before they moved into Eagle River three years ago. But his sister lived just west of Prosper, and kept him in the loop.

"Mabel told me it's a toss-up between some shade of light blue, and one of light green," Harvey said with a shrug. "Anyway, it's apparently the biggest blow-up there since ..."

"Auggie's plans for his gas pumps?" Max chortled. "Hoo, boy, that had everyone riled up."

Kate poured herself a cup of coffee. "Who's Auggie?"

His friends gasped in disbelief, and Grandpa Wayne slapped the table with one beefy hand. "Are you serious? You don't know?"

"Don't tell Auggie." Max chuckled. "He'll be offended to hear he's not the local celebrity he thinks he is."

Harvey passed Kate the bowl of sugar packets. “Auggie Kleinsbach runs the Prosper co-op, has for decades. He’s lived in this area all his life, too.”

“Isn’t that just about everyone, though?” Kate frowned when she realized a condescending tone may have slipped into her voice. “I mean, no offense.”

“You’re right, lots of families’ roots run deep around here.” Grandpa Wayne gave her a wink. “Including yours. But Auggie, he’s a bit of local legend. A colorful guy.”

Max peppered his eggs. “Opinionated and stubborn, you mean.” Then he laughed. “But like Kate said, that’s just about everyone.”

Joan was back with Wayne’s plate and her own. “Everyone at this table, for sure. Kate, yours will be up in a minute.”

“No problem.” She settled back in her chair, which was a rust shade of padded vinyl. “Where’s Lena today?”

“Up in Mason City, at her daughter’s,” Joan said. “And Chris is at the pharmacy, of course. He usually only joins us if we meet on the weekend.”

Lena Wakefield was a retired music teacher, and still gave private lessons in her home. At fifty-eight, Chris Everton was the youngster of the group. As the lone pharmacist at Eagle River’s only drug store, he was determined to stay on the job until he reached seventy.

Joan soon brought out Kate’s breakfast, and she tucked in with a groan of satisfaction. She’d want a nap when she got home, but this was worth it. Her family had been coming to Peabody’s since, well, as long as she could remember.

Being there was like wearing a comfortable, old sweater, one that you were never in a hurry to remove. And despite being so much younger than Grandpa and his friends, Kate felt warmly accepted at this table.

It was good to reconnect with these folks again. But it would be even better if she could find a way to bring up

Milton without seeming like she was fishing for information. Kate felt a bit guilty, given her main motive for showing up this morning, but she'd promised Bev not to reveal their connection to Sheriff Preston.

Her connection to Milton's farm, however, was certainly fair game. Half the town seemed to know she was out there Monday when it was discovered Milton might be missing. If she waited long enough, Grandpa's friends would ask her about work. And for the first time, Kate was eager to discuss her interesting afternoon.

The chatter soon turned to the goings-on in Eagle River. Most of the group's focus was on the sweet corn festival, which was held in mid-August. Grandpa Wayne was on the committee again, even though he no longer lived in Eagle River. He'd been involved with the event for decades, and reliable volunteers were always in demand.

Pretty soon, Max gave Kate the opening she needed.

"So, how's it going at the post office? You've been there, what, a month now?"

"Two months. It's been an adventure, moving back. I like it, though, getting to know everyone in the department, and meeting the residents."

"It's been a big change," Joan said gently. "Walking routes in a town as small as Eagle River must be very different from Chicago." Across the table, Harvey's cheerful expression dimmed slightly and Joan hurried on, eager to skirt that subject. "And now you're delivering on country roads, too."

"Good thing she's a farm girl." Wayne was proud. "Knows her way around a mile section, don't you?"

"That I do. But I'm sure it'll get very interesting when winter comes."

"Snow chains," her grandpa said. "We'll get you fixed up."

Max leaned down the table. "I bet Monday was interesting. Me, I'd like to hear all about it from someone who was actually there, for a change."

The group's questions focused mostly on Kate's role as bovine midwife. Karen had stopped by Milton's yesterday to give the new mother and baby a look-over, and Kate now passed along the news that both were doing well. Karen had also told Kate that Thomas kept insisting Milton's disappearance was suspicious, and she and Doc were already tired of listening to his conspiracy theories. But Kate wasn't about to share that at this table, or anywhere else.

It had been difficult, too, to not confide in Karen what Bev had discovered. But if Kate was going to keep tabs on Milton's disappearance, and pass along whatever she found to Sheriff Preston, she would have to get good at keeping a poker face. And secrets.

"Glad to hear the delivery turned out just fine." Harvey nodded his approval. "Most of them go off without a hitch, but you never know." Then he sighed. "It's just so strange about Milton, though."

Kate expected any mention of Milton would get her group's full attention. But she hadn't counted on the sudden cutoff of conversation at the next table, or the curious stares aimed at her grandpa's friends from across the aisle.

The people around them didn't seem merely curious, they were ... wary, she decided. Maybe a bit suspicious. It made her consider how many people in and around Eagle River suspected foul play could have been involved. And wondered which of their neighbors might be to blame.

Joan leaned in and lowered her voice. "I find it hard to believe he's on 'vacation.'" She put air quotes around the last word. "I don't see him sunning on a beach, or heading out West, or anything like that."

"He used to go over to the riverboat on the Mississippi, sometimes," Max said quietly. "Play the slots a little. But it's been years, I think, since he's bothered with that."

Interesting. What if Milton had a gambling problem? Kate hadn't considered that as a factor. But maybe she should. At this point, anything was possible. She busied herself refilling her coffee cup as she considered her next move. If she was going to directly ask for details, here was her best chance.

"I don't think I'd even heard of Milton until the other day. Do any of you know him? Or some of the other neighbors, like Jasper Tindall? Seems like he's the last stop before Milton's when I'm out that way."

Grandpa Wayne gave Harvey a look Kate couldn't quite read, then began to fiddle with the syrup dispenser.

"Well, Milton likes to keep to himself. A good guy, I suppose." And then he smirked. "Speaking of Auggie, his head must be spinning right about now. He and Milton are some sort of cousins."

"Really?" Kate was all ears.

"The distant kind." Grandpa shrugged. "I don't know exactly how they fit together."

Max turned toward Harvey. "You used to live out that way."

"Yeah." Harvey seemed to choose his words carefully. "Wayne's right, Milton's the quiet type. I know Jasper a little bit. Not much," he added quickly. "He's a nice kid." Then he laughed. "OK, so he's in his fifties. But a youngster to me. I knew his dad better."

"Oh? Is he still around?" Kate tried to keep her tone light. Maybe she was getting somewhere with this.

"He's at the nursing home, over in Elm Springs," Harvey explained. "Jasper's sister lives there. Their mom and dad were older when they finally had kids, so Oscar is, let's see ... oh, over ninety now. And she passed, several years ago."

"God rest her soul." Joan's expression was somber. "Oscar's had dementia for a very long time. He got it way early, compared to most people. I shouldn't say this, but maybe he had it coming."

"Joan!" Max whispered. "Watch what you say. People might be listening."

"You know they are." But Joan kept her voice low. "And I don't care. Most people around here know the truth. How could they not?"

Harvey leaned down the table toward Kate, who was now hanging on every word. "Oscar was always, well, he was one mean mister."

His immediate family took the brunt of Oscar's rages, Harvey said. But the neighbors knew better than to get in his way, or cross him about anything. He could hold a grudge for years, and one of his long-standing resentments focused on Fredrick Benniger, Milton's father.

Fredrick was as mild-mannered as Oscar was hotheaded, so the grudge had been rather one-sided. Fredrick was quite a bit older than his neighbor, but even that didn't seem to earn Oscar's respect. The feud actually went back to the generation before them, or maybe even the one prior to that. No one was sure, but everything boiled down to what it often did: money. The Tindalls claimed the Bennigers once cheated them out of the chance to buy forty acres from another neighbor, and Oscar never let Fredrick forget it.

"But Jasper's a good guy, not like his dad," Harvey claimed. "He's just helping a neighbor out. I don't think there's anything more to it than that."

Wayne turned to his granddaughter. "Word is, Milton just said he'd be gone for a couple of weeks, and he didn't say where he was going."

Kate gave the only reaction she could, which was to nod and pretend this was information she didn't already know.

Max set down his coffee cup. "That's weird, all the way around. Milton didn't give specifics, and Jasper didn't even ask? I don't think I believe it."

Kate waited to see if anyone would mention the cash that had allegedly changed hands, but no one did.

She realized that while Jasper had shared that detail with Deputy Collins, he likely hadn't told anyone else. Because if he had, it would have spread through Eagle River like wildfire. And subjected Jasper to even-more scrutiny. No wonder Sheriff Preston was keeping that information close to his vest.

The table's talk soon circled around to other topics, and Kate lingered for another half hour over her breakfast. She tried to work the rest of the way across her pancake, but its syrupy goodness turned to sawdust as she chewed.

Her nosy questions had unlocked a Pandora's box of information. She hadn't expected that. In fact, she'd had no idea what to expect. But it was now clear to Kate that if she kept searching for clues, she needed to be prepared for just about anything to come her way.

* 7 *

The suspicious stares from the other diners at Peabody's were a reminder that the longer Milton was missing, the more people around Eagle River would be creating, and spreading, their own theories about what happened to him.

Or was he just gone? Maybe nothing had happened to Milton ... other than whatever was his own choice.

Kate didn't know, but it was clear she and Bev needed to keep their tip-gathering as confidential as possible. When she called Bev that afternoon, they decided to swap detailed information only when they were off work. Because the post office was indeed filled with eyes and ears. Ones that sometimes started gossip, not just repeated it.

"A feud between the Bennigers and the Tindalls, huh?" Bev mulled that over. "You know, now that I think about it, one of the neighbors did mention it, back when we bought our place. But that was years ago. I haven't heard anything like that recently."

"It seemed credible. But the thing about the gambling?" Kate shook her head. "I don't know if that's relevant. The guy has a right to have a little fun now and then. Do you think Jeff would be interested in that?"

"I'll pass it on. But let's not get disappointed if we don't get many more tidbits like the ones I got yesterday. We've opened that door, but I think we should assume that, most of the time, it's only going to swing one way."

Bev's assumption turned out to be correct. The next morning, as they sorted their deliveries, Kate simply asked, "how did it go last night?"

Jack was pretending to check his route list at the far end of the counter, so Kate felt the need to be careful. Or maybe, he wasn't paying any attention to them at all. Was this how things were going to be? That she would have to start second-guessing everyone, and everything?

"Oh, it was fine." Bev raised an eyebrow, then leaned in and switched to a whisper. "I think he already knew."

Even though the air conditioner was running full blast, the post office's large back room was already stuffy at this early hour. Kate never bothered with makeup when she was working, only a heavy-duty sunscreen. Which she'd have to reapply several times today, as the heat and humidity were sure to sweat off a little more of it every time she rolled down Bertha's window. With her letters and parcels now in order, she reached into her personal tote bag and lined up her still-empty water bottles along the counter's edge.

"Better fill those up." Marge ambled over with a knowing grin. "It's going to be a scorcher."

"Speaking of which, Clyde's home all day today," Bev told Marge. "Just in case you need to drop by."

"Glad to hear it." Mae would be back Friday, and Roberta had asked Marge to pick up that route until then. "We need to stay hydrated. I hope I can hold out until my lunch break, but you never know."

Kate felt a little guilty, as she was Mae's usual backup, but was secretly relieved she wouldn't have to relive Monday's events until sometime next week. Today was Jared's day off, and Kate had instead been tapped to take his southern loop.

Although in-town routes offered easy access to the post office as well as Eagle River's businesses, answering nature's call could be a real challenge for rural mail carriers. Carriers were allowed to drive off their regular routes if needed for this necessity, but were encouraged to seek out facilities at public buildings or businesses, not private residences. But when your route was mile after mile of gravel dotted with farms, those officially approved options were hard to find.

The route northeast of Eagle River, through Union township, had no public places other than a rural church that was usually locked. The southeastern loop had the best accommodations, thanks to the unincorporated hamlet of Mapleville. There were only a handful of houses, but thankfully the owner of Mapleville's small farmers' co-op had a generous open-door policy regarding federal employees. The fact that the carriers sometimes purchased a soda or chips from the guy's small snack selection seemed to help keep the "welcome" mat out.

The only public place west of town was a county nature preserve situated halfway between Eagle River and Prosper. But it was as popular for winter hikes as it was in the warmer months, so the restroom shed was unlocked all year long.

Because of these challenges, the Eagle River post office had longstanding, off-the-record agreements with a few local farmers. Most were the family or friends of current or past carriers. And in an emergency, rural-route drivers were prepared to answer nature's call directly in nature.

"You could always handle it like the guys," Bev said now. "Jack just pees in his truck." The room erupted in laughter.

"In a bottle!" Jack jokingly shook a finger at Bev. "And that's just when it's twenty below. Desperate times only."

"When I signed on here, my grandpa bought me a little booklet with lovely illustrations of both native and invasive plants," Kate said. "And I have no plans to become a botanist."

Jack clapped her on the shoulder. "Gotta watch where you're going when you're on duty, in more ways than one."

Satisfied he'd capped off the conversation with the best pun of all time, he picked up his mail case and started for the door.

"It's never dull around here." Bev shouldered her tote bag. "But Marge is right. Drink as much water as you can today, then do what you have to do. We've all been there."

By mid-afternoon, Kate was very sweaty and very tired. It had been a rather-uneventful shift, thank goodness, but the heat was starting to wear her down. Despite Bertha's blasts of Freon-cooled air, it had been a welcome respite to circle back to the post office for her lunch break.

Since then, she'd had two parcel deliveries along with the usual mail. The Alberstons' dog, who was normally overeager to greet visitors, hadn't bothered to leave his spot of shade, so Kate was able to drop their box without having to fend off Luke's slobbery greetings. A half-mile lane separated the Grangers' farmstead from the road, but the playhouse where their children waited for the school bus years ago continued to serve as a weather-proof place to stash packages.

Just an hour to go. But now, she had to cool her heels thanks to road construction. While most of this route was gravel, Kate still had a few miles here and there on the blacktop that ran west to Prosper. Working in sections, crews were adding a fresh layer of asphalt to the much-used road. Many locals had created their own off-highway detours, but this section of pavement crossed a creek and it was just as fast (or slow) to wait for the pilot car.

There weren't many vehicles waiting on the east side of the bridge, just two trucks and Bertha. Kate turned up the air conditioning and the radio, and tried to relax. Before she knew it, she'd be on her way back to the post office. Then home for a shower, and clean clothes ...

Suddenly, a shadow blocked her side window.

Rap rap rap!

Kate jumped. Through the glaring sunshine and the dust, she glimpsed a man towering over her door. He motioned for her to roll down her window and, for a second, she was somewhere else.

Come on, pull yourself together. Kate took a deep breath and powered down the glass.

"Hey there!" His orange vest, and the sign-capped pole in his hand, told her everything she needed to know. But Kate's heart still beat double time when the crew member poked his head inside.

"My family's going on vacation next week," he shouted over the roar of the machinery just down the road. "What do we do to stop our mail?"

Kate somehow found a smile. She had to stay calm. Even out here, she was a representative of the post office. Besides, this guy meant her no harm.

"Sure, it's easy. Just go online, all the info you need is there. You can do it on the website, or stop at your post office to fill out the form."

"Thanks!" He finally backed off. The pilot car was about to cross the bridge, and he had to return to his post. "I knew you would know."

Her heart pounding wildly, she nodded and buzzed up the window. A wave of dust settled over Bertha as the parade of eastbound vehicles passed by. The pilot car circled back, and her new friend soon turned his sign and gestured for the truck in front of Kate to fall in line.

She followed the truck through the construction zone, kept her speed low and watched out for the workers toiling away in this sweltering heat. But once she was through the gauntlet, Kate noticed her hands were shaking. Just a bit.

Here was her corner, at last. She flipped the blinker and turned off on the gravel.

Just focus on the route, she told herself. *The Smiths are next. There's that catalog along with the first-class stuff.*

Kate made it through four more stops before she realized she had to pull over. The panic, no matter how unnecessary, wouldn't leave her alone. Down in the next mile was a township cemetery, a quiet, restful place with a circle drive where she could stop without worrying she was blocking access to someone's field.

The gate under the arch was closed, but she didn't mind. It was too hot to get out and open it, and all she needed was a moment to collect herself. Kate rolled Bertha off the road and breathed a sigh of relief when she shifted into "park."

She closed her eyes and took a deep breath. Held it, then let it out for twice as long. *It's OK. That guy didn't mean to scare you. He had a question, that's all, and you were able to help him.*

"Why did I think coming home would change things?" She slapped the steering wheel with one hand, then rested her forehead on it. "Because it hasn't. Not really."

Eagle River's small-town streets felt entirely different than those in Chicago. Other than the occasional overly excited dog, Kate didn't feel uneasy when she delivered in town. And out here, on these gravel roads under an open sky, with nothing surrounding her but gently rolling hills covered with corn and soybeans, she had all the breathing room she needed.

No one could sneak up on anyone out here. Or so she thought. Until today.

After she was attacked on the job, and after Ben confessed his infidelity, Kate had often felt the urge to run. But her morning routine, with its laced-up shoes and podcasts, didn't take her far enough. She'd had to get out, one way or another. When a spot opened up at the Eagle River post office, Kate suddenly had the escape route she'd needed.

But even here, way out here ... She tried to leave them in Chicago, but her troubles had followed her home.

She didn't want to go back. Which was good, because the

house closing was in less than two weeks and she had nowhere to go. She didn't want to go anywhere else, either. But no matter where she was, now or in the future, Kate knew she had to face up to everything this past year had thrown her way.

She lifted her forehead off the steering wheel, blinked through her tears, and stared at the orderly rows of headstones. This little cemetery wasn't abandoned, far from it. The grass had been recently mowed, and flowerpots and small flags decorated many of the graves. While there were some newer, modern stones, many of the markers had settled into the soil long ago.

Kate looked to the left, which seemed to be the oldest part of the cemetery. She couldn't make out the dates, not from here, but a few of the surnames were readable. Many of those people had likely spent their entire lives in this area. Most of them never had the chance to move away, experience new places and different people.

Did they ever feel hemmed in by their lives here? Or had they been content enough, their only expectations to marry, have children of their own and, if they were lucky, live to an old age?

Expectations. They made all the difference.

Kate wasn't sure what she wanted, not anymore. She was home, had been welcomed back to Eagle River with open arms. So why was she so restless, so unsure about the future? And maybe, just a little afraid?

She had to find her way through all this. But first, she had to deliver the rest of this mail. If she lingered here much longer, she'd have to explain to Roberta where she'd been.

Well, the flag guy scared me, and then I pulled off at the cemetery to feel sorry for myself.

Kate sat up straight and took another deep breath. There was work to be done, and she was supposed to be at her parents' farm by six. She took a large gulp from her closest water bottle, and realized another reason she had to get moving. If she wanted to make it to the nature preserve in time, she had to leave now.

Bertha inched back into the road and Kate, her hands placed exactly at ten and two, returned to her rounds.

What had Deputy Collins said? *Don't wait, don't let it build up inside you. I know, from experience, that's not the way you want to handle things.*

It was time, and Kate knew it.

Maybe she didn't need to sign up for a weekly appointment, not like before. But she had a phone number in her purse, tucked away in her wallet. When she got home this afternoon, she needed to reach out.

* * *

Kate called the therapist as soon as she got home, even before she hopped in the shower. With Charlie purring in her lap for support, they talked through several coping strategies and set a time to check in early next week.

By the time she left town, the heat had loosened its grip and the afternoon's stiff breeze had eased to a whisper. Her parents' farm sat on a small rise down a gravel road, and the sight of its gray-painted house and tidy outbuildings always told Kate that she was really home.

Waylon, who was some sort of black Lab mix, ran to Kate's car as soon as she pulled up by the front porch.

"Hey, buddy!" His wriggles of joy always raised Kate's spirits. "Am I glad to see you! It's been a long day. What's Dad making us for supper?"

Based on the wonderful aroma drifting around from the patio, Curtis Duncan had steaks on the grill. Which meant Waylon was certain to get a special dinner, too.

Along with Waylon, the Duncans' farm was populated by a herd of beef cows, a small flock of chickens and several well-fed barn cats. The family also raised corn and soybeans.

Charlotte, Kate's mom, worked as an administrative assistant at Prosper's elementary school.

Her brother, Bryan, and his wife farmed just a mile down the road. Bryan had taken over the Duncan homestead when Grandma Lillian and Grandpa James moved to Fort Dodge five years ago.

But it was just Kate and her parents tonight. And after the rough day she'd had, Kate was fine with a simple supper for three.

Or seven, if you counted Waylon and the trio of kitties that pretended to soak up rays on the patio's edge but were really waiting for tidbits fresh off the grill.

Charlotte gave her daughter a hug as soon as she walked into the kitchen. The room's color scheme was stuck in the 1990s, but that made Kate love it all the more.

No matter where she'd lived over the years, how far away she'd been, she could always come to the farm and take comfort in the fact that, at least out here, some things never changed.

"I think it's cooled off just enough that we can eat outside." Charlotte's brown, shoulder-length bob had a few streaks of silver, and her face was tanned from hours spent in her garden. "Want some iced tea?"

The savory steaks, along with heaping helpings of Mom's potato salad and ranch-dressed cucumbers, went a long way toward soothing Kate's jangled nerves.

"You've been through so much the past few months. Give it more time." Curtis passed the strawberries for the shortcake, and Kate was eager to accept both the dessert and the advice. "I'm so sorry that happened to you today. That flag guy had no idea what he was doing."

"I know. But I need to handle these things better when they come up."

Her mom passed Kate the pitcher of iced tea. "When we're done eating, why don't you take Waylon for a walk? We can clean up. You know how he loves to go down to the creek and see what's what."

Soon, it was just the crunch of her tennis shoes on the gravel, the rhythmic swish-swish of Waylon's somehow-fluffy tail, and the buzz of the cicadas.

One of the cats, a brown-tabby guy named Sammy, sauntered down the lane after Kate and Waylon but grew bored with the expedition before it reached the road. He flopped down in the grass on the side of the driveway, and waited for Kate and Waylon to return.

Waylon sniffed his way to the creek bridge at the bottom of the hill, content to be out and about on such a fine summer evening. All Kate had to do was follow his lead, and take in the peaceful scenery around her.

They paused at the bridge, which wasn't more than metal siderails and thick wooden beams coated with packed gravel. Kate dropped to the rail and planted her shoes in the dust, and watched the sun gently lower itself into a haze of pink and amber.

And before she knew it, the tears were back. Because the first time she'd brought Ben home to the farm, they'd come down here to the bridge to take in this very scene. It had been a warm, humid night exactly like this one. But it wasn't just the romantic memory that hurt Kate now; it was the fact that, on that night a decade ago, everything, and anything, had seemed possible.

She had to forget about Ben, although that was easier said than done. What did the rest of her life hold? Kate had no idea and, right now, she wasn't sure she wanted to know.

All she could do was put one foot in front of the other. One day at a time.

And as she rested there, kept an eye on Waylon as he wriggled through the thick grass and weeds along the creek's banks, she counted up how long Milton had been gone.

Eight days. Because it was one week ago today that she'd

left that box on his side porch and, if Jasper was to be believed, the day before that was when Milton left home.

Or disappeared, depending on how you looked at things.

She wondered how Sheriff Preston was looking at things these days, but it seemed clear that even Bev wasn't going to get a straight answer on that one. All that was left to do, at least until some new lead arrived, was to watch and wait.

Kate was ready to be patient, if she had to. To not give up. Sure, Milton might turn up tomorrow, or call someone, and none of this would matter anymore.

But as the days went by, her feeling that something wasn't quite right seemed to grow.

Waylon was now on his way up through the ditch, his feet muddy and his furry face alight with his adventures. It was time to head home. As they reached the driveway, where Sammy waited to rub his whiskered greeting against Kate's bare legs, she decided the case would only go cold if she let it.

She had an errand to run tomorrow afternoon. If she played her cards right, maybe she'd uncover something that could get it moving again.

* 8 *

After hours spent sitting on the wrong side of things, it always took Kate a few moments to adjust back to her personal vehicle. She powered the windows down to let out some of the hot air and, for the first time in weeks, didn't bother to put them up again. It was surprisingly pleasant for a late-July afternoon, perfect for taking a little drive.

Prosper wasn't far, about ten miles. But Kate had been too busy lately to even get over there to visit Grandpa Wayne and Grandma Ida, so this was going to be a bit of a treat. With the radio up and the windows still down, she took a left at the stoplight and headed west on the county highway.

Charlie wasn't yet out of his favorite specialty cat food, but word was Prosper Feed Co. carried some high-end brands. That, combined with Grandpa Wayne's mention of Auggie's ties to Milton, had Kate eager to head over to Prosper and check things out.

She didn't know much about Auggie, other than he was a bit of a know-it-all and prided himself on being a straight shooter.

Kate hoped that meant two things: If Auggie had any details that could help the case, he might spill them. And the chance to hear about Kate's adventures at Milton's farm, direct from the source? He wouldn't be able to resist.

All she had to do was drop in at the co-op, find Auggie, chat him up, and see what she could dig up.

Without attracting too much attention from nosy customers. And without offending the high ethical standards he apparently applied to himself. Because if she did, he was likely to huff and puff and tell her to leave.

The car's windows had to go back up at the construction zone. This time, her wait was thankfully short. But it was long enough for her to be in line, just like yesterday, and notice the same flag guy was on the job. Nothing unusual happened this time, of course, but that was a positive for Kate. It did her good to replay yesterday's situation and have a different outcome.

So as the blacktop meandered west and south toward Prosper, she had a clear mind to consider the best way to get Auggie alone.

It was only about four in the afternoon, so he should still be around. She'd heard Auggie was an observer for the National Weather Service; hopefully he wasn't up in his lab, which was in one of the co-op's towers, working on his reports. It would be easiest if he was wandering the aisles or stationed behind the counter.

The highway eventually coasted down a small hill to cross the Shell Rock River, then curved a bit northwest to come in on Prosper's east side. Its four-block Main Street seemed to have more empty storefronts than thriving businesses, but there were some welcome signs of progress. A former bank on one corner had recently been transformed into a community center, and there was a relatively new gift shop Kate was eager to explore another day. Farther down, she spotted a sign for a new barber shop.

The intersection of Third and Main held the most memories for Kate, as the post office was on its southwest corner. Next to it was Prosper Hardware, which had been operated by the same family for over a century. Grandpa

Wayne was still postmaster in Prosper during Kate's college years, and whenever she stopped in to see him, it was always fun to go next door and take in the variety of goods Prosper Hardware had to offer. Even better was a visit to the vintage pop machine chained to a tree in the store's back parking lot. It was stocked with fresh soda during the warmer months, and the price hadn't been raised in decades.

It didn't take long to travel through Prosper and, after she bumped over the railroad tracks, Kate took a left into the co-op's parking lot. The one-story shop's beige siding didn't accurately convey its status in the community, because even on a Friday afternoon, the place buzzed with activity.

Adding to the commotion was the backhoe tearing up the ground just north of the main building, which was where the long-awaited gas pumps would be installed. She wondered about the "duck crossing" sign posted along the main drive, then laughed when she spotted a pair of Mallards sunning themselves in the patch of lawn on the building's south side. She finally found a parking spot, took a deep breath, and started for the door.

The farmers gathered around the coffee pot looked up in surprise when they spotted a stranger in their midst. Although the place was packed, there were only a few other women walking the aisles. As the old-timers eyed her with a mix of curiosity and guarded suspicion, Kate wondered if this was a good idea.

How likely was she to get a quiet moment with Auggie among all this chaos? And if he refused to talk to her, public embarrassment seemed very likely. But she was already here, so Kate grabbed a hand basket and did her best to blend in while she scoped out the scene.

A younger man with a coppery beard was at the register, chatting with customers as he rang up their purchases. And there, at his left elbow, a fat buff-and-white cat lounged on the counter and accepted a few pets from its admirers. Kate was so taken with the novelty of Auggie having a shop cat that she temporarily set aside her errands. She was about to approach the counter, both to greet the cat and casually inquire about Auggie's whereabouts, when a booming laugh a few aisles away caught her attention.

She rounded the bend to find an open office door, and an older man behind the desk. It had to be Auggie. He looked to be almost sixty, with sharp brown eyes behind a pair of rounded glasses. And like the owl he almost resembled, it didn't take him long to spot Kate.

"Well, you must be new." He pointed at her before she could even say hello. "Find everything you need?"

The man who had been loitering by Auggie's desk gave Kate a quick nod on his way out.

"I hear you have a nice selection of cat food. My Charlie is very particular." She popped through the door, then looked Auggie right in the eye. "I'm Kate Duncan. Wayne Burberry's granddaughter."

That was all it took. Auggie's eyebrows shot up in interest. He knew exactly who she was, personally and professionally. She smiled and waited, wondered what Auggie would do next.

"Well, then, Wayne's granddaughter, huh? Sounds like you had quite the afternoon on Monday."

Kate almost laughed at how easy this was going to be. In his quest to get the scoop, Auggie seemed to have already forgotten she had shopping to do.

"It was a wild day, for sure." She leaned in and lowered her voice. "Grandpa says Milton is your cousin. You must be so worried about him."

Auggie's chin dipped lower, and Kate caught the flash of concern in his eyes. "Yes," was all he said.

He waited. She waited.

Finally, Kate closed the door behind her and took the battered chair in front of Auggie's desk. He was no fool. She might as well be clear about her real errand.

"As you can imagine, it was a hard day." She shifted her basket and purse to the floor. Another plump cat, this one with a plush gray coat, appeared from under Auggie's desk to inspect Kate's things.

"I've been pretty upset about what happened. I just wish Milton would come home, or call someone." She squared her shoulders. "I guess I feel bad that, even though I grew up around here, I never even heard of Milton until this week. What's he like?"

Auggie nodded and settled back in his chair. He loved to talk, she already knew that, and he seemed poised to start in on a long-winded character assessment. But suddenly, he crossed his arms.

"I didn't have anything to do with it," he blurted out.

Kate's mouth fell open. She hadn't expected this, hadn't meant to imply anything. But what was "it?" Had something actually *happened* to Milton? "I'm sorry, I didn't mean to ..."

"Yeah, you and half the county." Auggie rolled his eyes. The gray cat had made her way back around the desk and jumped into his lap. "I already talked to the sheriff. Three times."

As Kate pondered why the sheriff felt the need to take more than one run at Auggie, he lifted his chin.

"Just for the record, Milton is my second cousin, once removed. I gave Sheriff Preston the photo for that missing person notice he sent out to regional authorities. It's five years old, from a family reunion, but it's better than those driver's license mugshots we all suffer through. They make everyone look like a felon."

Kate had to laugh. Her new Iowa photo wasn't any more flattering than the Illinois one she'd had for years. "So, he's not one, then? I mean, a shady guy?"

"No way." Auggie absentmindedly stroked the cat's back. "Salt of the earth, you know the type. I was glad to help out. Milton's only shirttail relation, but family is always family.

Isn't that right, Pebbles?" The cat closed her eyes in bliss and lowered her chin to her paws.

Auggie turned again to Kate. "I bet you met Mr. Checkers, out front. He's Dan's best buddy."

"I love that you have cats here, they really add something to the place."

Auggie was willing to talk, obviously, but he was already trying to steer the conversation off course. He was probably too shrewd to let anything useful slip out, but she decided to try again. "I'm glad the two of you stayed in touch. Milton didn't have many close relatives around here, seems like."

"I'm about it, these days. We chat from time to time. The Bennigers haven't been prominent around here for several decades." Then his eyes twinkled. "The Kleinsbachs, now, that's another story."

What followed was a ten-minute overview of Auggie's immediate family's history, which seemed to slant heavily toward his own accomplishments.

He'd worked at Prosper Hardware in high school, then moved over here to the co-op. When the former owner retired, he bought the business. He was content enough being a leader in the business community, Auggie said, but one could never rule out the possibility of serving on the city council, or running for mayor. Of course, his good friend Jerry Simmons held that post, and he did a fine job.

Kate glanced at the clock. She'd better get to the point.

"What do you think happened to Milton, then? I mean, would he really take off like that, especially at his age? It just bothers me. What if he's stuck somewhere, needing help?"

Auggie's lined face softened. "I can see you're really worried. Milton's getting up there in years, but he can still take care of himself. He has his mind; I guess, as much as any of us do as we get older. I take comfort in the fact that they've looked everywhere for him, and he hasn't turned up. Now, if they ever find his truck, abandoned ..."

Auggie shook his head. "That's the day I really start to worry."

"The corn's so tall this time of year," Kate said. "Would be difficult to find someone if they wandered into a field."

"I've thought the same," Auggie admitted. "Still, that just doesn't seem like something he'd do, go off in there alone. They've been all over the original Benniger homestead, too, although I can't imagine he went there. All the barns, and that big old house."

"Where's that?" Kate's curiosity was raised for another reason: she loved history. "I don't think I've heard of it before."

The place had been vacant for years, Auggie explained. Another distant cousin from over by Dubuque owned the farm, ended up with it almost by default. The fields were rented out, but the once-grand house needed so many repairs that no one had found the motivation, or the money, to shine it up again.

As for Milton, Auggie did have one bit of news he was willing to share with Kate.

"It's been almost ten days, as you know. Sheriff Preston's hoping something breaks over the weekend. But if it doesn't, he'll soon have justification to widen the search."

Milton allegedly told Jasper Tindall he'd be away "a couple of weeks," and it was the only timeline the sheriff had at his disposal. Wednesday was the two-week mark and, if Milton didn't call someone or show up by then, Sheriff Preston planned to step up his efforts with local media, and post flyers at businesses and community buildings.

This bit of insider information made Kate wonder what else Auggie had in his back pocket. Had he heard about the money that allegedly exchanged hands? Did he know about the neighborhood feud?

But this was her most-pressing question right now: Did Auggie share this detail, which was interesting but rather obvious, to satisfy her curiosity and send her on her way? Before she could figure out how to find out more, Auggie quickly changed the subject.

"Your grandpa said you're wanting to buy a place." He gave her a conspiratorial smile. "Why don't you drop by the old home farm, give it a look? It's up on a hill, has an amazing view. I'm sure David would give you a sweet deal." His eyes sparkled with interest. "Besides, Chicago real estate is outrageous. I bet you'll see quite the profit from your share of the house there. Plenty of cash for renovations."

Kate stopped herself, just in time. Auggie would love nothing more than to confirm his hunch about her impending windfall, then blab it around. She also realized he'd yet to pump her for details about her afternoon at Milton's farm. That could only mean one thing: he'd long ago gleaned so many bits of gossip that he didn't feel the need to hear any facts from her.

"I am looking for a house," was all she said. "I need to get some cat food, and head out. But maybe I could swing by there, just for fun."

"I'll give you my number. You want to talk to David, let me know." Auggie grabbed a sheet of scrap paper off his cluttered desk and started to draw a map. "So, you'll head back out of town the way you came. First gravel, take a left. There's an old iron bridge over the river, then you'll take another left ..."

* * *

Half an hour later, Kate was on a gravel road she'd never traveled before. Despite the unfamiliar surroundings, she found herself humming along to the radio as she followed Auggie's quickly sketched map. This was going to be an adventure.

"Here's the iron bridge! Auggie's right, it's certainly an antique." The river was low and lazy under the historic structure, but the woods along its banks were lush with the bounty of summer. A sizeable hill met her at the three-way intersection, and she turned north to follow the slope's base through the river bottoms. She easily found the next crossroads, and another, then turned east and started up the steep grade.

She passed a few farms and field drives before she spotted the substantial grove on the north side of the road. While most people never gave mailboxes a second thought, Kate always looked them over. And the rusted, dented cubicle at the end of the next lane told her she had the right place.

"No delivery here for years. That thing's not even up to code, anymore."

She hesitated for only a second before turning up the drive. The weeds were high and dense on both sides, but the crushed gravel was plentiful enough on this lane that she was confident her car could make the trip. She couldn't get arrested for trespassing; Auggie had given her his blessing.

And around here, she was quickly learning, that counted for something.

The grove of trees was farther away than it first seemed. The western view down the slope was breathtaking, but the lane would quickly fill in with drifts once the snow came. Anyone living here would need a blade-mounted tractor, or a reliable neighbor with some serious machinery, to keep this driveway passable.

When she finally reached the farmstead, Kate gasped. What she found was both awe-inspiring and overwhelming.

Auggie said the house was built in the late 1800s, when the original Bennigers became wealthy farmers due to the heritage breed of cattle they raised. He hadn't exaggerated when he'd claimed the farm was a real showplace back in the day.

The house was all brick, with heavy white cornices over the tall windows and under the wide eaves. Two full stories, with a generous attic above. Several of the downstairs windows were crowned with stained-glass transoms. A grand porch with ornate scrollwork brackets greeted visitors arriving via the circle drive, which also opened toward a side portico where guests could dismount out of the weather.

And the weather up on this hill would certainly be a factor. Even today, on what was a pleasant summer afternoon, a bracing breeze blew across the yard. Winter would be so much worse.

While the place was obviously deserted, someone had come through in the past few weeks to give the grassy areas close to the house and outbuildings a shaggy haircut. The rest of the yard, however, was a wild tangle of vegetation. It was as if time had stopped here, long ago, and no one had bothered to start it up again.

But the place intrigued her, and Auggie had all-but-insisted she give it a look.

Even in her off-duty vehicle, Kate was always prepared. She reached in the backseat for a floppy straw hat and a cannister of bug spray. In her shorts, she'd better not venture too far across the estate's grounds. At least she was wearing sensible tennis shoes, not sandals.

As grand as the place had once been, Kate saw decay everywhere she looked. The porch was about to part ways with the house; the tiled roof was worn, and gap-toothed from missing pieces. Some of the windows were cracked, and a few of the others were covered with weathered plywood. A carriage house slumped in a tangle of weeds near the driveway.

The barn must have been magnificent in its prime. But its slanted boards and busted windows warned Kate to stay away. Three sheds were also on the property. One resembled a chicken house, but the roof sagged so badly it was hard to be sure. The other two were in much-better condition, and probably once housed other animals and equipment. Kate cautiously approached the structure that looked like a machine shed, and tried the iron handle on its roller door.

The panel gave way with surprising ease, as if the track had been oiled. The biggest shock, however, was the "moos" that greeted her when she peered inside. Two well-fed cows stared at her from the other side of a board fence. The shed's back door was open to the pasture, and several more cows grazed on its grass. "I'm not here to feed you, sorry."

Kate backtracked to an area by the chicken house that offered a sizeable gap in the windbreak, and discovered another angle of the farm's stunning views. The pasture slid gently away to the west, down the grade to where she could just make out the gravel road along the river. Beyond that, low on the horizon, she found the compact grid of Prosper's streets.

No wonder the original Bennigers picked this place. The choice location, and its once-grand home, had made a strong statement: *We're here, we've prospered, and we're staying.*

Kate wasn't sure what had happened, when the family's fortunes had taken a downturn and why so many of its descendants moved away. But as she walked back to the car, she knew she wasn't the right person to bring this historic farm back to life.

"It's way too big." Holding her straw hat low against the wind, she stared up at the house one last time. "I'd be lonely here, all by myself." Despite the warm breeze, she shivered. "All those big, empty rooms. And it's raw and wild up here on stormy nights, it has to be."

Kate loved Charlie, but she was thinking about getting a dog, too. Especially if her new home had some outside room to roam. She could have a few chickens, maybe. But this wasn't the place.

"If I want to play farmer, I can go out to Mom and Dad's. And while this house is amazing, it has to be a money pit. If not, someone would have pounced on it before now."

It was all too much, in more ways than one. And then, for just a second, Kate decided maybe she could see herself living at this restored acreage … if she wasn't alone.

Ben loved to work with his hands. Between the two of them, they could have tackled something like this. It would have been an adventure, one to experience together. And when they would have started a family, the old house would have been filled with shouts and laughter. That big front window was surely in the parlor, and it was the perfect backdrop for a Christmas tree …

She had to look away. Kate didn't know what might come next, or where she'd live, but it wouldn't be here.

"I'd better get going." She reached for her keys. "Charlie's going to wonder where I am, and someone might turn up soon to check on these cows. Auggie's well-known around here, but I'd still have a lot of explaining to do."

Kate got behind the wheel, turned down the lane, and didn't look back.

* 9 *

Kate's visit with Auggie didn't net her any leads in Milton's case, but the nosy proprietor of Prosper's co-op definitely helped her in another way.

Despite mulling over her options for a few weeks now, Kate had yet to visit any of the properties available on the local market. But her visit to the Benniger farm, with all its challenges and possibilities, inspired her to move forward with her search.

She was getting restless in her little apartment, as cozy as it was, and hoped that was a good sign. Kate had been back in Eagle River for just over two months now, and maybe she'd become comfortable enough in her day-to-day groove to take some steps forward in this part of her life.

Of course, there was that windfall soon to be wired to her bank account. One thing she knew for sure: it was time to start looking. It was late July, and it would be best to find a place in the next few months so she could move before winter set in.

Scratch that. The sooner she found a place, the better. It would be ideal to have several weeks of pleasant fall weather to get settled, inside and out. Kate needed to find a realtor; she needed someone she could trust, who would be patient while she figured out what she wanted.

Karen moved to Prosper just two years ago; had she enjoyed working with her agent? One quick call to her new friend, and Kate had a name, a number, and a glowing recommendation. Donna Stevens was eager to get Kate's house hunt started, and they'd made plans to see a few properties on Tuesday, Kate's next weekday off.

Despite the upheaval of the past two weeks, Kate found herself humming as she washed the breakfast dishes that morning. There weren't many but, given the grumpiness of her apartment's window air-conditioning units and the day's steamy forecast, she didn't want stuck-on food sitting around while she was away on a jam-packed day.

"We have work to do," she told Charlie, who'd already breakfasted and now lounged at Kate's feet while she ate her cereal and studied her errands list.

Return library books. Groceries. Find a house. (?!)

"Or, should I say, I have work to do. Your job is to look cute and nap." She gestured at the front windows with her spoon. "And keep an eye on everyone, and everything, moving along Main Street."

Make more friends should be on the list as well, but there was enough to do today. That last item was going to take some time, and probably even more effort, than finding a new place to call her own.

While it was good to be near family again, and she'd been warmly welcomed at the post office, Kate was lonelier than she'd expected. At first, she chalked it up to the stress of moving and starting a new job. And of course, there was a gaping hole in her heart that, for so many years, had been filled by Ben.

Kate really missed her Chicago friends, even though they'd stayed in touch. She longed for girlfriends to share her thoughts with, a few people to meet for drinks or dinner. Her closest companions from high school moved away years ago, just as she had, and hadn't returned. Other classmates were around, and she kept up with a few of them through social media. But she wasn't sure how much they had in common these days, and hadn't really had time to find out. Or maybe, to be honest, she hadn't made the time.

Her limited connections in Eagle River these days turned her thoughts toward Milton.

He certainly had little family, especially around here. But what about friends? It was rather sad that the only person with a photo (and one that was five years old, no less) of Milton to share with the sheriff was a second cousin, once removed.

Everyone said Milton lived a quiet life. But someone had to have more knowledge of this man and where he might be. Maybe Milton had more friends than Kate, or most other people, suspected. Maybe they were also private, and had talked to authorities but hadn't wanted to spread Milton's business all over the community. They'd be true friends, in that case. Small towns were full of gossip, and they knew Milton wouldn't want to be in the spotlight any more than necessary.

Another weekend had passed, and there was still no news. Tomorrow was the two-week mark for when Milton allegedly left home. If Auggie was correct, Sheriff Preston was preparing to step up his efforts.

Of course, there was also the possibility someone knew something, but was keeping it hidden to protect themselves.

What had Auggie said?

I didn't have anything to do with it.

Kate didn't know Auggie well, hardly at all. But she considered herself a pretty good judge of character, and he didn't seem like he'd harm a fly. Talk it to death, maybe.

His sudden defensiveness was likely an instinctive reaction to being scrutinized by a stranger. Because the people who loved to gossip the most usually bristled when they became the topic of conversation.

No, she decided, Auggie wasn't part of some sinister plot to harm his cousin. Even so, he probably knew more about Milton than he was willing to divulge, especially to a near-stranger like herself.

Either way, she would certainly be willing to drive to Prosper to pick up food for Charlie in the future. Auggie's prices, surprisingly, weren't much higher than what Kate would have paid online, and she liked to "shop local" when she could.

Even better, those dog treats he talked her into buying would be a sure-fire hit with the canines on her routes. Auggie said so.

As it was just past nine, Eagle River had yet to wilt from the heat. Kate decided to embrace the remaining hour or so of tolerable air, and walked to the library.

Clusters of vehicles were parked in several spots along Main Street, and she spotted a man watering the flowering planters that dotted the curbs. Kate couldn't be sure, but he might have been one of the city's handful of full-time employees. City hall was a squat, beige-brick building just up the street from the post office, but she hadn't spent much time there other than when she switched her apartment's utilities into her name.

The library, however, was an architectural marvel. It was one of the Carnegie buildings constructed in the early 1900s in small towns all across the country.

Towering windows wrapped around its main floor, and the basement rose high enough for generous amounts of light to circulate through the lower level. A gabled portico flanked with columns welcomed visitors up the wide stone steps. It was both outrageously ornate for a little town like Eagle River, and the perfect complement to the dozens of other red-brick buildings that lined the business district.

The building was one of Kate's favorite places, and she smiled as she tugged open one of the front doors. She was greeted by the comforting aroma of old books and wood polish, as well as shrieks of laughter from a meeting room where children's story time was in full swing.

She dropped her books in the return slot in the lobby, and wandered into the high-ceilinged main space. Hardwood floors ran the length of the library, but plush carpets anchored reading areas occupied by overstuffed chairs and couches. The original pendant lights still dropped from the ceiling, which featured a grid of white-painted beams.

"Can I help you find something?" A man looked up from the main counter, which was built from solid walnut. "It's sure lively in here today, with all the kids."

"I do have some holds to pick up." Kate moved in his direction, and tried to come up with his name. He was the new librarian, just started in May. He and his wife and their two young children moved to Eagle River from Cedar Rapids, if she remembered right.

"I'm Kate Duncan." She extended her hand, and he shook it. He looked to be in his mid-thirties, with sandy-blond hair.

"Kyle Gibson. I'm not sure I know you. And in a town this small, that's a feat in and of itself."

She laughed. "I grew up around here, but I moved back two months ago. I lived in Chicago for several years."

"Chicago?" He was intrigued. "I grew up in Freeport, by the way. Chicago's fine and all, but my wife and I, we like the small-town life. Good for raising children." He slid a few books across the scanner built into the counter. "How about you? Any kids?"

"Oh, no. Well, not yet." Kate decided this was one road she didn't want to travel today. "I know your family's new in town, so I guess I have a question for you."

Kyle nodded, but there was a twinkle in his eyes. "If you're going to ask us to join a club or a committee, I think we're going to hold off until we get more settled. Everyone's looking for volunteers for everything."

"No, it's not that." Kate laughed. "But I know just how you feel. Actually, I'm looking to buy a house. I have the name of a realtor, I'm meeting up with her today. But if you don't mind me asking, who did you use?"

Kyle raised his eyebrows. "Well, that's a new one. I mean, I'm the reference librarian as well as the children's department coordinator, and sometimes the janitor." He rolled his eyes toward a five-gallon bucket just behind his desk. "I'd fix the roof, too, if I knew how. It's going to cost us a fortune."

He reached for a piece of scrap paper. "Donna Stevens. She lives between here and Charles City, has worked around the area for years. No-nonsense type. Sees through the B.S., if you know what I mean. But I have to warn you, if you're looking for someone super aggressive, she's not your gal."

Kate's smile stretched from ear to ear. This was a rural area, to be sure, but there were certainly more than a few realtors to choose from. If two people recommended Donna, Kate knew this was going to be a good experience.

"Perfect! Thanks so much. We ... I ... just sold my house in Chicago. That was stressful and hectic, I always felt like I was swimming with sharks. I'm so glad it's over. I'd rather work with someone who's laid back. Knowledgeable, of course."

"She'd be perfect, then. How soon do you want to move? We had a hard time finding something."

"Before winter. I'm renting right now, above the furniture store. Month to month, so I don't have a tight deadline."

"Good luck in your search!" Kyle gave her a thumbs-up. "I guess I have a question for you, too. I know you just moved back, but what do people our age do around here for fun? We've been so busy settling into our jobs, and getting the kids ready to start school in the fall. I think we found a church we like, but that's it so far."

"To tell you the truth, I have no idea." Kate shook her head. "Been wondering that, myself. The next big event is the sweet corn festival."

"We've heard all about it, and are looking forward to it. Do you know Austin Freitag, who runs the coffee shop? I went to college with him, down in Iowa City. He's from here, as you probably know. So I've been hearing for years what a big deal the festival is."

"Austin went to school with my brother. And yes, the festival really puts Eagle River on the map. For two days."

Kate needed to run errands in Swanton yet this morning, as her first house showing was right after lunch. But maybe there was something else she needed to check out at the library. "Where are the high school yearbooks these days? Are they still along the far wall?"

Kyle pointed to one corner. "You got it."

A woman cradling a tall stack of books was on her way toward the counter. "Thanks again!" She waved at Kyle. "Maybe I'll run into you at the festival."

Kate wasn't sure what the yearbooks would offer, but she had to look. Milton would have graduated from Eagle River High School, what if there was something ...

Based on his age, she calculated backward. The late fifties, then. Milton should be in here, somewhere. She pulled out the volume from Milton's senior year, and admired the wildcat illustration on its embossed cover.

Local lore said when the high school began to offer sports, sometime around 1900, community leaders decided an eagle was a too-obvious mascot. Mountain lions and bobcats were occasionally still spotted in the fields and ravines, so a feline representative was chosen instead. The district's spirit colors were royal blue, white and black, with the dominant shade a nod to the river that ran through town.

Kate's fingers pulsed with anticipation as she turned the yearbook's yellowed pages. It didn't take long to find what she was looking for. Kate stared at Milton's photo for several moments, and felt a little disappointed.

But what had she expected? The snapshot was similar to those of many of the other young men in his class, most of them farm boys like himself. Crew-cut hair, black-rimmed glasses, button-down shirt, a small smile for the camera. His list of clubs and activities wasn't of much note, either. He was a member of the local chapter of Future Farmers of America, played basketball. No arts activities, not on the student council. Not a mover and shaker at Eagle River High School. Just one of the guys, probably too busy helping his dad run their farm to have time for much else.

She tapped the faded photo with a gentle finger. "What happened to you?" she whispered. "Where are you?"

Kate sighed, put the yearbook back in its rightful place, and checked the round clock high on the wall above the fiction section. She needed to grab her books off the holds shelf and run them over the scanner. Kyle was deep in conversation with another patron, and there wasn't a minute to spare.

* * *

Kate looked up at the water-stained ceiling and down at the scratched hardwood floors, and shook her head.

"I don't know," she mused. "It has character, I guess. But it might be more than I want to take on."

"It's a dump, honey." Donna was a petite woman, and her bright paisley scarf set off her chic pantsuit and silver hair. "Do you want to move on? I thought we might as well see anything with potential. Maybe that wasn't the best plan."

This was only the second house they'd visited, and Kate was already painfully aware of what was available: not much.

Their first stop had been a small subdivision on Eagle River's southwest side, by the middle- and high-school complex. It was the only area of town with newer housing, and its lone on-the-market property was chic, expensive and terribly boring. Even worse, Kate sensed the place wasn't quality construction. A few of the windows wouldn't open, despite the home only being five years old, and the kitchen cabinets seemed cheap and flimsy. It only took fifteen minutes to cross that one off the list.

This house was a story-and-a-half on the northwest side of town, built in the 1890s. It had tall, narrow windows, but not many of them. There were cramped rooms, narrow hallways and shallow closets. Kate might be able to get past the quirks, but the mess was another thing entirely.

The current owner bought it as a foreclosure a few years ago, and started an ambitious remodel. But based on the half-finished projects that littered every room, he'd hit several dead ends. It was as if the more he tried to help the old house, the more it fought back with uneven floors, rusting pipes and nasty surprises. Could it even be saved?

Her dad might be able to give Kate an answer, but she hadn't brought him, or anyone else, along today. She just wanted to get a feel for what was out there. And despite this old house's hidden charm, it wasn't worthy of a second visit.

"It's just too much," she told Donna. "I wouldn't even know where to start."

"I'm afraid it wouldn't matter. The current owner started here, and there, and over there." Donna pointed around them. "And he's given up." She reached into her stylish tote bag and pulled out two surgical masks, then a flashlight. "Since we're already here, should we stay for the haunted-house part of the tour?"

"Why not?" Kate wrenched open a wooden door and peered down the basement stairwell. There was an outdated light switch at the top, and she was pleasantly surprised when the yawning darkness below them took on a faint glow.

"Well, that's a point in its favor." Donna rolled her eyes. "Let's see if the mice are home."

A gigantic metal air tube, which would have served the house's first coal-fired furnace, still snaked its way to the large grate in the kitchen floor above. One tiny room was so filled with cobwebs, the women refused to enter. Donna's flashlight showed dirt-smudged shelves littered with empty canning jars. Except for a few filled ones of indeterminate age hiding in a back corner. A bowing foundation wall and asbestos-wrapped pipes completed the tour.

Kate brushed off her arms and ran her hands through her hair once they made it back to the comparative civilization of the kitchen, then made sure the door was shut tight behind them. "Wow, that was ..."

"There are no words." Donna pocketed her flashlight. "Even if you were interested, and I know you're not, he'd have to come way down on price given what we've seen. He doesn't have a lot of competition these days, but this is a money pit."

"I wish it wasn't." Kate lingered on the porch while Donna locked up. "The yard is beautiful, with all these perennials and trees. And the neighborhood? It's so charming."

"I know. Close to the river, but not so close you have to worry about flooding. Main Street's within easy walking distance. But then, you could say that about most of this town." Donna shrugged. "Two down, two to go. This next one's historical, but I think in a good way. I'll see you soon!"

Kate considered her options as she drove the three miles south to Mapleville. Old homes, new homes. A house in town, an acreage. There were so many ways she could go with this. But what did she really want?

Like so many things these days, Kate wasn't sure. And she was afraid that, in the end, the tight real-estate market was going to decide for her. Sure, she could stay in her apartment a while longer, but that no longer felt like the right option. Kate needed her own place, she'd opened that door the moment she and Donna made their first stop today. She just had to keep looking.

Her thoughts kept circling back to Ben, no matter how hard she tried to stop them. How excited they'd been when they started looking for a house in Chicago! They'd spent countless hours walking neighborhoods, studying online listings, dreaming about the future. Everything was planned out, just the way they wanted it to be, hoped it would be. They'd expected to spend the rest of their lives together, but only made it a decade. How could things have changed so much in so few months?

And then, everything else changed, too. And here she was, back home, trying to start over.

The Mapleville house had started out as a country school, then turned into a storage shed for the adjoining property when the school closed in the 1950s. It had been boarded up and vacant for a time, then was purchased in the 1990s and converted into a single-family home.

Unlike the last place, the renovations here were quality and period appropriate. The house had high ceilings and lots of natural light. There was a cozy yard out back, with a thriving vegetable garden. But despite its charms, Kate didn't love it. The flow of the rooms was odd, thanks to the retrofit of the building's initial use. On top of that, she wasn't sure she wanted to be right on the busy blacktop. Mapleville wasn't a hopping hamlet, except for the co-op, but this highway was the go-to route through this part of the county.

"I can tell this isn't the one." Donna gave Kate an understanding smile. "It's cute, but maybe it's too quirky. I know you're looking to put down deep roots somewhere, but you never know what life's going to throw your way. Not everyone is going to be interested in something this unique. Resale could be an issue when the market turns."

Donna raised an eyebrow. "Notice I said 'when,' not 'if.' Because it always does."

"I can't do it. It's charming, but you're right. I have to think about making a good investment."

She took a deep breath and tried for a smile. “One more?”

“One more. Let’s go.”

A little farm north of Eagle River had come on the market over the weekend. A house with seven acres of pasture, outbuildings, everything. It was probably too much, and too much money, but Kate wanted to see it, just in case. She kept saying town life was probably best for her. Where would she find the time and energy for an acreage?

But it was love at first sight. A classic T-frame farmhouse, with two open porches. Fully renovated inside, top-notch everything, like something out of a glossy magazine. The barn had been lovingly cared for over the years, even though it currently housed just a few horses. A big garden plot, lots of perennials, a sturdy windbreak. Kate could see herself here, with a few goats or sheep, some chickens, a dog ...

However, this fabulous-farmhouse fantasy didn’t come cheap. Even in a market this rural, primped properties still brought top dollar. Kate could swing it, she really could, but there wouldn’t be anything left to sock away in her retirement accounts. Besides, even at a place so carefully restored, something was bound to break, sooner or later.

“I wish I could,” she told Donna as they lingered by their cars. “I love it. But do I really want to look after this much stuff? I have to say, though, that it’s stunning. So much time and effort has gone into this place.”

“That’s just it.” Donna looked around them. “It’s perfect. Too perfect, maybe.” She thought for a moment. “I could see you with a little acreage, but nothing this big. And while the upgrades are impressive, they don’t leave you any opportunity to put your personal touch on things.”

“You’re right. Would I really feel at home, or like I was just the caretaker for someone else’s dream?”

Donna stuffed the listing printout in her tote. “I didn’t want to tell you, right off the bat, but I think there’s another offer coming on this place, tonight or tomorrow. They’ve had several showings already, and it's sure to go fast. I don't want to push you," she added quickly. "This is a big decision, so you need to take your time."

"Then this isn't the one." They'd been out for almost three hours, and Kate was exhausted. "I can't believe how tired I am. All we did was cruise around, see some interesting houses; it was fun. But there's so much to think about."

"That's why we are going to take this slow." Donna reached for her keys. "This fancy place has someone else's name on it. Your home is out there; we'll find it. And you never know when it'll turn up."

Kate knew Donna was right. She'd only visited a few homes on this first day, and surely, more and better properties would come on the market soon. But by the time Kate made it back to town, she was already feeling discouraged. Along with hot, tired, and thirsty. She deserved a treat after this whirlwind of a day, and decided The Daily Grind would be her final stop before heading home.

And her apartment, after all, was still home. Even if it wouldn't be for much longer. She just had to give it time.

There was a line at the coffee shop, but Kate was glad to wait. The place had only been open a few years, and was one of the most progressive businesses in Eagle River. Of course, that wasn't saying much, but Kate loved it all the same. It reminded her of when she attended college in Madison, as well as a few of the bistros she'd enjoyed in Chicago.

The coffee shop was housed in an old brick storefront, with oversized glass windows that flooded the space with light. Linen shades could be drawn down when the heat was too much, as it was on this afternoon.

The interior, with its hardwood floors, high ceilings and exposed-brick walls, was refreshingly cool ... just like those coffee-ice cream confections that were so in-demand this time of year. Kate could hardly wait to get her hands on one.

"Hey, Kate!" Austin called out as he bused one of the small round tables along the windows. "Is it your day off?"

"Sure is. I got my errands done. I'm exhausted, so I had to come in. I need some caffeine."

"You've come to the right place." Austin smirked as he stacked ceramic cups and saucers in his plastic dish tote. "Because we have the best coffee in town."

"The *only* coffee in town," Cordelia added from behind the counter. Austin's assistant handed one woman her drink, motioned to the next person in line, then gave her short, blue-streaked brown hair a defiant flip before she started the next order. "Because I don't count the sludge that comes out of those cannisters down at the gas station."

"You got that right," Austin insisted. He was in his mid-thirties, tall and wiry with dark hair and funky-framed glasses. Given the years he'd spent in Iowa City, which had extended far beyond college, he was the epitome of what folks around Eagle River would call a hipster. While some of them would mean that in a snide way, Kate thought what Austin had done with this once-empty storefront was admirable. The place had the kind of energy this town needed.

And Austin wasn't satisfied with the coffee, sweets and sandwiches. The first time Kate stopped in this summer, he'd shared his plans to convert one corner into a micro bookstore. And the upstairs? Well, it was just storage for now, but someday it would make the perfect art gallery.

The rent was cheap, as commercial properties weren't in demand in a town this small, so he might as well dream big, right? The landlord, an elderly man from out of town, was just relieved someone was interested in using the space.

As Kate waited for her turn at the counter, Austin sidled up to her with his dish pan under his arm and a sly grin on his face. "Now, don't be shy. You know what I'm going to ask you. I hope you'll say yes."

The woman ahead of Kate turned and smiled broadly at her, as if she had all this figured out. How cute! Austin was surely going to ask Kate out on a date.

Not so fast. Kate and Austin had never been more than distant friends. Even so, she knew what he wanted.

"Oh, OK." She sighed. "I have to work that Saturday, so I can't take on too much. But put me down for the corn-shucking chores."

The annual sweet corn festival was held the third weekend in August, from Friday evening through Saturday night. Which meant that on Friday afternoon, a crowd of local residents would gather in the auction barn's parking lot to peel the husks off thousands of ears of sweet corn. It was sticky, messy work, but Kate had to admit it was sort of fun.

"The corn-shucking *event*," Austin corrected her. "It's the kickoff to the whole festival! You know you need to be there. I'm sure you've missed helping out. Your grandpa would be despondent if you turned us down."

Kate hadn't participated in this ritual since high school. And Austin was right about the possibility of a family-based guilt trip. Austin was president of the small-but-mighty chamber of commerce, and he'd been after Kate for weeks to volunteer at the festival. Now that he'd extracted one promise from her, he tried again.

"Oh, I almost forgot," he added casually. "We also need a few more people to sign up for the competitive portion of the corn shucking."

When Kate shook her head in the negative, he tried again. "How about the eating contest, Saturday afternoon?"

"I have to work, remember? Besides, I like an ear or two, and that's enough for me."

"You know, being public employees and all, I think someone from the post office should participate in one of those events." Austin wasn't about to give up. "Can you ask around? You know, butter up a few people?"

Kate had to laugh at that. "Fine. I'll bring it up, but I can't promise anything."

"Excellent."

Kate paid for her mocha ice cream shake, then moved to the end of the counter while Cordelia set to work with the blender. Austin's excitement about the festival was infectious. She kept saying she wanted to meet more people, feel a part of the community again. This was the perfect opportunity to take a few small steps toward that goal.

"Kate Duncan! Is it really you?"

She turned to find a woman about her age in the to-order line. Kate scanned her memory bank but, while this person looked vaguely familiar, she couldn't come up with a name.

"Oh, I'm so sorry." The woman was suddenly flustered. Or maybe just eager for gossip. "It's 'Duncan' again, right? I mean, I heard that ..."

"Yes, you're right." Kate interjected before the word "divorce" crossed the woman's lips. With nothing else to do but wait, people in line had started to stare. Kate wasn't about to explain how her last name had never changed.

And thankfully, she now had the first name she needed. "Hey, Vanessa, how are you?"

"It's been a while." Vanessa's smile was bright, but a bit forced. "Our five-year reunion, I think. And where were you, for our tenth? We all thought you'd be there, with your parents still in town and all."

"I couldn't make it." Kate tried to sound disappointed. "Work, you know. The postal service never stops."

"Well, I'm a receptionist over in Charles City." Vanessa leaned on the freshly wiped counter, and Cordelia shot her an annoyed look. "Crazy-busy, of course. And then with the kids, thank goodness for those summer camps offered through the school, you know? I don't know what else we'd do."

Vanessa gave her order to Austin, who'd joined Cordelia behind the counter to get the line moving, then turned back to

Kate. When Vanessa lowered her voice, Kate knew what was coming next.

"So, is it true? I heard you were the one who discovered Milton was missing." Vanessa shook her head, her gesture almost sincere. "It must have been such a shock."

"Well, it wasn't just me. And he'd told his neighbor ..."

Vanessa rolled her eyes. "Oh, Jasper's not a reliable source, let me tell you. My dad's known him for years."

She had all of Kate's attention now. "Huh. Why is that?"

"Well, it's the whole family, really." Vanessa glanced around and began to whisper. "Always one step ahead of the taxman, if you know what I'm saying. So deep in debt, I can't imagine how they've held on to that farm for as long as they have."

"I haven't met Jasper," Kate said evenly. She waited for Vanessa to say she knew him well. Or that she knew him, at all.

When she didn't, Kate's frustration flared. Vanessa's observations weren't based on any personal knowledge. Like too many people in a small town, she merely parroted what she heard.

"Well, anyway, it just upsets me that Milton's disappeared." Vanessa wouldn't let the subject drop. "That day, when you were out there, it must have been so upsetting for you. Did you notice anything strange? There must be ..."

Cordelia arrived with Kate's shake, just in time. "Here you go." Along with the to-go cup, she passed Kate a look that said, *run while you can.* "Vanessa, yours is just about ready."

"Oh, wait, there is something else," Vanessa said before Kate could start for the door. "Almost forgot. My mom's in the Red Hat Society here in town, and they're thinking of allowing us younger ladies to join. Other chapters do, you know. What do you think?"

Kate was aware of the group. While her mom wasn't a member, she knew several older women who enjoyed the social time and volunteer opportunities that came with being in the club.

"I don't know." Kate smiled and took a step back. Suddenly, her schedule was jam-packed. "I'm really busy."

"You think about it." Vanessa patted her on the arm. "It wouldn't start until fall, at least. Just something they're kicking around, a way to get more members. Isn't that exciting?" And with her coffee in hand, Vanessa finally left Kate alone.

Austin laughed as he topped off an iced coffee with whipped cream. "Kate, you remember how things go around here, right? Don't let people know you have any free time on your hands, or they'll rope you into every little thing that comes along."

"Well, you would know." She took the first sip through her straw, and it was heavenly.

"Oh, don't put me in that category. The sweet corn festival's a big deal. More than worthy of your efforts."

"Let me know what time I need to be there." She waved and headed out into the heat.

As she reached for her car keys, Kate decided maybe she wasn't as lonely as she'd thought. Eagle River's pool of potential friends was shallower than Chicago's, but it still might be wise to fish for quality over quantity.

10

Just as Auggie predicted, Sheriff Preston stepped up his public-awareness campaign the day Milton's disappearance hit the two-week mark. Kate arrived at the post office Wednesday morning to find a freshly printed poster waiting on Roberta's desk.

"Deputy Collins dropped it off a few minutes ago." Mae held it up for everyone to see. "He was waiting in the parking lot when I got here, said they'll have them posted all over the region today. I'll take it up and get it on the bulletin board, front and center."

An article was on the Swanton newspaper's website before noon, and the case was featured on the regional television stations' evening newscasts. With a sinking heart, Kate couldn't help but notice that, just like with Milton's personal life, there didn't seem to be much to say: He was elderly, he'd been gone for two weeks now, authorities weren't sure if he was truly missing or just out of town. Call the sheriff's office if you know anything, or see his truck, or want to volunteer for the renewed effort to walk the secluded areas near his farm.

"That's it?" Bev was exasperated that night on the phone. "That's all Jeff can do?" Then she sighed. "I guess it is, from what he told me today. There's no sign of suspicious activity, no proof that someone's harmed the poor man. Not much to go on."

"Well, I suppose that's true," Kate admitted. "And this isn't a movie, it's real life. I don't know what I expected. A team of search-and-rescue dogs? Helicopters buzzing over town? A dramatic press conference with Jeff making heartfelt pleas to the camera?"

"That's just it. All that stuff costs money, he says, incredible amounts of money. Well, except for the press conference. But he's not one for public displays of emotion, and there isn't anything more to share, anyway. Without enough proof that something's truly wrong, he can't call out the calvary. Or justify the bill to us taxpayers."

Several days had gone by with no word from Jeff, so Bev had called him to see what new details she could uncover. As it turned out, not much.

Jasper was sticking to his initial statements about Milton's departure, and authorities hadn't uncovered anything that made them believe Jasper was lying. If his resolve would weaken as the weeks went on, well, that remained to be seen. And the only other thing Jeff had obtained so far also pointed back to Jasper, which left the sheriff turning in a circle.

Jeff wouldn't say which regional medical clinic Milton went to, but did tell Bev he'd been able to get access to Milton's emergency contact form. With no close family nearby, and the Tindalls just down the road, he'd given the front office Jasper's information.

Milton's health records, however, were another matter entirely. Sheriff Preston had no reason to believe Milton had any serious medical conditions, especially anything that might affect his cognitive ability. Jasper's timeline was the only one the sheriff had at his disposal so, up until today, he hadn't had any serious leverage to demand the clinic turn over copies of those files.

"He's going to make a run at those now," Bev reported to Kate. "But even if he gets them, it was pretty clear he can't share what they contain."

Auggie had been right when he claimed Milton didn't have a cell phone, and there was no sign of an internet-service account, either. That left the house phone and, while Jeff said those records would be easier to obtain than Milton's medical files, the process could still take time.

"So we wait," Bev said sadly. "And hope someone comes forward with something that can help Jeff find Milton."

Thursday brought a pleasant change of pace for Kate, and not just because the hot, humid weather had mellowed a bit. It was Aaron Thatcher's day off, and Roberta had asked Kate to take his route on the west side of town.

Kate enjoyed the rural routes the best. Bertha was old but she was still reliable, and driving the back roads cleared Kate's mind. Even so, it was fun to drive an in-town mail truck again, just like she had in Chicago. Eagle River only had two official vehicles, and one of them had been up for grabs this morning. It would save hiking back to the post office for more of her items, and also meant her bag would be lighter.

Walking a section of Eagle River gave Kate the chance to interact with more residents. But it also made her think about the customers along her last Chicago route. How she missed them! There was Ted Jackson, whose Lab puppy had finally learned to sit for one of the treats Kate always carried in her pocket. And elderly Opal Grafton, who always met Kate at the mailbox, as eager for a visit as she was her daily delivery.

As she parked the mail truck along Oakland Avenue, Kate wondered who she'd meet today. And looked forward to the blocks of historic homes that made up this route.

Long ago, this neighborhood had been home to Eagle River's most-prosperous residents, the mill owners and mercantile operators who founded the town. Their former homes were impressive in their size and grandeur, at least for a town this small, and walking this section made Kate feel like she was stepping back in time.

But over the decades, some of the houses fell into the wrong hands, or just into disrepair. Maintaining a historic property was very expensive, and not all of these were lucky enough to be tapped for restoration. The ones that had were recognized by Eagle River's small-but-vocal historical commission, and the others had to settle for a little paint and some substitute shingles now and then.

Kate loved these old houses. But she wasn't up to the task of caring for one, and none were for sale. So she admired them from the sidewalk, enjoyed the grand old ladies' interesting features and passed an understanding eye over their faded front doors and peeling trim.

Eagle River might be a world away from her former life in Chicago, but Kate still implemented the checklist her old crew used before dismounting from the truck.

Mail organized. Hat and phone. Keys. Dog treats.

And then she laughed. For there was a foe here on Oakland Avenue that she'd nearly forgotten about, one that wasn't easily befriended with a snack. Up ahead was one of the town's oldest trees, a towering specimen that graced the front yard of a three-story Italianate-style home. None of the neighbors recalled exactly how long this particular squirrel had lived in that oak, but everyone knew he (or she) was as territorial as they could be.

Kate liked to think this squirrel was female, and that she'd become so accustomed to defending her nest when it was filled with little ones that she now was on guard all year long. But whatever the reason, one thing was clear: this critter hated mail carriers.

The people living on her street were tolerated. Some of them set out corn for her and her fluffy-tailed friends, and more snacks were available on the ground under their bird feeders. The neighborhood dogs and cats were generally ignored, as a swift scramble up the trunk of a tree kept her out of their reach.

But those people who dressed alike, and invited themselves into everyone's yard, day after day?

They were the enemy.

The scolding started before Kate left the neighbor's porch. By the time she was next to the tree, Mrs. Squirrel was stationed at the far end of the biggest branch that shadowed the sidewalk, her sharp eyes trained on the trespasser below.

It's not the one from yesterday, she could see that!

Sometimes, the squirrel skittered down the tree trunk to face these foes head-on. The critter was also known to meet carriers on the front walk and run ahead of them to the porch, scolding all the way. Post-office lore said more than one carrier had been ambushed when the squirrel jumped out at them from around the corner of the house.

The most-dramatic story came from Jack and, as one might suspect, that tale starred himself. Back before he switched to a rural route, Jack was on his way down the sidewalk one day when the scolding started up in the tree. Before he turned up the walk, something went *thump* on the crown of his straw hat.

It was a walnut. Launched from the limb of an oak tree in early summer.

Jack insisted that meant only one thing: this territorial beast had such a grudge against the Eagle River post office, that it had carried out a sneak attack with a projectile from the previous winter's food stash.

Kate had her own approach to this situation, and it had worked so far. What was the saying? You can charm more squirrels with honey than with vinegar?

Jack had a big ego, and he wore it like an ill-fitting suit. Kate suspected this smart squirrel could sense that, even from high up in her tree, and had felt the urge to take him down a peg. After all, there were days Kate wanted to chuck a walnut at Jack's head, too.

"Good afternoon to you," Kate trilled at the squirrel. "Aren't you looking cute today? It's such a nice afternoon!"

Maybe a little acknowledgement was all the squirrel wanted. She flicked her tail in a half-hearted warning, then pivoted to keep a keen eye on Kate all the way up the front walk. But Mrs. Squirrel remained at her post, and Kate was allowed to deliver the day's mail without incident.

With that potential crisis out of the way, Kate continued on her route. Most of the deliveries were made up of the usual stuff, but there was a handful of pastel-colored envelopes for the elderly widow in the next block. Aaron had let Kate know that Myrtle Bradford's ninety-second birthday was tomorrow, and greetings had been rolling in for almost a week.

Like Mrs. Squirrel, Myrtle always kept an eye out for the mail carrier. She just happened to be watering her front-stoop planters by the time Kate left the neighbor's yard. Myrtle must have been at the front room's picture window before that, because Kate spied the chair pulled up to the other side of the glass. Percival, Myrtle's little terrier, had since claimed the seat for himself.

"Well, hello! Anything for me today?" Myrtle shuffled in Kate's direction, a cane in one hand and her watering can in the other. It was likely empty by now, but Kate still cringed at how Myrtle tried so hard to keep her balance.

Kate quickened her steps and reached Myrtle before the old woman could go much farther. "Of course! Lots of good mail for the birthday girl." She gently took the watering can from Myrtle's veined hand. "Here, let me help you with that. Should I put it back inside the house? I'll set it there on the table, with the mail."

"Well, that's really nice of you." Myrtle seemed pleasantly surprised by this suggestion. Kate wasn't sure if that was an effort to maintain dignity, or if Myrtle honestly didn't remember Aaron often did the same.

Myrtle's once-grand home had a cozy vestibule with a closet, a built-in bench, and a small credenza just inside the door. She was too proud to fill out the form to have her mail brought to the entrance, rather than left in the box at the curb. But the carriers often carried it inside, especially during the winter months, to lessen Myrtle's chances of falling when she hobbled out to meet them. Because just like it was for Opal Grafton back in Chicago, the mail's arrival was a highlight of Myrtle's day.

Once she was safely back inside, Myrtle had an offer to make. "I baked some cookies this morning. Maybe you need one? And a glass of lemonade?"

Kate knew Myrtle hadn't baked the cookies herself. Her home health aide stopped by every morning, and Patty's considerable baking skills were well-known among the post office's crew.

"I really should move on soon," Kate said gently, then reached down to give Percival a pet. "But I can smell how good the cookies are. How about I take one with me?"

She lingered inside the door while Myrtle shuffled into the kitchen and came back with a folded paper napkin in her hand. "Here's two. To keep up your strength."

"Thanks." Kate laughed and tucked the cookies in her bag. Oatmeal-chocolate chip, she guessed by their mouthwatering aroma. "I hope you have a good birthday tomorrow. Aaron will be back, so he'll come by with your mail."

"Oh, it will be good to see him. It's been so long." Aaron had been there just yesterday. "My family is coming for dinner tomorrow night. We're going to have lasagna and cake!"

"I'm so glad you'll have company here to help you celebrate. Happy birthday, Myrtle! And thanks again for the cookies."

Kate finished the rest of the block, then returned to the truck and drove to where this neighborhood met up with the back of the business district.

There weren't as many of them, but these once-grand homes had been chopped into apartments decades ago and fallen on harder times. Apparently one guy from Mason City owned most of the properties and, while they weren't exactly blighted, this area didn't offer the genteel appeal of Myrtle's street.

As Kate prepped for the rest of the route, she was reminded of how grateful she'd been to snag the vacancy in Roland's building. There weren't many apartments in a town as small as Eagle River, and she'd toured one on this street that was dreary and depressing. It had been carved out of the second floor of a Queen Anne-style house, and its main features were a stale-smelling kitchen and tiny, awkward rooms.

Still, these residents made the best of what they had. All the houses had porches, and patio chairs and tables were arranged to take advantage of summer breezes. The lawns were mowed and relatively free of debris. Hanging baskets swayed on their hooks, and old-time flowers still bloomed along the foundations.

All these houses had multi-compartment mailboxes in their lobbies, which had been gracious front halls during more-prosperous times. Kate was just locking up one building's depository when a woman came down the wide front stairwell.

"Oh, am I glad to see you!" She started for the wall, mail key in hand. "Been looking for something. Where's Aaron?"

"Off today, back tomorrow."

The woman opened her box and riffled through its contents. "Hmm. Well, maybe it'll turn up by the end of the week." She glanced back at Kate and studied her closely. "You're the new carrier, right?"

Kate smiled and introduced herself. The Eagle River crew was small, and she'd learned fast that, while they weren't exactly local celebrities, they were close enough. People saw them walking around town, and driving the back roads, and depended on them for so much.

It was an honor to serve, even though people's curiosity sometimes was more than Kate was used to dealing with. She hadn't heard the next question in several days, but it was the one she expected to hear. Especially after Sheriff Preston's renewed efforts to drum up awareness about the case.

"So, you're the one that found Milton?" The woman quickly corrected herself. "Sorry. I mean, you're the one who realized he was missing. That must have been very upsetting."

She seemed sincere enough. Kate was about to point out, once again, that it was still possible this was all a huge misunderstanding. But with a sinking heart, she realized that explanation was losing potential as the days slipped by.

"Yes, it was unexpected, for sure. But we called the sheriff right away, and the deputy he sent out was so kind and understanding. We turned everything over to him, and went on with our day."

"I'm sure they're doing all they can." The woman leaned in closer, as if sharing a secret. "But they should have found that poor old man by now. I mean, where could he be, and gone this long? That's just my point, I guess. Milton never really went anywhere."

Kate was eager to get back to her rounds, but maybe she could spare a few minutes. Especially if this woman had something interesting to share.

"Oh?" was all she said, and leaned against the wall. Kate was learning that sometimes, the best way to get a lot of information was to say as little as possible.

"Well, you know, he didn't go far, just errands and such." The woman tucked her mail against her side, and crossed her arms.

"This whole thing about Milton, it just bothers me. See, my husband and his buddies go down to Paul's Place a few nights a week, after work. The beer's cheap and I guess the burgers are decent. Decent enough that I don't have to cook him dinner when he gets home." She frowned. "Which is just as well, as the kids are ready for bed by the time he turns up."

"I haven't been there yet, since I got back," Kate admitted. "Actually, I don't think I've ever set foot in the door."

"You're not missing much." The woman rolled her eyes. "Well, Jake says Milton used to come in, every once in a while. Not enough to be one of the gang, but a bit of a regular. He's quiet, you know the type. But I guess he loosened up after a beer or two. Nice guy."

Kate nodded, and the gears turned in her mind. Did the sheriff know about this?

Maybe. If so, his deputies had already canvassed the bar and prodded the usual hangers-on for tidbits regarding Milton's personality and habits. But what if he didn't? Or, just as likely, Sheriff Preston had taken a run at the regulars, but they clammed up as soon as someone in uniform walked in the door.

Maybe it was worth a try. But Kate wasn't about to go there alone.

"We shouldn't give up hope yet." She shouldered her mail bag and started for the door. "Maybe something will shake loose, and soon."

And thanks for the best tip I've gotten yet, she thought but didn't say. *Walking a town route certainly has its advantages.*

* 11 *

Karen scooped peanuts out of the plastic bowl at her elbow. “OK, so what’s our game plan?”

“I don’t really have one.” Kate already had two peanuts unshelled. She gave them a try, and made a face.

“Eww, these are stale. I guess we’re here for the ambience, not the snacks.” Classic rock wafted from speakers perched in the small bar’s corners, their volume kept low so they wouldn’t compete with the robust conversation that circled around the dark-paneled room.

“Well, the AC’s cranked, and there’s music.” Karen shifted on the cracked pleather that covered the sagging booth’s seat. “Ouch. Maybe I shouldn’t have worn shorts. The lights are low enough that you can’t really tell how clean this place is.”

Kate pulled a miniature bottle of hand sanitizer from her purse, wiped her palms, and passed the disinfectant across the scratched laminate table. “Let’s assume it’s filthy, and try not to use the ladies’ room.”

She’d almost set her purse on the floor by her feet, but had decided against it. And it’d been wise to not wear open-toed sandals.

Something sticky was keeping the bottom of one tennis shoe from sliding across the worn linoleum, but she didn’t want to look close enough to find out what it might be.

Bev had loved Kate's idea to take a run at the Paul's Place crowd. Sheriff Preston, however, was less enthusiastic. Deputies had already stopped in a few times, he'd told Bev, and didn't drum up any solid leads.

But if someone else wanted to soak up the atmosphere, they were welcome to try. After all, "everyday folks" might have better luck talking up the regulars.

Bev wasn't about to set foot in this bar. She'd been here only once, many years ago when it was under different ownership, and it was already a dive back then. Karen and Kate had been planning to get together for lunch, and Karen wanted to introduce Kate to Melinda.

When Kate suggested a change in plans, and shared the real reason she wanted to check out Paul's Place, Karen had laughed and said, "why not?"

Although it was difficult, Kate didn't reveal her inside track to Sheriff Preston. She simply promised to alert authorities if this bar visit netted any gossip that backed up what she'd heard while on Aaron's route.

It was Friday happy hour, and the place was packed. All the bar stools were taken, and only two of the eight booths had been vacant when Kate arrived ten minutes ago. Stares of curiosity, if not outright hostility, had met her when she walked through the door, and she'd been glad when Karen arrived only a moment later.

The lion's share of the patrons were men, most of them in trucker hats and all of them wearing tee shirts and jeans. Only a few appeared to have cleaned up after work before they'd assumed their usual perches. The few women milling around wore weary smiles and too much makeup. Just as one might expect, the aroma of stale beer and cooking grease seemed to hang in the air.

Kate tried hard not to judge, but she couldn't help it. This certainly wasn't her crowd. And it didn't seem like Milton's, either. But then she remembered how Max said Milton liked to go to the riverboat casino sometimes; or at least, he used to. Maybe her take on Milton hadn't been entirely accurate.

Which meant, if the ladies played their cards right, they might get something out of this visit other than fresh-grilled burgers and fries. Actually, those sounded really good right about now.

"Oh, there's Melinda!" Karen waved in the direction of the door. "I can't wait for you to meet her."

Melinda Foster moved back from Minneapolis two years ago to help her aunt and uncle run Prosper Hardware. From what Karen said, Melinda had a bumpy transition when she returned home, and hadn't planned to stay.

But now, she was poised to take over the family business someday when her aunt and uncle retired. In addition to her little farm and her animals, Melinda had someone special in her life: Josh Vogel, a veterinarian over in Swanton. At forty-one, Melinda wasn't likely to have kids, and she was fine with that.

She and Josh had been dating only seven months now but, according to Karen, he looked to be "the one."

After several twists and turns, it sounded like Melinda was now on a solid, comfortable path. Kate was very curious to discover how she'd done it. The closing for the Chicago house was Monday and, even though Kate's part of the process would be completed online, it was still a significant step in her efforts to rebuild her life.

"Hey, girls!" Melinda slid in next to Karen. Her brown hair was pulled back in a ponytail, and she'd gotten the memo about attire: old shorts and a tee shirt. "Sorry I'm late. Pepper was in a snit when I got home, wanted some extra attention and bugged me until I gave it to him. I think the sheep teased him quite a bit today."

Kate nudged the peanut bowl across the table. "If you're feeling adventurous. Is Pepper your dog?"

"Her donkey," Karen put in with a grin.

"Hobo's my dog," Melinda explained. "But my donkey shares his pasture with the ewes. Most of the time, they get along. But not always."

Along with the donkey and the dog, Melinda's acreage was home to eight sheep, two outside cats, two inside cats, and over a dozen chickens. Kate thought of the perfectly restored acreage she'd visited the other day, and knew she'd made the right choice to let it go. Two potential buyers started a bidding war, and the place was now under contract for far over list price. Besides, she didn't need room for that many critters. Right?

"Kate's just starting to look at properties," Karen told Melinda. "She had quite the adventure the other day."

Melinda shook her head in sympathy over Kate's string of house tours. "I guess I had it easy, then. My place practically fell into my lap, and I rented it at first. When Horace was ready to sell, I was ready to buy."

"How is Horace?" Karen wanted to know. "You haven't mentioned him lately."

"He's doing great. Won the Scenic Vista checkers tournament last weekend, second year in a row."

Kate was stunned to hear that Horace Schermann, a lifelong bachelor, had remained at his home farm until he was nearly ninety. He'd only left it when his brother's roommate moved to another nursing home. Kate immediately thought of Milton. Would he be able, or even willing, to live alone in the country for another decade?

Melinda leaned over the table and lowered her voice. "You know, when I heard about Milton Benniger, I thought of Horace right away. Their situations are similar; or at least, they were until ..." She frowned, worried. "Oh, I hope Milton's not in the past tense, if you know what I mean."

"Why are we whispering?" But Karen did the same. "Aren't we here to drum up leads? If someone hears us talking about Milton, maybe they'll chime in."

"Well, I don't know," Kate admitted. "I heard he came in here, but this crowd seems too young." Some looked to be her age, some a generation older. But still, not exactly Milton's demographic.

"Maybe it's different at other times of the week," Karen suggested. "On other nights, or even in the afternoons, there could be a different clientele."

Melinda laughed. "Excellent observation. You have a knack for this stuff."

"Thank you. I'm feeling pretty good about it, myself."

Kate sighed. "I think I'd feel better if someone would come by and take our order."

Karen looked around. The guy behind the bar seemed to be the only staff member on duty, other than the teenaged dude flipping burgers in the back. She motioned to the bartender, and he gave her an annoyed look.

"What's with him?" Melinda wondered. "You think he'd want to make some money off us."

With another scowl, he tucked his towel into the waist of his apron and came out from behind the crowded bar.

"Oh, my," Karen whispered. "Don't tell Eric, but I might be in love."

She didn't have to say more. It was obvious the bartender worked out, as his efforts were clearly visible beneath his snug-fitting gray tee shirt. Kate guessed he was in his thirties and, while she wasn't going to admit it to Melinda and Karen, she'd noticed him as soon as she walked in. Just a little.

Thick brown hair, soulful brown eyes. Maybe the best way to describe him was "ruggedly handsome." Or just hot. Either way, right now, he was steaming angry.

He stopped at their booth and crossed his arms. "You girls want something?"

Kate looked at Karen and Melinda in shock, then turned back to their impatient visitor. "Well, yeah, we'd like to order some drinks and food."

He jerked his thumb at the bar. "We don't wait on people here. You gotta come up front if you want stuff."

His dark eyes scanned them with a piercing look Kate couldn't quite read. "You ladies must be new." It wasn't meant as a gesture of welcome.

Melinda sighed with irritation. "Look, Paul ..."

He barked out a laugh. "Seriously? That's not my name."

"Are you sure?" Melinda stared at him. "It's on the sign."

"She's from Prosper," Kate said quickly, as if it were a hundred miles away instead of ten.

"Figures. No, I just decided that name had a nice ring to it. Paul's Place. It fits the vibe, don't you think?"

Kate didn't know *what* to think. Other than he was the rudest, and best-looking, bartender she'd ever met. Then, it started to make sense. If this guy really was the police chief's cousin, as she'd heard, he could probably do as he pleased in this town.

"So, who exactly are you, then?" Karen was back to tracking down answers. Or at least, getting them some dinner.

"Alex Walsh." He shrugged. "Alex's Place doesn't have quite the same ring, huh? Now, I gotta get back. What do you want?"

Kate was going to ask for a menu, but decided it wasn't worth the hassle. And she was starting to think they didn't exist. She was right.

All they had were burgers, Alex said. Fries or coleslaw on the side. It cost extra if you wanted both. Beer on tap or in bottles, three kinds total. Mixed drinks, too, as long as you didn't want anything fancy. The women gave him their orders, and he just nodded.

Melinda smiled. "Well, aren't you going to write those down?"

Kate bit back a laugh, as Melinda was clearly tired of this guy's attitude. Kate was, too, but maybe she could overlook it.

Especially when there was so much to look *at*. She was a long way from being ready to date again. But if she could feel any attraction to a guy other than Ben, that was a good sign.

"Gee, I think I can remember them, they're all the same." Alex was about to leave. "Oh, for the beer: Do you want a bucket?"

Kate couldn't hold back this time. She burst out laughing. "OK, Paul, or Alex, or whoever you are."

He glared at her, a sudden hint of suspicion in his eyes. "It's Alex."

"Yeah, Alex. We're hungry and we just want one round, OK? I don't know about my friends, but it's been a very long time since I've drank so much that I needed to throw up."

"Are the burgers that bad?" Karen asked innocently.

"I think there is something sticky under this table," Melinda put in.

"That's not what I meant." Alex was doing his best to keep a straight face. Kate realized that, just maybe, this gruff exterior was for show. At least a little bit.

"No, see, we have a special where you get six bottles in a bucket of ice." Alex evaluated the trio again. "And there's a bigger discount for a dozen, but I wouldn't recommend it for this table."

"I'll take that as a compliment," Melinda said.

"I'll bring your beers out." Alex acted as if this was a great concession on his part, reserved for only his favorite patrons. "But when the food's ready, you'll need to come get it."

He slid away, and the women were silent for a moment.

"Wow, he's interesting," Karen finally said.

"He's cute, that's what he is." Melinda reached for the peanut bowl. "Has that bad-boy vibe about him."

"You got that right," Karen said. "But seriously, how does he expect to win and keep customers with that attitude?"

Kate tried to study Alex further without being too obvious about it. If she was going to find out what happened to

Milton, she needed to learn the players in this game. At least, that's what she told herself.

Alex didn't even give them a nod when he left their bottles on the edge of the table. But when a woman at the end of the bar beckoned to him, he hurried right over and gave her a disarming smile. Kate felt a flicker of irritation and looked away.

"I'm starting to think some of this is for show," she said. "Not all of it, but some. The crowd in here's a little tough, but look how happy everyone is. And the longer they stay, the more money they spend. The only other bar in town is too preppy. Where else would they go?"

"True." Melinda nodded. "Maybe he's smarter than we think."

Kate wondered if she should even try to unearth any clues about Milton. It would be awkward to randomly ask people, and could even arouse suspicion. Because she was starting to think there were people in town with things they could say, but hadn't.

And then she remembered that in a small town, good gossip was a valuable currency.

She'd been relieved when the questions and comments about her afternoon at Milton's farm had dwindled, but maybe it was time to rehash the situation. Karen had been there, of course, and she was here right now. And while Melinda had heard about the incident from Karen, she'd just met Kate.

Oh, this was going to be easy. Anyone around them with even a smidge of curiosity wouldn't be able to stop themselves from joining the conversation and mining Kate and Karen for details. And maybe, they'd let something useful slip. The alcohol flowing through this bar certainly wouldn't hurt.

Karen and Melinda were all-in on the idea. "You're right," Karen said. "Two eyewitnesses, right here at this table? They won't be able to help themselves."

"Hey!" Alex shouted from the other side of the bar. "Your burgers are up."

Karen and Melinda fetched the baskets while Kate held down the booth. More people had wandered in, which meant the little bar was now standing-room only. The noise level had grown as well, between the increase in patrons and the Chicago Cubs game now showing on the two screens behind the bar.

The burgers were excellent. Kate didn't know where Alex had found the young guy in the kitchen, but he knew his way around bar food. After the ladies finished most of their meals, it was time to start the show.

"Well, Kate," Melinda said in a voice just loud enough to carry into the next booth. "You and Karen had quite the adventure out at Milton Benniger's last week! I want to hear all about it."

As Karen and Kate began to rehash their story, Kate sensed their conversation had attracted at least a few listeners. The trap was set. Who might step into it?

"I just can't imagine," Melinda said now, with an overheated gasp. "I mean, when you realized that Milton was missing? How scary!"

Karen stifled a smile. "We called the sheriff right away, didn't we?"

Kate nodded vigorously. "Oh, yes. It was the right thing to do." A man leaning against the bar was watching them out of the corner of his eye, she was sure of it. "We weren't about to start snooping around on our own. It could have been dangerous!"

"We didn't know what had happened," Karen told Melinda. "Milton could have been there in the house, dead, for all we knew!"

Then she leaned toward Kate and raised her voice a bit more. "Do you remember what a relief it was when the deputy came up the lane, all those flashing lights?"

Deputy Collins hadn't needed to turn on his emergency flashers. But Kate thought, why not? It upped the drama. "He was so helpful, put us right at ease. When it was time to give him my statement, I ..."

"Hello, ladies." The guy from the bar was now at their table. Just as Kate had hoped he would, he plopped down on the edge of the booth, beer in hand, and said his name was Clark.

Kate guessed him to be around fifty. Not Milton's age but, judging by his weathered expression and how drunk he was, he probably hung out at Paul's Place more often than not.

"I couldn't help but overhear." Clark slurred his words a little, but his eyes glittered with curiosity. "Am I in the presence of the two heroes who brought Milton's plight to the attention of the authorities?"

"You certainly are." Kate was eager to pounce on Clark's insinuation that Milton was in trouble. But instead, she forced a smile. "Do you know him?"

"Oh, sure." Clark stretched his legs out into the aisle and settled in. "He came around here some. Not always, you know, but some."

"I feel so left out that I never knew Milton," Melinda said. "Everyone else around here seems to. What's he like?"

Clark started to ramble. Kate hoped for something of use, something interesting, but came up empty-handed.

Milton was a nice guy. Not too chatty, but more so once he had a beer or two, like most folks. Lived around here his whole life, you know. He loved that old truck of his. Everyone told him to trade up, but he wouldn't. He'd taken it hard when his dog passed away three years ago, said he wasn't going to get another one.

"What about his family?" Karen gave a frown of sympathy. "They must be so worried."

"Oh, his sister moved to California a long time ago. She died a few years back." Clark shrugged and chugged his beer.

That seemed to be all he had, and Kate started to review her options to get this guy to leave. An empty seat was the best chance they had to draw in someone else.

"Hey, Todd!" Clark suddenly called across the room. "Come over here!"

Todd was a little younger than Clark, but just as drunk. "Hey, what's goin' on?" With no place to sit, he put his hands on the table for a little support.

"They're the ones that found out Milton was missing!" Clark pointed at Kate. "That's the mail carrier, and the other one's that lady vet."

Karen's jaw tightened with annoyance, but she wisely kept silent.

"You don't say!" Todd shook his head. "Well, we sure miss Milton around here. I really hope he comes back soon."

"So he's just gone, then?" Kate leaned in. "You don't think something's happened to him?"

"Naw. Who'd hurt a guy like Milton? He was everybody's friend."

"Well, maybe not everyone," Clark said. "I mean, he had some pointed opinions from time to time."

Before Kate could press Clark on that observation, Todd crouched next to the table, like he had something really interesting to share. "Most everyone likes him, though. I mean, everyone around here. And for good reason."

Clark rolled his eyes. "Are you on that kick again? You don't know anything about it."

"I sure do." Todd was indignant. "My dad always said so." He turned back to the women. "See, sometimes, when Milton came in? He'd buy everybody a round. And he could afford it, too. He's rich, you know."

"Rich." Karen gave Melinda and Kate a doubtful look. Then she laughed. "Just because he bought some drinks once in a while? I've never been here before, but I have to say, the prices are pretty cheap."

"No, no." Todd was whispering now. "I mean, *loaded*. See, his family had all this money, and ..."

"Like a hundred years ago," Clark interrupted. "The Bennigers raised this one kind of cattle, made serious cash. I can't remember the details, but whatever. They went bankrupt, eventually. And that was way, way back. I mean, long before the depression."

Kate thought of the old Benniger farm, and how grand the house would have been in its heyday. No wonder some people might think the family was still flush. But too often, legend was far more interesting than reality.

"I still say it's true." Todd used the edge of the table to lift himself up. "But no one believes me. No matter how many times I tell them."

When Todd wandered off, Clark pointed his beer bottle at Kate. "Just ignore him. I mean, he's into all those conspiracy theories and such. Since Milton disappeared, Todd's mind, or what's left of it, has been working overtime." Then he smiled. "Milton's a great guy. But it's just being neighborly to buy a round, now and then. People did it for him, why wouldn't he reciprocate?"

Alex appeared to be busy pouring drinks behind the bar, but Kate sensed he was watching their booth closely. It made her uneasy.

Or maybe it was just that Clark didn't have anything else to share, but was in no hurry to move on.

Melinda and Karen seemed to be thinking the same thing. "Well, it was nice to meet you," Melinda said briskly. "But we need to settle our tab and get going."

"I'm tired," Karen added quickly. "My husband will be wondering where I've been." She and Eric were only dating.

"Mine, too," Kate said.

That did the trick.

Clark suddenly spotted another friend on the other side of the room.

"Nice touch," Kate told Karen after their guest melted back into the crowd.

"Oh, I really am tired; that part is true. But this was so much fun! We have to get together again, and soon." Then Karen grimaced. "I'd rather not, but I think I'd better use the little girls' room before I head out."

As Karen started off through the crowd to the back of the bar, Melinda asked Kate about the next steps in her house search.

"I'm feeling a little overwhelmed," Kate admitted. "Which is funny, since there's not much to pick from around here. I have to ask: How did you know that you'd made the right decision, moving back?"

Melinda thought for a moment.

"Well, I didn't at first. It was supposed to be temporary. And then, it just seemed I was meant to stay. Are you having second thoughts?"

"No. I don't know. I grew up here, but it's been harder than I thought it would be, to settle back in. It's different, I know. I'm not the person I was when I left for college."

"That's the key, I think. Or at least it was for me. I had to give myself permission to start fresh, even though I was back where I started."

There was a sudden commotion in one corner of the room. A woman and a man started to argue, then another guy stepped between them. The two men were soon in each other's faces, shouting profanities that drew bemused looks from nearby patrons, while the woman added her two cents.

"You're just in time for the real drama," Melinda told Karen when she returned. "How is the bathroom?"

"Gross, as expected." Karen sat down, but she didn't seem to want to stay for long. "I think we should get out of here."

Kate agreed it was probably time to call it a night. All they'd netted was a bit of gossip that didn't seem to hold water. "The facilities are that bad, huh?"

Karen leaned in so she could be heard over the growing uproar across the room. One guy had just shoved the other in the chest, and a few bystanders looked as if they were about to jump into the fray.

"Oh, it's not the bathroom. On the way back, I got a good look behind the bar. Alex keeps a baseball bat on the shelf under the cash register. Which makes me think he's no stranger to trouble."

Kate grabbed her purse. "In that case, I'm glad his cousin's the police chief. Let's go."

12

Kate was tapped to work the front counter on Tuesday, since Roberta had a regional manager's meeting in the morning and planned to take the afternoon off.

The post office didn't open to the public until nine, so Kate's first task of the morning was to tidy up the back area and the break room.

As the other carriers sorted their mail on the main space's tables, she pulled on a pair of rubber gloves and stared down the mysterious items lurking in the staff's refrigerator. Most of them might have been edible at one time, but Kate could no longer be sure.

It was a messy, smelly job, but Kate didn't mind. The Chicago house's sale was finalized yesterday, and she was in the mood to make a clean sweep.

"I've got something for you." Bev came into the kitchen as Kate pawed through the far reaches of the top shelf. "Something good. Or bad, maybe. I don't know."

Without pulling her head out of the refrigerator, Kate gestured toward the garbage can at her side. "Did Jared leave the rest of his sandwich on the counter again? Roberta's been after him to stop being such a slob. Toss it in. It's all going out to the dumpster, first-class priority rush, before the mice can find it."

Bev's steps crossed the room in double time, which caused Kate to finally look up. There was something in Bev's hand, all right. And it wasn't a disintegrating turkey-on-wheat.

A business-sized envelope, whose fine fibers and soft cream color hinted at great expense and weighty purpose. Bev held it up. "Exhibit A. Mae just found it."

As Kate peeled off her gloves and washed her hands at the deep sink, she couldn't take her eyes off the envelope. She didn't need to hold it, however, because the front of it told her what she needed to know.

It was from an attorney's office in Des Moines. Addressed to Milton Benniger.

"This was in with the rest of her route's stuff." Then Bev smiled at her own foolishness. "Of course it was, that's her usual turf. What I mean is, well, what do you think it's for? And more importantly, what should we do about it?"

As Kate stared at the innocuous envelope, she sensed it was actually the opposite. This was important, one way or another. Far more so than any of the gossip she'd netted Friday night at Paul's Place. Over the past few days, she'd studied that conversation several times. She'd thought about Alex, too, but never mind that.

Todd's claim that Milton was rich had been quickly shot down by his buddy. But even if it happened to be true, did it have any bearing on why Milton was missing? Kate took comfort in the fact that, if Milton was financially comfortable, there was at least a small possibility he'd gotten a whim to book a long cruise or jet off to Europe. Or, if he was as low-key as everyone said, found a luxurious island resort where he could soak up the sun in relative solitude.

Even so, that didn't explain his secretiveness about where he was going. And when, or maybe if, he planned to return.

Of course, piles of cash could mean someone had a motivation to harm the old man. But who would stand to benefit from Milton's passing? Or at a minimum, the chance he could eventually be declared dead? Kate didn't have a handle on that sort of thing, but decided it might be possible.

Her mind worked through all those scenarios again as she studied the elegant envelope. Its contents surely held clues to Milton's life, even if they didn't shed light on his disappearance. Of course, this sort of mail wasn't always good news. Kate had delivered enough legal-based items over the years to know they were far-more likely to be about money woes than secret riches.

If nothing else, this attorney's office held the key to finding more people with connections to Milton. Oh, if only they could ...

"Well, we definitely can't open it," she said with a sigh.

Kate's voice was so full of disappointment that Bev laughed. "We sure can't. But I'm dying to know what's inside." She blinked. "OK, maybe that's not a good word to use, in this instance."

Mae popped into the break room and shut the door behind her. "Kate! I can't believe it. When I saw it in my pile, I just knew it was important."

"Can we hold it, for any reason?" Kate hated the idea of this envelope leaving the post office. At least, not yet. If only Roberta wasn't at that meeting! She'd know just what they could, and couldn't, do.

"I don't think we can." Bev shook her head. "Although I suspect the sheriff would like to get a look at this."

The front of every piece of mail was digitally scanned as it went through the postal system, so it could be automatically sorted by zip code and street address. The process made the carriers' work infinitely easier, but they still had to organize and double-check their delivery stacks to be sure nothing was out of line.

While the scans weren't permanently stored by the post office, they remained available for a period of time and law-enforcement officers could request to review that information if they believed it might help solve a case. Even so, it was illegal for the post office to open someone's mail, except under very-rare circumstances when there were concerns about a suspicious package. And even then, there were strict procedures to follow.

"Well, Mae," Kate said, "you're the senior staffer among the three of us. Any ideas?"

"I want to steam that thing open as much as you both do, but we can't." She threw her arms up in frustration.

"If Milton planned to be gone for this long, why didn't he just fill out the hold form? That would mean it was all here, and secure." Then she shook her head. "It's just one more reason I'm worried this absence wasn't his idea, after all."

Because Milton hadn't requested his mail be held at the post office, the drivers could only cease delivery if the box became too full. Mae kept a close watch over Milton's mailbox and reported Jasper had been emptying it twice a week, per Milton's instructions.

But given the increased publicity about Milton's disappearance, maybe that wasn't often enough. His continued absence could draw less-than-savory people to snoop around at his farm, especially at night. Such folks wouldn't be above popping the mailbox open and rifling through its contents.

So with Roberta's blessing, Bev had stopped by the Tindalls' farm on Saturday and asked Jasper to pick up the mail every day. It was the best possible solution until something changed.

However, there was still the chance Jasper wasn't telling everything straight. And a piece of mail like this one might be too tempting to leave alone.

"I don't know Jasper," Kate said, "but do you think he's honorable enough to not open this? Or anything else, for that matter?"

Bev shrugged. "He's the only ally we have right now. Most people's mail is pretty boring, day after day. But this?" She held up the envelope again. "This just screams, 'I'm important.'"

Bev reluctantly handed the envelope to Mae. "You have to get going, as do I. I'm not sure if this is the right thing to do, but I feel like we need to pass this information to the sheriff."

Kate reached into her back pocket, then changed her mind. "It doesn't feel right to take a photo of the front, especially with my personal phone." She grabbed a scrap of paper and a pen off the break room table. "How about I just write the firm's info down?"

"It's already in the system," Bev reasoned. "This just saves us from having to search for it if the sheriff filed a request."

"I concur." Mae raised an eyebrow. "We're not playing by the rule book, but I don't know what the rules exactly are."

"Maybe it's just as well that Roberta's out," Bev said. "We can always beg for forgiveness later."

After Mae hurried out of the break room, Kate and Bev huddled at the table.

"I don't like this," Kate whispered. "And I don't mean taking down that name and address. We needed to save the information. It's just that Jasper ..."

"Could be more involved in all this than what he's saying," Bev finished the thought. "I hate the idea of handing that letter over to anyone but Jeff at this point, other than Milton himself."

"And he doesn't seem to be around." Kate put her head in her hands. "Oh, none of this adds up!"

"Don't get discouraged." Bev reached across the corner of the table and squeezed Kate's shoulder. "Remember how pleased Jeff was with what you girls gathered at the bar the other night? He's so grateful you're helping out. That maneuver was something his deputies never could have pulled off. They are so well-recognized in the community, even out of uniform, that those guys never would have opened up to them."

"A lot of good it did." Kate rubbed her eyes. "A couple of drunks with a silly story. And I think we narrowly escaped getting caught in a bar fight." She had to smile. "I hadn't realized such a simple undercover assignment could be so dangerous."

"That gossip may or may not be useful to Jeff. The important thing is, you tried." Bev thought for a moment. "I hope Milton's off enjoying himself, but if he's not ..."

She shook her head. "I don't know him well, but I think he'd be touched that a stranger's making such an effort on his behalf. Actually, even if he left under his own power, I believe he'd still feel the same."

Bev looked Kate in the eye. "You care, and that's what's important. I know you're still young, but as we get older ... someone who cares? Well, that means more and more as the years go by."

Kate nodded slowly. "Especially for someone like Milton, who doesn't have many people in his life."

"Exactly." Bev stood up. "Now, if you'd be so kind as to hand me that slip of paper, I'll send the details to Jeff right away." She squared her shoulders.

"I'll tell Roberta what we've done. I don't think the fur's going to fly, but you never know."

* * *

Roberta's return text praised the ladies for noticing the letter and getting the contact information to the sheriff as quickly as possible. Maybe it had been an unorthodox move, but Kate took heart in that, in the larger scheme of things, they'd done what was right.

She hurried through the rest of her cleaning duties with a lighter heart. Bev was right; this wasn't the time to let up on the search. That envelope was the perfect example of how quickly the situation could change, how suddenly a solid clue could fall right into their laps. Or, in this instance, Mae's mail case.

Milton stayed on Kate's mind as she worked the counter that morning, and not only because of the new clue the carriers uncovered. Thanks to the flyer on the post office's bulletin board, the old man's shy smile was on full display in the lobby.

The "Have you seen me?" plea across the top of the poster deepened Kate's resolve to stick with the case. If everyone in the community stayed vigilant, and passed on anything that seemed unusual or noteworthy, it could bring the authorities one step closer to solving this mystery.

Kate hadn't worked the post office's counter for several weeks; the last time had been just days before her wild afternoon at Milton's farm. So she wondered if he would be a topic of conversation and concern. But by noon, there hadn't been one word.

How was that possible? If Jasper was telling the truth, Milton had been gone three weeks as of tomorrow. Every day that passed without word from the old man was one more sign something wasn't right. And it had been only six days since the sheriff raised the case's public profile. Were people really so caught up in their own lives that Milton had already been forgotten?

Despite people's dependence on digital communication, the post office's bulletin board was still a popular hangout for notices on everything from lost pets to church suppers and kids looking to mow lawns for extra cash.

Maybe that was the problem, Kate decided during one lull in the action. Several new flyers had crowded in on Milton's real estate. She took a few moments to rearrange the board, remove posters for now-past activities, and straighten the items that were left. Milton stayed front and center, right where his notice could catch people's attention.

The afternoon brought a steady stream of visitors to the counter, but next week's sweet corn festival and the start of school at the end of the month were at the top of customers' minds.

"Fifteen thousand ears of corn, can you believe it?" one man asked Kate. "Why, that's so much, it has to be some kind of record."

Kate shrugged. With Grandpa Wayne so involved in the festival, she recalled years where the haul was even higher than that. "Well, if five thousand people show up, like last year, that's three ears per person. Either way, it's going to be a great time."

"And that band!" The woman behind him was eager to join the conversation. "I hear they cut a demo down in Nashville, just last month. Poised to break into the big time, my neighbor says." She smiled proudly. "Her son knows the drummer, from college down at Ames. It was a stroke of luck the committee booked them six months ago. They're sure to draw a huge crowd."

"Me, I'm leaving town that night," grumbled another man. "I love the festival, too, but we're just off Main, over there on Fourth. I swear, the noise from that street dance gets louder every year."

The woman laughed. "Harold, maybe you're just old."

"I guess anything's possible. But seriously. They should do something about that, make them turn down those amps. This city has a noise ordinance, you know."

"The dance brings people to town from all over," Kate reminded him. "The festival really keeps Eagle River on the map."

Another man with a parcel had just come in the door. "I know what you mean about noise. They started up marching-band practice last week over at the high school. Two-a-days, sometimes. The kids are out there, blasting away, the minute the sun comes up."

Kate motioned for the guy to put his box on the counter. He might as well, as this rambling conversation was bound to go on for several more minutes.

"It won't be long before Friday-night football will be back in action. My nephew says he's starting this year."

"Did you hear, the council might not let us burn leaves any longer? Who wants to bag all that stuff up? This isn't Swanton. I don't see why we have to change how we do things around here."

"You been to the library lately? That roof leak is something terrible. It's such an elegant building. Can't someone do something?"

Kate smiled and nodded and waited on her customers, all the while hoping someone would mention the fact that Milton was still missing. She'd chime in if they did, throw out something that might prompt them to drop a crumb of useful information or even just express concern for the elderly man's fate.

But when the group finally dispersed, still chattering about the ins and outs of everyday life in Eagle River, Kate was left alone with her thoughts and concerns. And that poster in her line of sight.

The envelope. It had to turn up some kind of lead. Because it was starting to look like the case was in desperate need of one.

* * *

Milton wasn't top-of-mind for some residents, but the handling of his mail quickly became the focus of the post office's weekly staff meeting Wednesday afternoon.

"OK, everyone, let's get started." Roberta rubbed her hands together and took her seat at the head of the break room's table. "I won't keep us long. It's not beastly hot, for once. We all want to go home and get stuff done outside, especially if it's going to rain tomorrow."

"My garden's a weed pile," Marge muttered. "I think I'd rather stay and sweep up the office."

"Suit yourself," Mae said. "Hey, Bev, how are those tomatoes coming along?"

Jack leaned down the table. "What she really means is, when will you bring us some more? They're the best I've ever had. What are they called, again?"

"German Pinks. They're going gangbusters and we're canning like crazy. I'd say the final surplus starts next week."

Roberta adjusted her reading glasses and studied her notes. "That's an important announcement. Far-more exciting than what I have to share. And Bev, I'll take as many of those tomatoes off your hands as you're willing to give me."

Bev elbowed Kate. "I'll be sure to keep back several dozen for next Saturday," she whispered.

Kate had asked her new friend to join the Duncan ladies for their annual tomato-canning marathon. The Stewarts only lived a few miles from Kate's parents, but they didn't know each other well. Kate was eager to bring the neighbors together, and gather with her relatives, all at the same time. And put up some jars of those heirloom tomatoes before the growing season ended.

Roberta ran through several announcements for her team, whose members listened intently but without much comment.

This wasn't an especially busy time of year, although more parcels were expected in the coming weeks as families prepped for the start of school. Many area residents were trying to pack in their last vacations of the summer, and the number of hold requests remained high.

"And that brings me to one other topic." Roberta sighed, as if she expected a bit of resistance from her staff. Then she glared at Jack, and Kate knew resistance had already been raised. And likely in a rather-vocal fashion.

"As you all know, Milton Benniger is still missing." Worry

flashed in Roberta's eyes, and Kate was glad at least some people were still concerned about him. "Milton went to high school with my dad, I hear he's a nice guy. Anyway, that's neither here nor there."

Jack gave a grunt that could be read as skepticism. Roberta ignored him.

"I had a chat with the sheriff this morning. He wants us to keep an eye on Milton's mail. We had something come through yesterday that, while it may be of no use whatsoever, could possibly provide a lead on someone who might know where Milton is."

Jack stared at Kate from across the table. She raised her chin, but stayed silent. By now, everyone knew she'd written down what was on the front of that envelope. She wasn't sorry, not one bit.

"Well, we already sort everyone's stuff." Allison didn't seem to have an issue with the sheriff's request. "But I don't really pay attention to it. Too much volume to look after." There were nods of agreement around the table. "What exactly are we looking for?"

"Mae will handle most of it, since he's on her regular route, with Kate filling in," Roberta explained. "But I wanted everyone to be aware. He's been getting mostly junk mail, the newspaper. Electric and phone bills, the usual. We just need to watch for things that stand out. Like that item from an attorney's office in Des Moines. There could be other things as well, such as anything that looks like a greeting card, or a letter."

"People are still writing letters these days?" Jared asked in mock surprise.

"Milton's old, so he's probably old-school," Allison reminded him. "I heard he doesn't even have a cell phone."

Jack crossed his arms. "What Roberta means is, we're looking for anything that's personal. Private. You know, stuff that's really not our business."

"A man is missing." Bev sat up straighter. "I'd say that's our business."

"We have a duty to the community." Roberta tapped the table for emphasis. "The sheriff needs our help, and we're going to give it."

"Look, I don't want anything bad to happen to anyone, either." Jack frowned.

"But I hate to say it: It's been, what? Three weeks now? Either something bad's happened to Milton, and it's too late for anyone to help him. Or, most likely, he's got a damn fine reason for being gone."

Mae narrowed her eyes at Jack. "Like what? He's over eighty."

"I have no idea, and that's exactly my point! It's not our business. I just want to go on the record as saying I'm opposed to spying on people's mail."

Randy let out a bark of a laugh. "Duly noted. Or it would be, if anyone ever bothered to take notes at these things."

Mae sighed. "Jack, I can sort of see your point." She held up a hand. "But I'm worried about Milton, too. This is an unusual situation, so we need to do it. Of course, this speaks to the broader issue of customer privacy. Do things like this blur the line between public and private? I mean, where does this stop?"

"What does the handbook say?" Aaron asked. Laughter erupted around the table and dispersed some of the tension.

"There's one on my desk, and I know you all have a copy," Roberta intoned in her best schoolmarm voice. "Without referencing the depths of its great knowledge, I'll remind all of you that the front of every piece of mail is automatically scanned into the system."

"That's different." Jack tried another tactic. "I think most people would be livid if they thought we were studying what they sent out, and what came in. And I say, let the sheriff fill out one of those review requests if he's so nosy."

"That's just a pile of red tape." Marge dismissed the idea with a wave of one hand.

"How long could it take to process that? Every minute counts, if there's even a chance Milton is in some sort of trouble. And the sheriff's not asking to see every piece of Milton's mail for the past how-many months, he just wants us to keep an eye out. That's all."

Kate wanted to jump into the fray, but decided against it. She'd worked hard to build camaraderie with Jack, but his resistance on this issue could cause their goodwill to unravel in a matter of minutes.

And it wasn't just because she'd taken down the address from the front of that letter.

When Grandpa Wayne retired from the Prosper post office, he'd put in a good word for his top carrier, Glenn Hanson, to take over the shop. Jack had eyed that post for himself, had seen the much-smaller town's lead position as his best chance to break into management.

From what Grandpa had said, Jack still held a bit of a grudge over the perceived snub. Kate was trying her best to stay out of the way.

Besides, it already seemed as if most of the team agreed with the sheriff's request. Or at least, didn't object to it.

"People probably already think we're peeking at their mail," Randy said. "You all know how people badger us for whatever gossip they can get. Why do you think that is?"

Jack wouldn't let it drop. "But it's not right!" He turned back to Roberta. "Your dad knows Milton. High-school buddy, right?"

"I didn't say that. They weren't friends."

"What does it matter?" Mae wanted to know. "Everyone knows everybody. Here in town, or out in the country. We all have to set our personal relationships aside, sometimes. As for Milton, if we went around the table, I'm sure some of us, even in an indirect way, have some tie to him or this case."

Kate felt Bev stiffen at this sudden turn in the discussion. Did anyone here know Bev and the sheriff had been high-school sweethearts? Kate held her breath and waited. But it seemed that even Jack, as nosy as he was, either had no idea or was keeping that one under his hat.

Roberta glanced at the clock, then steered the conversation back to her original premise.

"I promised Sheriff Preston we would continue to be vigilant as we make our rounds. And we will immediately alert him about anything of note we come across related to Milton." She shot Jack a look. "And that includes the outwardly facing, already-scanned portion of his mail."

"We owe it to him," Jared said. "Milton, I mean. I guess the sheriff, too."

There were nods around the table. Even Jack finally gave a curt dip of the chin.

"Now, that's what I like to see." Roberta smiled and stood up. "Teamwork, community service, the whole nine yards. Let's get out of here and head home. Tomorrow morning will come soon enough."

13

The mail drop in Mapleville was Kate's favorite part of the route southeast of town, as it was a nice break from the gravel roads. With only eight houses and the co-op to visit, it was a good opportunity to get out and stretch her legs.

Eagle River's post office had serviced this tiny community for over a century. Although it was never incorporated, Mapleville had a post office until the early 1900s. It was housed in the front room of one of the now-vacant stores at the community's only crossroads. Grandpa Wayne probably knew which one, but Kate couldn't be sure.

The "for sale" sign was still in the yard of the converted schoolhouse on Friday, but Kate knew she'd made the right decision to pass it by. And she was even-more certain when Donna called to say there was a property on the outskirts of Eagle River that Kate needed to see. Right away.

"It'll go fast, I'm afraid. Honey, this could be the one. Nice house, not too big. Mature trees in the yard, garden plot, a couple sheds, just over an acre of land."

"An acre?" Kate gasped as she lingered in one house's driveway. "That seems like too much to look after. I don't know, maybe I'm better off right in town."

She and Donna had viewed just two properties since their marathon session last week, and neither had felt right to Kate.

But the more she considered her options, Kate wasn't sure she wanted the country life. At least, not right now.

She was single, living alone. Would she feel too isolated, out on some gravel road? Especially at night. Sure, it was wonderful at her parents' farm, but there were always other people around.

Grandpa Wayne had cheerfully suggested firearms training. And Ben, when she'd talked to him the other night about the last of the house-sale paperwork, had said the same. Kate considered herself to be a resourceful woman and, until she'd been attacked on her Chicago route, hadn't been one to flinch at a challenge. But she doubted a gun was the answer.

Getting her own place, however, increasingly seemed like a great idea. One of her neighbors was moving out at the end of the month, and Roland was looking for another tenant to take that unit.

The three current renters got along well, but there was always a chance that would change with someone new in the mix. And with that apartment's living room on the other side of her bedroom wall, Kate was getting anxious to find a new home.

So when Donna gushed about the sort-of-rural property with the too-big lot, she was eager to see it.

"I hear the house is a little dated, but it's cozy," Donna promised. "And while it's on the gravel, you can see the edge of Eagle River from your front yard. It's not out in the middle of nowhere."

"How soon can we get in?"

Their slot was set for four that afternoon. Starting work as early as she did, Kate had the advantage of being off sooner as well. And with some locals working in Charles City, or even Mason City or Waterloo, being employed right in Eagle River had its benefits. From what Donna said, Kate would be the first to see the place.

And in this hot market, every hour would count. If Kate loved it, she wasn't going to get days to make up her mind. Other offers would likely be on the table in the morning, Donna had cautioned her, and the listing was sure to be under contract before the weekend was out.

When Kate made it back to Bertha, the dash clock showed it was nearly two. Just a few hours to go, and Kate would know what's what.

She noshed an energy bar, swigged some more of her water, and left Mapleville in her rearview mirror.

As the gravel dust billowed behind Bertha, Kate wondered again at the wisdom of buying a home in the country. Her mail car was always desperate for a bath, and that couldn't be helped. But what about her personal vehicle?

For over a decade, trips to her parents' farm had been the only time she'd had to really think about how clean her car was, or if there was too much gravel gunk stuck to its undercarriage.

Even so, Kate marveled at the views outside Bertha's windows and wondered what it would feel like to wake up to such scenes once again. A carpet of rolling, rich pastures and wide blue skies. The rich colors of fall, when the combines hummed in the fields until well after dark. Blankets of sparkling snow. The fresh green of new growth in the spring.

"And the mud," she reminded herself as she pulled up to the next mailbox. A hot breeze slapped her face when she rolled down the window. "And the wind. The icy roads in the winter. What am I getting myself into?"

Had she already decided? She hadn't even seen the place yet. But something about Donna's excitement was contagious. Was this was the place where Kate would make a fresh start?

* * *

She rushed home from the post office to change her clothes, then hugged Charlie on her way out. A right at the stoplight, then a short meander to the east edge of town. As soon as the blacktop left the city limits, she watched for the first gravel intersection and turned south. Two acreages slid past, both of them seemingly well-kept. So neighbors were close, at least on this side of the property. She crested a slight rise in the road, and there it was.

The vintage house was a foursquare, with a wide front porch and a hip roof. All brick, with white trim. There was the realty sign at the end of the driveway, which made a little bend as it entered the yard. A two-car garage sat comfortably next to the house, and three outbuildings were just on this side of the pasture fence.

The barn was gone. Donna said it was taken down years ago when it became too difficult, and too costly, to repair it. But that was fine with Kate. A green expanse of lawn, dotted with flower beds and large trees, was what caught her eye.

Donna was already out of her car, pacing with excitement, when Kate pulled up in front of the garage.

"Well, what do you think?" Then Donna laughed. "Oh, I can tell that easily enough by the look on your face. Isn't it adorable?"

"Where do I sign? If the inside's half as stunning as the outside, I think I'm in love."

Donna held up a cautionary hand. "It's in solid condition, as I said, but things indoors are very outdated. Cosmetic only, but there's a lot of it. Unless your personal style is 1970s Grandma."

"Oh." Kate nodded. "So that's the secret. I thought the price was really fair, given the market."

"But you have the cash," Donna reminded her. "And if you can find good help, and the time it'll take, you could really make this place special." She dangled the front-door key in her hand. "Let's take a peek."

The front porch stretched the entire length of the house, and its swing looked west across the front lawn. A row of sturdy evergreens partially screened the yard from the road. Inside, a small foyer held the staircase, a closet, and a cute built-in bench.

The home was built in 1924, in the Craftsman style that was so popular then. Donna couldn't be sure, but the plans likely came from one of the do-it-yourself house companies popular during that time. The entry hall opened into the living room, where a large picture window fronted the porch and a double window looked south over more of the lawn. The tile around the fireplace looked to be original.

The living and dining rooms were connected by an oak-trim opening with built-in bookcases and columns on each side. But there was no built-in buffet in the dining room.

This style, in a different form, was popular in many Chicago brownstones, and Kate was a little disappointed to discover this long-ago farmer hadn't splurged for some of the extra details. But there was so much natural light, and a little pantry. The kitchen also opened into the front hall, and its back door was protected by a closed-in porch.

Upstairs, the three bedrooms weren't terribly spacious, but one of them had a charming window seat. The only bathroom was right by the top of the stairs, above the kitchen. There was a small sleeping porch, currently enclosed with screens, on one corner.

"Not an inch of space wasted," Donna said as she opened the built-in linen bureau in the upstairs hallway. "Unfortunately, that includes the closets. But I'm glad someone found a way to put an extra, modern one in the front room. That's the master."

As Kate took it all in, her bright smile started to fade. "It's cute, and not too big. But I see what you mean about the outdated finishes. They are everywhere."

Sage-green carpet filled most of the house, with a sculpted rust-brown version tacked down in the smallest bedroom. The only other flooring on display was the faux-square linoleum that filled the kitchen and bathroom. The kitchen's cabinets were coated in a dark stain, and looked to be the product of a forty-year-old remodeling job. Wallpaper was everywhere, and none of it was especially pretty.

But Kate looked past the dusty, pinch-pleated draperies and the jarring paint colors. The house was a grand lady, if not a showy one. Kate could see herself here, even in its current, dated state. For once, she wasn't scared off by the basement, which had solid walls and a surprisingly current heating-and-cooling system.

The yard was wonderful. There was a small garden plot, although its vegetable plants were becoming crowded by weeds. An elderly couple had lived here for years before the husband died a while back, Donna reported. The woman had tired of trying to keep this place up with the help of her adult children, and had found herself a little ranch house in Eagle River. Which, true to Donna's word, was visible beyond the farm fields across the road.

"She's moving into town, and you'd be doing the opposite." Donna looked around the yard and gave it a nod of approval. "Trading places, if you will."

They inspected a tiny building that Donna guessed had once been the well-pump house, then toured a still-sturdy chicken house with a surprisingly high ceiling. Up under its tall, steep peak, a bank of south-facing windows mimicked the ones in the wall below.

"This is a nice building." Kate looked around and inhaled the still-lingering scent of straw. The structure was sort-of swept out, with just some crates and old lawn implements sitting here and there. "And that big machine shed looks solid, too."

"There are even a few stalls in there." Donna made sure the chicken house's door was securely latched, then gave Kate a knowing smile. "The pasture's not large, but the fence is sturdy enough."

"I see what you're about. Just enough room for a handful of something furry and four-legged."

"Or maybe just feathered and two-legged." Donna jerked her chin toward the elaborate chicken house. "There's a little grove of apple and pear trees over there, behind the garden. And a bit of creek runs through the back corner of the pasture. Let's go see."

By the time they returned to their cars, Kate had made up her mind.

"Are you sure?" Donna hedged a bit. "I can tell you love it, and the price is fair. But this is still a big decision. Just because it'll sell fast, doesn't mean you have to jump in right now. Do you want to wait until after dinner, even? First thing in the morning?"

Kate considered that, then shook her head. "I'd rather make an offer and see how it goes. If too many people jump in, I might have to bow out, but ..." She grinned from ear to ear. "This is the place! Or at least, I hope it is. Being out here reminds me how much I missed the country, all those years in Chicago."

"I'm sure this woman would love to have someone like you take it over." Donna reached into her car for her laptop, and the ladies wandered back to the front porch and sat in the scroll-iron chairs across from the swing. Donna started the offer paperwork, then suddenly stopped.

Kate gave her a quizzical look. "What? Oh, no! Is there something you forgot to tell me? It seems too good to be true. It's haunted, or the septic line's about to burst."

"Don't worry, we're good." Donna leaned in with a smile. "But something just occurred to me. We'll come in with a strong price, it'd be foolish to underbid in this market. But I think something else, something personal, might make your offer stand out."

* * *

Kate had to admit, it was a great idea. Donna filled out the paperwork and sent it to the listing agent, with the promise of another document to come yet that evening.

"Just put some feeling into it," Donna told Kate as they lingered in the yard. "Tell this woman exactly why you love the place so much. She's emotionally attached, I hear, which is understandable after living here half of her life. She'll get a great deal no matter who she chooses, so why not pick the young lady who promises to take good care of it?"

Another car was about to turn up the lane, and Donna reached for her keys.

"Time's up. That's the agent for the next showing. Say what's in your heart. Either way, you can't go wrong."

Kate hurried home and, with Charlie next to her on the couch, tried to do exactly that. As she typed away, a lump formed in her throat. She wanted this little farm, more than she'd wanted anything in quite some time. Things had been so difficult this past year; change, even when it was for the best, was always hard.

"You should see it," she told Charlie, who was nearly asleep. Once Kate made it clear he couldn't sit on the keyboard, he'd quickly lost interest. "There's a window seat that you're going to love. And the views! We'll set up a bird feeder or two, right there by the house. OK, scratch all that for now. Let's not get ahead of ourselves."

Kate read her letter over, twice. Then she reheated some leftovers for dinner, and gave it another go. She closed her eyes, offered up a quick prayer, and sent it off to Donna.

Sleep came easily that night, quicker than Kate expected. She woke Saturday morning with a sense of excitement, and a little trepidation. Her note to the acreage's owner, which felt so meaningful and personal last night, now seemed pushy and dramatic. And was she really going to buy a property after seeing it only once? She could afford it, but that wasn't the point.

Donna was right; this was a big decision. But Kate had already thrown her hat, and her heart, in the ring.

Other bids would come in today, that was certain. Her initial offer, no matter how meaningful it might be, was sure to be challenged in price. Kate could bow out gracefully if it came to that. And besides, there would still be the obligatory inspections if she did get the nod.

Kate always kept her phone in her purse when she was on her rounds, so its beeps wouldn't tempt her while she was driving. But she turned the radio's volume a bit lower than usual, and watched Bertha's dash clock as the afternoon dragged on. Donna promised to call as soon as there was any news, either way.

Kate was out southwest of town and, just before she came upon the country church where Grandma and Grandpa Burberry had been members for years, her phone rang. She pulled off into the wide patch of gravel where cars parked for Sunday services.

The letter had moved the acreage's current owner to happy tears, Donna said. Two other candidates entered bids higher than Kate's, but not by much. Would she be willing to come up a little more and match the highest current offer? If so, the place was hers.

"She won't even allow the others a chance to counter." Donna was so excited she was almost shouting. "Kate, she wants you to have it. What do you say?"

"Yes. Absolutely yes!"

After a few more minutes of conversation and celebration, Kate got back on the road. As the miles added up and the letters in her mail case dwindled, her mind ran ahead to all that was to come. Sometime in September, the little acreage would be hers. Plenty of time to make some changes during the fall, be really settled before winter arrived again.

Kate was home, had been for a few months now. And soon, she'd have her own home, too.

* 14 *

Everything happened quickly after that, and Kate took it as a sign it was meant to be.

With the updated offer accepted, Donna lined up the needed inspections. Kate knew Roland would be disappointed to lose another tenant in such a short span of time, but that wasn't the reason she decided to keep the good news quiet, at least for a few weeks.

There was always the chance something would go wrong, that the deal could fall through. And as excited as Kate was about this acreage, she knew there was little else available if something didn't pan out.

So she kept her announcement limited to family and close friends. But as she waited to meet with the loan officer at Eagle River Savings Bank, where she'd had accounts since she was a girl, Kate realized word of her impending purchase might soon be spread far and wide.

"You're buying a house? That's so exciting!"

Lindsey's nameplate was new and bright. As the receptionist for the main officials of the bank, she prepped paperwork for their meetings as well.

Which was unfortunate, since her desk was right out in the open. And Lindsey apparently didn't know the meaning of the word "discretion."

"Well, I have an offer in." Kate kept her voice down, and hoped Lindsey would take the hint. "So we'll see."

"Oh, don't worry, things will sail right through." Lindsey waved it all away with the abundant confidence of a woman barely in her twenties. "Of course, every once in a while ... I mean, look at the Carlsons' deal, last week." She snapped her fingers. "Fell apart at the last second. Shouldn't have taken out that truck loan while they were in escrow."

The woman at the next desk stared at Lindsey in horror.

"But you don't have a thing to worry about," Lindsey assured Kate. "Gosh, your credit is excellent: 805!" She was studying something on her computer screen that Kate couldn't see, which made Kate very nervous.

"And wow, what a haul from that house in Chicago! Just huge, even after you paid off the rest of the old loan." She leaned over her carefully organized desk and smiled. "You know, you always hear how outrageously expensive properties are in those big cities, and I can see that it's true. I mean, with your divorce you only got half the proceeds, but still."

Kate was rarely speechless. But right now, she didn't know where to begin.

Not only was this girl rude, but she was likely also violating an ethics policy. Did this place have one? It should, and Kate now wanted to see it for herself. Besides, the feds had a zillion regulations for everything, anyone with the post office knew that. She wondered what they would say about little Lindsey here. Kate briefly entertained herself with the idea of several men in expensive suits marching in and escorting Lindsey out of the building.

Finally, she gave the younger woman an icy smile. "Have you worked here long?"

"Oh, no, just three weeks or so." Lindsey shrugged, then sashayed over to the nearby printer. "But it's amazing what you see, working at a place like this. And hear."

"Really."

Lindsey began to sort the printouts with the careful eye of the inexperienced. "Let's see, this goes with this. And these go here." She looked up, her blue eyes filled with curiosity. "You did get half, right?"

"Half?"

"The money from the house. Your ex isn't one of those dirtbags, I hope. My sister, she was married to one. Not anymore, you see, and I told her that ..."

"I got my share." Kate glanced at the clock, then at the closed door to the loan officer's suite. He wasn't the most personable guy, but he seemed knowledgeable and fair. Kate had briefly considered one of those online mortgage companies, then decided she wanted to stay local.

But a faceless corporate entity looked pretty good right now.

"Glad to hear it." Lindsey stacked the papers with an air of oversized authority. "I mean, what a huge wire transfer!" She shook her head in awe. "We don't get many of those."

Kate blinked. "It wasn't that much."

Lindsey leaned over her desk again. At least this time, she kept her voice down. "You're just about rich! It's like, before you moved back, Milton Benniger was our only high roller."

Milton.

"Oh, really?" Kate's sudden curiosity was genuine, and Lindsey apparently loved a captive audience.

"Well, it's not for me to say." The younger woman was whispering now. "But he's loaded, from what I hear. Oh, he's not flashy about it. I think he just draws on his Social Security, like most old people. But there's so much more than that." She nodded gravely. "He's old money."

"Old money." Kate couldn't help but play along. "Like what? Do you mean steel, or railroads?"

Lindsey didn't grasp the sarcasm. Those two ways to become filthy rich hadn't been common for over a hundred years, and now were only found in historical melodramas.

"Maybe, I'm not sure. But that old truck he scoots around in? It's all for show."

This was the second time Kate had heard a version of this story, which had her wondering if there was any possibility it was true.

She then pondered who was more credible, a drunk guy in a bar or a young woman who maybe read too many silly novels. It was a toss-up, and she was glad she didn't have to choose.

And then, her curiosity about Lindsey's gossip quickly turned to frustration.

Milton was still missing, and here this girl was babbling about his personal finances to a total stranger. His money, no matter how much he had, wasn't anyone's business but his own. As was hers.

Kate's irritation was further fueled by what she'd discovered online last night, when she was so excited about her acreage that she hadn't been able to fall asleep.

She finally had time to make a deep digital dive regarding the attorney's office that sent Milton that letter, and was shocked at what she found. One of the firm's now-retired partners was investigated for financial fraud several years ago. The case had been dropped for lack of evidence, but ...

Was nothing sacred anymore? Could you trust anyone, anywhere, to just show up and do the right thing? Maybe Milton's ties to that firm hadn't been affected, but she couldn't be sure. If he was working with them in any way, he'd trusted them to handle his affairs in a professional, legal manner.

Just as she'd assumed her hometown bank would look out for her interests. But maybe she'd been too trusting. With someone like Lindsey on their payroll, she had to wonder. This young woman interacted with several clients every day. How many other confidential details had she blabbed during her few weeks in this job?

Although it looked like she might not have it much longer. The woman at the adjacent desk was no longer in her chair. Kate spotted her in a glass-walled office on the other side of the bank, and she and a grim-faced man soon started toward Lindsey's desk.

"You know, I don't care what kind of truck Milton Benniger drives." Kate snatched away the stack of papers before Lindsey could even react. "But I do care that he's still missing."

"Hey! I need those to ..."

"No, you don't." Kate stuffed them in her tote bag.

"Miss Duncan?" The loan officer was now at his door. "I'm sorry to keep you waiting."

"Don't worry. I needed a few minutes to sort some things out." Kate started toward the bank's entrance. Or in this case, her exit.

"Where are you going?" Lindsey called after her.

Kate didn't even bother to answer. She marched out into the humid sunshine, then leaned against the brick for a moment and closed her eyes.

Keep asking questions, Ben always said. *The first answer isn't always the real one.*

There hadn't been a bank in Prosper for years, but there were two in Swanton and more in Charles City. Pre-approval was a quick process these days, and Kate was willing to start over.

She pulled out her phone and texted Karen. *When you bought your house, where did you get your loan?*

Kate went home to change into shorts and a tee shirt, and had a new lead five minutes after she walked through the door. One of the banks in Swanton had top-notch customer service, and its manager was the husband of a Prosper book club member.

Melinda used them, too, Karen reported. Their longtime loan officer had been solid, if a little gruff, but that didn't even matter since he'd retired at the end of June. The new guy was Tony Bevins, the chief of Prosper's paid-on-call emergency department. Kate called Tony right away and, after a few minutes of conversation, set up a meeting for late that afternoon.

"Good thing it's my day off," she told Charlie, who insisted on his second brushing of the day before Kate left for more errands. "It's important to get this right."

Kate looked around her apartment and felt a pang of sadness under her excitement. This had been her home, if only for a few months. And in some ways, it was going to be hard to say goodbye. She had several more weeks, though, before that time would come.

However, she was likely to get possession ahead of closing since the current owner had already moved to town. Kate wouldn't put much effort into the place until the deal was officially done, but she could at least fine-tune her renovation ideas.

Charlie had jumped down from the couch and disappeared. Just as Kate was about to pick up her purse and leave, he returned with his favorite toy mouse in his teeth. His chirps and trills made it clear he wanted a game of toss-and-seek before she left.

Kate threw the stuffed critter halfway to the bedroom door, and Charlie gamely ran after it. "There are no long hallways at the farmhouse, buddy. But I promise you, there'll be so many other cool places to explore."

She treated herself to lunch at The Daily Grind, which further lifted her spirits. And while she was on her way to Swanton in a few hours, she had some shopping to do in Eagle River first.

Maybe she wouldn't get her loan at her hometown bank, but she could still support local businesses.

Eagle River Pharmacy was in the next block down from the coffee shop, and its grand storefront harkened back to the town's early days. Chris Everton had operated it for several years, as he'd bought the place when his former boss retired.

While the pharmacy's five short aisles contained many of the everyday items local residents needed, some of it was in very small quantities. Kate was reminded of this on her first visit after she'd moved back, when she spent a good five minutes debating if she should take the last bar of one brand of face soap.

Chris had given her a hard time, and told her not to be shy. He'd had four more in the back, which would tide his customers over until the next shipment arrived in a few weeks.

His wife, Janet, managed the floral department that was tucked into one front corner of the store. It had a steady flow of business through the one funeral home in Eagle River, along with the usual requests related to holidays and special occasions. A single rack of greeting cards nearby hit all the seasonal highlights.

The shop's lofty ceilings gave it a gracious air, and the industrial gray carpet on the floor helped muffle the rounds of chatter that echoed through the space. Kate usually had to gently interrupt at least one conversation as she made her way through the aisles, but she didn't mind. It was great to see the place thriving, and that people took the time to say hello to neighbors and strangers alike.

Janet wasn't at the floral counter this afternoon, so the only greeting came from the bell above the door.

"I'm in the back if you need anything!" Chris called up from the pharmacy counter.

"Thanks." Kate lifted a basket from the stack inside the door, as all three shopping carts were apparently in use. She consulted her list, and started down the first aisle. Laundry detergent, dish soap, maybe some new sponges ...

She was nearly out of cereal. Could it wait until the end of the week? The pharmacy's grocery selection was small, but popular with local residents. Especially since Chris tried his best to meet, or slightly beat, the prices at Eagle River's lone gas station/convenience store, which was owned by a large franchise chain.

It was worth a look. Kate rounded the aisle's end display, which was loaded with notebooks and pens for back-to-school shoppers, and stopped in her tracks.

Alex was in the grocery aisle with one of the prized carts. Kate's heart gave a little skip when she spotted him, standing there in what appeared to be another of his perfectly snug tee shirts as he studied the small selection of boxed dinner kits. She was a bit annoyed by her school-girl reaction to his presence, but he was just as handsome in daylight as he'd been in the nocturnal habitat of his bar.

Why had he commandeered one of the carts when it only had two items in it? Yes, that was why she was irritated, Kate decided.

Local code called for only taking a cart if you really needed it. And she needed to stock up on paper towels.

She stepped back, but it was too late.

"Hey," she heard from down the aisle. "Do I know you?"

Well, he was nothing if not direct. Kate gritted her teeth and strolled in his direction.

"What an odd thing to say." She instantly cringed inside, as her comment was just as inane. What was wrong with her today? Lack of sleep, she decided. Too much excitement about the acreage.

"I'm Kate Duncan. I work at the post office."

She made a show of shifting her basket, which was already mostly full, to extend her hand. But Alex didn't make a move to meet her halfway, so she pulled it back.

"Oh, that's right." Alex ran a hand through his hair as his dark eyes danced with amusement. "You're one of the thespians from a while back. Quite the dramatic reenactment you ladies had going on."

She must have blinked in surprise, because he rolled his eyes. "I know everything that goes on in that bar. So, did you get the dirt you were looking for?"

"I don't know what you mean."

"Here's a word of advice: Let the real detectives handle the case." He dropped a tuna-skillet meal into his cart. "You just happened to be in the right place, at the right time. Or maybe, the wrong time. Whatever. But it's not up to you to figure out what happened to Milton."

"So you think something's happened to him, then?"

When Alex ignored her question in favor of studying the single shelf of canned fruit, he stepped on Kate's last nerve. What was it with people today?

"You're taking the fifth, huh? Well, I have a word of advice for you, too."

His laugh was sarcastic and short. "Oh, really?"

"Yeah. Don't take one of the carts if you only need a few things. It's kind of the rule around here."

That got his attention. "I'm well aware of 'the rules' of this town. How do you know where I'm driving this thing to next? Oh, wait, you're a super sleuth." He tucked his list into the pocket of his cargo shorts. "Now, tell me what else I'm going to buy."

"All I'm saying is, I could use the cart if you don't need it." An older woman was about to turn down their aisle, but she decided to move on. Kate had a feeling every ear in the shop was tuned into this conversation.

Apparently, so did Alex.

"Put your basket in my cart," he whispered. Kate caught his drift, and they rolled on together. She found her cereal, and Alex lifted it from her hand and added it to the cart. His fingers brushed against hers, just for a second, and a tingle went down her spine.

"So, what else is new?" he asked. "What are you doing when you're not running around, trying to rescue everyone from their own problems?"

There was another insult in there, but she decided to let it pass.

"I'm buying a house," she heard herself say. "Or rather, an acreage. Just east of town." Why was she telling Alex this? The rule was, family and close friends only. He certainly didn't qualify.

"Oh, the Trowbridge farm. Just went on the market Friday, but I knew it would go fast." He nodded his approval, and Kate was surprised to find she liked that.

But then, this was a big decision. And Alex wasn't exactly easy to please. If he thought the place had merit, she surely had picked a winner.

She told him about the letter she wrote, and a genuine smile appeared on his handsome face.

"Way to go. Flattery and persuasion will get you far in life." He seemed to know this firsthand; in fact, Kate suspected it might be his personal motto. Which made her curious about the guy who was still holding her soap and cereal hostage.

He steered them into the next aisle, and reached for two large packs of toilet paper. "See, told you I needed the cart. Hey, Chris!" he called over his shoulder. "I'm good to go."

"Be right up."

Alex chatted with Chris for a moment, paid for his items and then, with his toilet paper bundles under one arm and his reusable tote bag in the other hand, headed out without even acknowledging Kate was still there by the register. Chris watched her for a moment, then snickered.

"It's a lost cause, you know. Trying to figure him out."

Kate shrugged. "No, I just ..."

"He's not so bad, really." Chris leaned on the counter, eager for a bit of a break before heading back to the pharmacy. Kate guessed with Janet out this afternoon, he'd been on the run most of the time. "Hard to get to know, though."

"So you know him, then?"

"As much as might be possible. See, he moved here, oh, maybe five years ago, to take over that bar. From up by Albert Lea, I guess. With his cousin being the police chief, I suppose he heard of a good opportunity here to make a fresh start."

Or run away from his past, Kate thought but didn't say.

There was something off about Alex, but she couldn't put a finger on it.

Of course, putting her hands on him, well ...

Chris's laugh pulled her back to the present. "Hey, that sounds like someone else I know."

"I don't get it." Kate lifted her items to the counter. "I mean, the name of the bar. If he didn't want to name it after himself, fine. What he chose has a ring to it, but why not just pick something else altogether? It would be less confusing."

"I think he likes it that way. It throws people off." Chris shrugged.

"I guess you wouldn't know, you were gone when he bought the place, but the name's actually in honor of the man who first operated a bar there. It was a roadhouse, way back in the twenties and thirties. Sometime after World War II, everyone says, there was a fire and it burnt down. This Paul guy built it back; smaller, of course. He wasn't going to let that setback stop him."

"Interesting. I had no idea." Why didn't Alex just say something that night at the bar? It was a cool story, a bit of local history that should be preserved.

Kate thought of Melinda's knack for marketing. She'd have a tee shirt designed in no time flat, and get a story in the local newspaper to drum up sales.

"I couldn't help but overhear," Chris started to say, and Kate hid a smile. Of course he had. In a place this small, in a town like Eagle River, everyone did. “Alex thinks you should stop asking around about Milton, huh?”

“Maybe he’s right.” Kate sighed and reached for her wallet. “Maybe I should stay out of it.” Especially when she hadn’t turned up anything really useful.

“Aw, I don’t know about that.” Chris handed over her receipt.

“You have a good heart, Kate Duncan,” he called after her as she started for the door. “We need more people like you in this town.”

15

Saturday dawned warm and clear. Kate went for her usual morning run, but changed into her oldest, worn-out shorts and tee shirt after her shower. It was canning day, and her clothes were sure to be splattered with tomato juice long before lunchtime.

Grandma Ida would be there, along with Anna, Kate's sister-in-law. And Bev, with a few crates of her prized German Pinks.

"We're making tomato juice, chopped tomatoes, and salsa. Maybe even some spaghetti sauce if we have time," Kate told Charlie as she packed all her large mixing bowls and her favorite paring knife into canvas totes. Her mom had a farmhouse kitchen well-stocked with supplies, but an event of this magnitude called for reinforcements.

As she waited at the stoplight to turn left on the county highway toward her parents' farm, Kate couldn't help but smile. And not just about how much fun this day was going to be. Because in a matter of weeks, she'd begin making a lot of turns in the opposite direction to reach her new home.

One small step toward that future had already been made, as two dozen new canning jars waited in the back seat of Kate's car. Her mom had offered to share from her stash, but Kate was adamant she'd provide her own. After all, it would be a good start toward building reserves for next year. Because she hoped to cultivate a small garden that provided enough tomatoes to can for herself, and to bring to this annual party. Bev had already promised Kate a flat of seedlings come spring, and Kate could imagine the wooden shelves in her farmhouse's basement laundry room filled with rows of glowing jars.

Alex's insistence that Kate quit trying to fix other people's problems had cut a little deeper than she expected. Maybe he was right; maybe it was time to put more focus on herself, at least for a while. Because even though she only had an apartment's worth of stuff to transport to her new farm, moving was always stressful and time-consuming. So last night, in an effort to focus on her own future, she'd started the fascinating task of researching the history of her little acreage.

But even then, Milton wasn't far from her thoughts. Because as she worked back through the vintage plat maps she found online, something interesting caught her eye. While the current owner and her husband had owned the place since the 1980s, the property had belonged to several families before that. One surname stood out from the rest. And at first, Kate wasn't sure why.

She was familiar with her own family tree, and it wasn't from there. And then, she remembered the Benniger research from a few weeks ago. Kate popped open the file and, sure enough, the family that owned the farm in the late 1890s was on one branch of Milton's family tree.

If she had it figured right, Milton's great-grandmother lived at the next farm up the road as a girl, and her father owned the acres that became Kate's farm when the house was built in 1924. The abstract, which would be in her possession once she owned the property, should include all the details.

Maybe she shouldn't be surprised, but this find still gave Kate a thrill of excitement. People didn't move far from home back then, and families often had several children. So the odds were rather good there could be some connection to Milton's deep-rooted family. Even so, was it one more sign Kate had found the perfect place?

She couldn't wait to share her discovery with her own family, as well as Bev. And by the extra vehicles already parked in her parents' yard, she'd have quite the audience when she walked in the door.

Waylon's happy bark said even he knew today was going to be special. "Hey, there!" Kate reached out to pet him before she gathered up her totes. "Are you the official greeter today?"

"That would be me." Her dad came through the porch's screen door and held out a hand. "Here, let me take those jars. Everyone's in the kitchen, about to get started."

"And what about you?" Kate gave him a half-hug as they went up the sidewalk, Waylon leading the way. "What's your task going to be?"

"Performing my special disappearing act. Tee time's at nine, before it gets too hot. Then lunch with the guys at Peabody's. But I've promised to help with the dishes when I get home, and I'm in charge of grilling out tonight."

"Mom's going to be too tired to cook, I'm sure. I know I will be."

"Yep. I was told if we want to eat anything other than frozen pizza, I'll need to come up with something."

Charlotte waved from her post by the kitchen sink. The counter was smothered with cookie sheets stocked with ripe tomatoes, and more waited in tubs by the back porch door.

"All the work is going to be worth it." She gestured for her husband to take Kate's jars into the dining room, and for Kate to set the rest of her things on one end of the kitchen table, which had all its leaves installed and was covered with a vinyl-coated tablecloth. "When it's snowing and cold, and we go down into the basement and grab a jar of homemade salsa off the shelf, we'll be glad we put in the time today."

"Where's Grandma?" Kate looked around.

Charlotte pointed with her paring knife. "In the dining room. The great jar organization has begun."

That table was also stretched to its limit. Bev, Grandma Ida and Anna had all brought some of their own jars to take home their part of the bounty, but the rest of the glass containers belonged to Charlotte.

These jars were all empty, at least for now. And there were dozens and dozens of them.

"Mostly quarts for juice and chopped, but we'll do some pints as well," Grandma Ida explained to Anna and Bev as they lined the jars up in rows. "Then these pints over here are for salsa. A few half-pints, too."

Ida was a petite woman with a cloud of snow-white hair, but her brown eyes were bright as she bustled around the table. "Kate! You're just in time. Mostly salsa this year?"

"Sounds good." Kate peered over her grandma's shoulder to study the breakdown on her notepad. "You have quite the system going there."

"Other than size, they'll all look alike once we get rolling," Bev said. "This way, there's no hard feelings." She glanced into the still-full boxes at her feet. "Anna, I have three more dozen here, all pints. Let's put them on the end of the table for now."

Thank goodness Kate's parents had a second, older stove in their basement. She and Bev would start their day sterilizing the already-washed jars in big pots of boiling water, then Anna would ferry them upstairs to be filled and processed in the kitchen.

Once Grandma Ida had her organizational system down pat, Bev and Kate each picked up a tray of jars and started down the stairs. Kate hadn't seen Bev since before her visit to the Eagle River bank, and the two of them had plenty to discuss. Even when they were in the post office at the same time, they were never alone; so the Duncans' basement was the perfect place to compare their most-current notes about Milton's disappearance.

Because despite Alex's comments, and Kate's excitement over her impending home purchase, she still couldn't set the case aside.

Too many people already had. If she were in Milton's shoes, and something had gone wrong, Kate would hope someone cared enough to not give up the search. And if Jasper was telling it straight, Milton had been gone for one month as of today.

With two oversized pots filled with water and the burners cranked high, Bev and Kate had a few minutes before it was time to add the first round of jars. Bev was fascinated by the history of Kate's little farm, but Lindsey's less-than-tactful assessment of Milton's financial situation drew a raised eyebrow. "First of all, does this girl even know what she's talking about?"

"I'd say she shouldn't be talking about it in the first place." Kate lined up jars on the nearby metal table, enough for the first two loads. "That's when I decided to take my business elsewhere."

Bev sighed. "I've banked there for years. But it does make you wonder who they are hiring these days. When old Mr. Creighton ran the bank, that sort of privacy breach never would have happened."

"So, let's say she's right. What might it mean?"

Bev crossed her arms. "In an ideal world, absolutely nothing. Milton's money is his concern and no one else's. However, if he's loaded, it could be a motive for someone to do him harm."

"It'd have to be someone who'd benefit from his death, like an heir to the estate. But who might that be? It doesn't make much sense, not when Milton has so little family."

Kate checked the stove and nodded her approval, and Bev picked up a pair of tongs and began to load jars into the pots.

"I hate to think about that." Bev was whispering now, even though they were alone. "But if someone could benefit financially from Milton's death, they would certainly try to accomplish that in some sneaky way. Map it out to a point where they'd feel confident they wouldn't get caught."

"Being charged with murder would make it difficult for someone to try to claim his estate." Kate frowned. "But with no body, no sign of a struggle at his farm, and no truck ..."

"It's the perfect crime. If that's what it really is."

"We don't know that," Kate said to herself as much as to Bev. "I keep hoping that ..."

Anna came downstairs with a large plastic dishpan in her arms. "I have some more jars. Are any ready to go up?"

"Maybe another fifteen minutes." Kate tipped her head toward the old clock on the wall. When her sister-in-law was gone, she turned back to Bev.

"I'm starting to wonder if there's a larger plot playing out here, something more sinister." She explained what she'd unearthed about one of the attorneys at that Des Moines firm.

Bev shook her head sadly. "First of all, I just hope Milton's OK. Beyond that, the idea of some shady folks taking advantage of someone like him? That just makes me mad. I'll pass it on to Jeff, but I suspect he's already found that out."

"That's why I didn't call you about it, right away. It was a routine online search." Kate took the first load of hot jars from their pot and arranged them on a cookie sheet. "What exactly has he told you? I mean, in the last few days?"

"Not a damn thing." Bev frowned. "That's just it. He has a case to protect, I understand that. But before, it seemed like he was willing to share bits, here and there, especially if he thought it would help us help him. But when I called the other day, he clammed up on me. And quick."

"That's a change, then. What do you think is going on?"

"I have no idea. But I don't like it." Bev blinked back sudden tears.

"What if he's uncovered something terrible, something that makes him think this isn't a misunderstanding?" She shook her head. "Every day, I wake up and I hope today's the day. Milton will show up, or call someone, and this will be resolved."

"I know, I feel the same way. What does Clyde think? He didn't know Milton well, but probably as much as most people around here."

Bev gave a bitter laugh. "That's just it. Clyde thinks I need to let this go. That *we* should let it go. 'Either he's dead, or he doesn't want to be found,' he told me last night. Can you imagine? I don't think that's being very neighborly."

As Kate added more jars to the boiling water, she told Bev how Alex had tried to steer her away, too.

"Well, there's two votes." Bev threw up her arms in frustration. "Is it time to hang it up? Maybe we've done all we can. Short of some new development, a new lead that comes in through the post office or some other way, I don't think there's much else for us to go on."

"Bev Stewart," Kate suddenly said with a smile. "I never thought you were a quitter. Besides, I'm not sure I'd put much stock in anything Alex says. And you know," she added with a laugh, "maybe Clyde's just jealous you're talking to Jeff so much."

"I never told him." Bev looked away. "Jeff made me promise, remember? I can't say anything now, I'd have to admit I've been keeping it from him, all these weeks. This is one of those times when a little white lie suddenly isn't so little, anymore."

Kate had also kept her word to not tell anyone she was feeding information to the sheriff. The closest she'd come to the truth was when she'd asked Melinda and Karen to meet up with her at Paul's Place.

It was a fine line, to be sure, but Kate felt she'd walked it as best she could.

She hadn't thought about it much until now, but she would have assumed Bev told Clyde the truth. He was her husband, after all. And Kate knew how secrets could fester, how much damage they could do. In any relationship, trust was everything.

Maybe, in this case, Bev's evasion wasn't too serious. But still, it was causing an issue in her marriage. Kate had never expected that to happen, for things to get so complicated.

It was just like that letter from the attorney's office. She'd done the right thing taking down the information, Kate still believed that, and Roberta had agreed. But even so, that effort to help the case had caused dissention within the post office's ranks.

And now, Kate wondered what Sheriff Preston had uncovered. There had to be something, given his change in behavior toward his former sweetheart. It was a small switch, but a telling one.

She thought again of Alex, and how adamant he'd been that Kate stop poking her nose into other people's lives. The sheriff's silence was one thing. But Alex's behavior? It could mean something else, entirely.

Nothing was ever simple. Kate knew that, had known it for a very long time. But she was starting to wonder how many layers of secrets stood between herself and the truth about what had really happened to Milton.

As Kate pulled another batch of jars from the water, another question came to mind. "If you don't want to talk about this, that's fine. But do you ever wonder what life would have been like if you and Jeff had stayed together?"

Bev blinked at this sudden change in conversation. "Well, I used to. Way back when. Did I do the right thing, breaking up with him? Yes. We were so young, just a couple of kids." A smile spread across her face. "And then Clyde came along, and it didn't matter anymore."

She studied Kate carefully. "Are you thinking about Ben?"

Kate nodded and looked away, surprised at how swiftly the tears formed in her eyes. She was excited about her little farm. One door closing, another opening, the usual. But sometimes, her courage faltered. She missed Ben. And why not? They'd been together for ten years. He'd been her best friend. Until ...

"It'll get easier," Bev said. "The hurt won't last forever."

"I'm trying. Really, I am. It's just that, some days, it's harder than others." She crossed her arms. "So, then, back to Milton. Do you want to stop? Jeff's capable enough. He has his own team. He doesn't really need us, right?"

"Oh, yeah, he does." Bev pulled on a pair of insulated oven mitts with the vigor of a boxer gearing up for a prizefight, and reached for a tray of sterilized jars. "And so does Milton. We need to see this through."

* * *

Kate was glad when their assembly line picked up speed, as it pulled her thoughts in a more-productive direction.

Soon there was near-constant traffic on the basement stairs, and the sounds of clanging pots and spoons echoed from the kitchen above. Once all the jars were sterilized, Kate and Bev joined the other ladies to finish peeling, chopping and cooking the best of summer's bounty.

There was a quick lunch break of sandwiches, potato salad, and sliced tomatoes (of course) before they returned to their labors. The dining room table was soon blanketed with thick towels, and row after row of filled jars glowed in the summer sunshine. Kate's tee shirt was stained with tomato pulp, and her hands and even her hair smelled like onions, but all the chopping and mixing and boiling was worth it.

Just before three, the last rack of jars was pulled from the canner and set on the kitchen counter to cool. Charlotte dropped into one of the kitchen chairs with a sigh of relief, and the other ladies followed.

"That was some good work today, everyone." She smiled at Bev. "And I'm so glad you could join us. Just think, you and Clyde have been only three miles away, all these years, and I'm sure we've only run into each other in town. Don't be a stranger."

"You and Curtis should come over for supper some night." Then Bev turned to Kate. "You, too." And then she laughed. "My tomatoes aren't done yet. I think in a few weeks, I could justify firing up my canner one last time for another, smaller round. Who's in?"

The silence around the table was telling. So were the groans that followed.

"I'm getting too old for all this," Grandma Ida said. "But I'm glad I'm still young enough to help out."

"Before you all go, there's chocolate cake and ice cream." Charlotte fought back a yawn. "If I can find the energy to get it out."

"Sounds wonderful." Bev left her chair. "Let me."

A silence settled around the table except for the *clink* of spoons in bowls. Just before they were done with their dessert, Anna raised her hand. "Everyone, I have an announcement to make."

"Should I leave?" Bev asked. "I'm not family."

"Oh, close enough." Anna smiled, her blue eyes alight with good news. "And besides, I can't keep this to myself one more minute."

Kate was pretty sure what this was going to be. Had expected it, actually, for the past year. But when Anna announced she and Bryan were expecting a baby sometime in March, it hit Kate harder than she thought it would.

"You're going to be a grandmother!" Bev exclaimed to Charlotte. "How exciting! I can tell you from experience, it's the best job in the world."

"We didn't want to tell anyone until we were really sure." Anna blinked back happy tears. "Oh, we're just thrilled!

Grandma Ida got up from her chair and wrapped her arms around Anna's shoulders. "I'll get started on that blanket as soon as I can." She loved to knit, and every grandchild and great-grandchild received a handmade gift.

"Any preferences on colors, let me know. Just think of it: There are three generations around this table, right now. And next year, we'll have a fourth."

Kate reached across the table and squeezed Anna's hand. "This is so exciting, I'm so happy for you!" And she meant it.

But when her mom asked her to run upstairs and get more clean towels from the linen closet, Kate was relieved for a chance to slip away, if only for a few minutes.

This wasn't a race, she knew that. But she'd gotten married before Bryan and had assumed a family would follow when she was ready. When it didn't happen, it was just one more thing Kate had adjusted her expectations about. And she'd made peace with it. Until Anna's announcement brought it all back.

Kate pulled a stack of towels from the hall closet, then paused at the door to her old bedroom.

It hadn't changed much since high school, simply because she was rarely there to use it. Or give it much thought, at all. But now she gazed at the peach-painted walls and matching checked curtains, and remembered the girl she used to be.

No, life hadn't turned out the way she'd planned. All the disappointment and heartache rushed back, so quickly that Kate had to take in a deep breath and then let it all go. Maybe it was time for this room to be turned into a nursery of sorts, a place for the new grandbaby to enjoy. And other siblings that were sure to follow.

Kate hadn't spent one night here since she'd moved back to Eagle River. And soon, she'd have her own little farm to look after, to love. She didn't need this room anymore, just as she had no more use for the dreams and expectations that filled it when she was younger.

She would stay; Eagle River was once again her home. But everything was different. Or, was it that she was different? The years away had changed her. She hoped it was for the better. But maybe, it was too soon to tell.

And then she thought of what Melinda said, that night at the bar.

I had to give myself permission to start fresh, even though I was back where I started.

Could she do it? Kate decided she had to. It wasn't just the best way to move forward, but probably the only way.

She wiped away a stray tear, set aside the complicated feelings coursing through her heart, and went back downstairs.

16

Roberta gathered her team around the back counters before everyone headed out. "I don't like the feel of this weather. It's too hot for this early hour. Jack, what does your knee say?"

He rubbed his left leg. "Hmmm. Thirty-percent chance of a twister today." Then he winced. "No, wait. More like fifty."

Roberta glanced out the two small windows that overlooked the parking lot, worry etched on her face. The sun was out, but barely; and the humid air draped over Eagle River like a thick blanket.

"We all know the drill, but let's review. Just so I can tell my bosses we were all up to speed if Jack's forecast is accurate. Because a mail vehicle, either government issued or privately owned, is not adequate shelter during a tornado."

Down on the end, Aaron yawned. Roberta pointed in his direction.

"Aaron, can you please remind everyone what they're supposed to do if there is severe weather?"

He frowned. "Why are you picking on me?"

"Because you seem to be paying the least amount of attention. And this is important. Maybe even lifesaving, but I hope it doesn't come to that."

Despite the stuffy air in the back room of the post office, Kate shivered. Roberta was right. Tornadoes were nearly unheard-of in Chicago; it was the same in most metro areas, come to think of it. Severe weather in general didn't seem to hit large population centers as hard as it could. And when it did, there was always a building nearby to offer shelter.

But severe weather was very common in rural Iowa, and Kate had experienced several terrible storms as a child. The thought of being caught out in one now, alone on some gravel road with only Bertha between herself and the elements, made her blood run cold.

"OK, fine." Aaron sat up straight. "Here's the drill: Those of us on the town routes, we're to head to the closest business or public building if we can't quickly get to home base. A private residence is a last resort, but do that if you must. Now, out in the country, that's your best bet. Beyond that, it's the shelter-in-a-ditch thing."

"And?" Roberta prompted him.

"And we all need to have our hard hats with us."

Roberta had dipped into the petty cash several years ago to purchase standard-issue construction safety hats for all her carriers. They were inexpensive, yet priceless at the same time.

Kate was handed one when she joined the team, and hoped she never needed to use it. But if any of them were ever caught out in severe weather without adequate shelter, it was their best chance to avoid head injury.

"I suppose we should talk about flooding," Roberta said. "Rural routes, you know this is most important for you. But it can happen in town, too, and I don't want anyone caught off guard. Never, ever drive through water running over a road!"

The safety guidelines were clear on this danger, on how even a few inches of water could sweep a vehicle away.

In the event of a gully-washer rain, the usually placid streams that meandered through the county could turn into raging rivers within a matter of minutes. They could easily rise out of their banks to engulf gravel roads and even damage the metal-railed creek bridges, which weren't much more than a layer of gravel packed over heavy timbers.

"That reminds me," Jack spoke up. "That culvert on Martin Avenue, three miles out from town? The bank erosion on the south side hasn't been fixed yet, and I emailed the county weeks ago."

Postal employees were encouraged, even expected, to file reports on any road or bridge maintenance issues they spotted as they made their rounds. And while there were well-known sayings about how the mail must always go through, carriers had the discretion to deviate from their mapped-out routes and, in worst-case scenarios, even suspend service if a situation was deemed too dangerous to safely make deliveries.

"I'll call them today," Roberta promised. "Thanks for reminding me. I suppose with road-construction season in full swing, those little jobs are still stuck in the queue. But today's a good reminder that we are never to risk our lives delivering the mail. If it gets rough this afternoon, and you no longer feel safe, just let me know and come back in."

It was Mae's day off, so Kate was taking her route. There was no mail for Milton, only the free, Charles City-area shopper that was dropped at everyone's place. But there was a parcel for Jasper Tindall.

As they organized their deliveries, Bev noticed the name on the box. "Interesting," she murmured to Kate. "Think anyone's going to be around?"

After their canning-day discussion, the ladies were determined to push on with whatever tidbits they could get. Even if the flow of information between them and Sheriff Preston had narrowed to a one-way street, they still felt an obligation to help. Kate wasn't planning any more visits to Paul's Place, or anywhere else, in a deliberate bid to gather information. But if something fell in her lap? Well, that was a different story.

And if something landed in her mail car? Even better.

"Who knows? I won't be by there until this afternoon. If the weather gets crazy, people might stick closer to home." But then she shrugged. "Even so, everyone has errands to run. And didn't you say his wife works in Charles City?"

Bev nodded. "She's not likely to be at the house. The kids might." Then she laughed.

"How heavy is the box? Maybe we need to be more concerned about it blowing away than who might be around to take it inside."

The parcel was fairly light and, given it was from a superstore known for using bigger-than-needed boxes, Kate decided that, if a thunderstorm popped up, this box could be a flight risk. She hadn't dropped a package at the Tindalls' before, and hoped there was a safe place to leave one on a day like today. It seemed like there was an enclosed porch on the back side of their house, at least.

Because while Kate had yet to have a reason to turn up their driveway, she'd found herself studying the Tindalls' farm from the road every time she filled in for Mae.

The morning passed uneventfully, but the heat and humidity remained oppressive. Kate worked up a sweat just leaning out the window a few times in every mile, and Bertha's air conditioner was cranked high and working overtime.

The sky was still blue, but the light was strange. Kate couldn't have explained the difference, not really, but like most Midwesterners, she knew exactly what it meant. Heavy clouds started to pile up in the west by the time she was halfway through her afternoon route, and her phone soon beeped with word of a severe thunderstorm watch until seven.

Her fingers tingled with anticipation as she neared the Tindall residence. Their parcel was the last one for today, sitting all alone in Bertha's back seat. She could simply drop the box and scoot back to the car, of course. But if someone was home, they were often eager to get their package right away, and also chat for a minute.

What might she say if one of the Tindalls came to the door? Mail carriers always had to walk a fine line between being friendly, yet respecting their customers' privacy. Maybe it would be best to not say much at all. Given how the Tindalls were tied to Milton's case, they might be on guard even if they had nothing to hide.

Kate would have to be careful. A quick comment about the impending weather was about all she could safely say.

"Hey, I know your neighbor is still missing," she muttered to herself as she guided Bertha into the last turn before their farm came into view. "Where do you think he is? And I have to ask: Did you tell the sheriff everything you know?"

She rolled her eyes. "Yeah, none of that's going to be well-received."

Her hopes were raised, however, when she spotted a truck in the Tindalls' yard. But as she drove Bertha up the lane, she was struck by how quiet the place seemed.

Their dog, which Mae had promised was of the friendly sort, lounged in the bed of ferns on the north side of the garage. He thumped his tail in greeting when he spotted Kate, but decided it was too hot to get up from his patch of shade.

Kate had been right about the enclosed porch. There it was, around on the back side of the house, and it looked to be the only safe option. The breeze had picked up, and was now blowing hot out of the southwest. A larger, west-side stoop, which likely accessed a room that long ago had been a formal parlor, had a roof over it but was soon going to turn into a wind tunnel.

As she walked around the corner of the Victorian-style farmhouse, Kate took in its bright-white vinyl siding and eyed the near-new truck by the garage. Neither gave any hint the Tindalls were in dire straits financially.

But then, Kate realized, maybe that was the problem. There was always a chance the Tindalls were overextended. Lines of credit were easy enough to get, and the bank didn't always care if there was a bad crop the next year, or if the markets were down.

She was in luck; the enclosed porch's storm door wasn't locked. With a wave to the dog, Kate climbed back into Bertha's climate-controlled interior and made sure the vents were all blowing directly on her sweat-drenched face.

Milton's farm was next. And as she approached the end of his lane, Kate wasn't sure if she should laugh or cry.

Because the big black cat with the white paws was right there next to the mailbox, sitting tall and proud in the shaggy grass where the gravel met the ditch.

Kate had seen him down by the road one other time in the past few weeks, when she covered for Mae. But Mae told her yesterday this "guard duty by the driveway" routine had turned into a daily occurrence over the past week or so.

At first, Mae assumed it was a simple matter of random timing. Most country cats liked to prowl the ditches and stalk striped gophers and birds, regardless of how full their humans kept their food dishes. And with it being the height of summer, the big guy surely loved to soak up the sun for as many hours as he could.

But when he started stationing himself next to the mailbox, afternoon in and afternoon out, Mae wondered if something else was going on.

With no dog at the farm and Milton still missing, did the cat think it was his duty to "wave the flag" and remind passerby that someone was on watch? After all, the cows in the front pasture certainly didn't seem to care.

On days when there were deliveries for Milton, Mae reported the cat often offered a "meow" of greeting when she stopped to pop the mailbox's door.

Jasper's family continued to do chores, but they only

needed to stop by once a day. The poor cat was probably lonely.

Because as a retired farmer, Milton was likely around most of the time. Any trip to the garden, or a step outside to hang something on the clothesline, would have provided this cat with an adventure or two. There would be some kind words, a pat on the head, maybe a treat of scraps from the kitchen.

"You'd think today, of all days, he wouldn't be out here." Kate frowned as she brought Bertha to a stop. "Look at that sky. I guess he's smart enough, and he can high-tail it up to the barn if he thinks it's going to storm. They say animals have a sixth sense about those things."

And then, she saw another cat emerge from the tall grass. This one was gray, with a white chest and paws, but smaller. So the tuxedo cat had a friend. That made Kate feel better, at least. Farms with cats usually had more than one. She didn't know how many were at Milton's place, but at least the big boy wasn't here alone.

Kate powered down the window. "Hello there, kitties. What are you doing out here? It's going to storm."

The black cat meowed, just as Mae said he would, while the gray cat only stared silently at the car. Kate had the distinct feeling she was being evaluated, and had at least partially passed the test.

She dropped the circular in the box and took comfort in that it was otherwise empty, which meant Jasper was picking up the mail every day as Roberta requested. Of course, that was only good if he could really be trusted. Oh, regulations ...

Just before she shifted the car into gear, the black cat did something Kate hadn't expected. With another "meow," this one louder than the last, he jumped out of the grass and stretched his big white paws up Bertha's door.

"No, no! Get away!" Kate leaned out and gently shooed him. "I have to go, and I don't want you to get hurt."

The gray cat was gone. And then, Kate saw it by the front tire. It made a few guttural noises before it ran around the fender, the black cat right behind.

"Hey!" Kate called after them. "Get out of the road!"

She honked the horn, and waited. She knew they hadn't moved, because neither showed up on one side of the car or the other, and they weren't visible past Bertha's hood, either.

The sky was turning darker by the minute; a storm was surely on the way. Kate needed to finish her rounds, and these kitties needed to get back to the shelter of their barn. She glanced at the pouch of dog treats in the back, and sighed. Did she need to start stocking cat snacks, too?

The felines finally came back around the fender, but were now rubbing their cheeks and tails along the side of the car. Kate didn't dare move Bertha until they were safely out of her path.

With another sigh, this one from irritation, she stepped out on the side of the road.

"Look, I'm sorry if you're lonely, but you need to get out of the way. I don't want to ..."

Before she could grasp what was happening, both cats came toward her, lickety-split, and launched themselves inside the car. Kate let out a sound somewhere between a gasp and a scream, and watched in horror as the kitties scampered over the mail case and catapulted into the back of her car.

"What are you doing?" She ran around Bertha and pulled open one of the back doors, which only sent the cats scrambling to the opposite side of the seat and down to the floor. They seemed determined to stay there, so Kate wasn't sure if it would do any good to open the other back door. As scared as they were, they would likely jump back in the car before she could close it up again.

If they didn't, they'd be out in the road, and they'd all be right back where they started.

Kate closed the back door, marched around the car, and climbed in. Then she turned in her seat to give both cats a stern stare.

"I have an idea. You're not going to like it, but I don't care. Hold on."

Kate put Bertha into gear and turned up the lane. She had to get these two inside the barn. Not just because a storm was coming, but because that would give her enough time to safely drive away before they could attempt to get back around Bertha's tires.

They'd have to run through the barn to the cows' open pasture door, slip around the foundation and squeeze through the fence. Kate wasn't sure how fast they could run, but was confident she and Bertha could make a safe getaway before the cats could make it that far.

"Why today?" She glanced in the rearview mirror out of habit, although her stowaways couldn't be seen. "What's changed? Mae said you just wanted to say hello, Mr. Tuxie. Now you have a friend with you, and you both act like you want to come with me."

All the sudden, Kate thought she knew why.

They say animals have a sixth sense about those things. And that wasn't just about the weather.

Tears formed in her eyes. She blinked them back, watched the driveway for any other cats that might be milling about. But Milton's yard was the same as the first time she'd been there: silent and empty. As Kate pulled Bertha up in front of the barn, she tried to collect her thoughts.

Sheriff Preston continued to stonewall Bev, and no new information about the case had been released for weeks. Surely, something had changed. An ominous feeling spread through Kate's chest, and it wasn't just because of the dark clouds advancing from the west.

"Oh, no! Is he dead?" She gripped the steering wheel tight. The radio played on, some country song she didn't recognize. A check of the back seat showed the two cats, still frightened and tense, huddled on the floor.

"Something's happened to Milton, hasn't it?"

The gray cat, unnerved by this stranger's voice, turned its head away. But the black cat stared into Kate's eyes and, while she couldn't be sure, especially in the dimming light, she thought she saw sadness along with fear.

"He's been gone for a long time now, huh?" she whispered. "Your caretaker, your friend. And I'm starting to think, you believe he's not coming home."

Kate wiped at her cheeks. Whatever had happened to Milton, whatever had gone wrong, she couldn't fix it. But she had to get these cats out of her mail car, and fast.

Her head dipped against the rising wind, she tried the latch on the barn door. The handle turned easily, which was a relief. With a struggling cat in one hand, she'd only have a second or two to jerk open the door and deposit the critter inside. She hoped the first cat would be surprised and disgusted enough that it wouldn't try to sneak out when she returned with its friend.

As she returned to the car, Kate remembered how Doc McFadden had boldly let himself in the barn that day, and how Karen had chastised him for potentially trespassing. How he'd insisted, despite any evidence to prove his hunch, that something wasn't right here at the Benniger farm.

It hadn't seemed very likely then, but now it seemed almost a certainty.

Kate pulled a pair of work gloves from Bertha's trunk, zipped on a sweatshirt despite the sweltering heat, and marched to the side of the car. She hoped to not get scratched or bit during this process, but at least her arms and hands were covered.

The black cat pinned back his ears when Kate opened the door. He could see he was right back where he started, which didn't seem to be his plan.

"Yeah, we haven't left. You're getting inside your barn, and your friend, too."

Kate took a deep breath, and nabbed him by the scruff of the neck. He flailed and howled, but she managed to get her other hand under his back legs to keep him from leaping away. Before she or the cat could really think about it, Kate had them both at the barn door.

"There! One down, one to go."

The gray cat, either due to shyness or observing the no-nonsense way Kate handled its friend, didn't put up much of a fight when Kate lifted it from the backseat. Only one small howl of protest was offered as they hurried to the barn.

"This is why peer pressure is a bad idea," she explained under her breath. "He's one crazy dude. Don't let him talk you into things, OK?"

Finally, it was done. Kate made it back to the car just as the first few wind-driven raindrops fell from the ominous sky. She pulled off her gloves and the suffocating sweatshirt, then checked Bertha's dash clock.

Fifteen minutes had passed. And once she got away from the barn and down the lane, she'd still have to stop and reorganize what was left of her mail case, which would probably take another five, at least. But Kate had done what she'd needed to do. The cats were in the barn, just in time, and she and Bertha could safely drive away.

"Well, that was probably a first." Kate shook her head as she considered the report that was to come. "A mail vehicle hijacked by two cats in need of a getaway car."

She wished she could laugh about it. And maybe someday, she would. But for now, her heart was heavy as she rolled down the lane.

* 17 *

The thunderstorms arrived before Kate even made it a mile from Milton's farm, and the heavy rain continued into the evening. Clear skies returned the next morning, and just in time. With only a few days left to prepare for the annual sweet corn festival, every hour was needed.

The auction barn's parking lot was half full of vehicles when Kate arrived late Friday afternoon. More than a hundred volunteers, wearing plastic gloves and with large buckets at their feet, took up most of the remaining space.

"Well, we pulled it off again." Grandpa Wayne handed Kate her volunteer tag. "No chance of rain in the forecast until at least Monday, so we're good to go."

"I'm so glad. It's not enough to have nice weather tonight and tomorrow. We need a clear day for cleanup, too."

"Oh, 'we' do?" Grandpa grinned. "Sounds like there's another volunteer willing to spend their Sunday morning picking up trash." He pointed toward the far row. "You'll be down on the end, right in there with the post office folks."

Kate hadn't volunteered since she was in high school, but she'd attended the festival several times after she moved away. Ben had always come home with her for this event, and they'd capped off their summers with carnival rides, funnel cakes and, of course, several ears of fresh sweet corn.

She set those memories of Ben aside as she carried her lawn chair across the parking lot. Instead, she recalled how fun it had been to help Grandpa when she was a child.

Bev waved from where the post office employees had pushed their chairs together. “Over here!” she called to Kate. “We’re about to get started.”

Randy scooted his buckets closer to his chair. “Can’t throw them as good as I used to. But I’m looking forward to an ear slathered with some of that chipotle-spice butter as soon as we’re done.”

He tipped his head toward a nearby tent where the volunteers would enjoy a free dinner, which included burgers, brats and all the sweet corn they could eat. “But I think by tomorrow night, I might be tired of even looking at this stuff.”

Several residents came around on lawn tractors with trailers hitched on behind. A large tub of fresh-picked corn was left with each handful of volunteers, who would shuck the husks and silks into empty pails and then drop the fresh corn into the sanitized buckets that were half-filled with water.

The prepped corn would be sealed in containers and stored at one of the handful of walk-in coolers in town, ready to be dispersed to the various cooking stations as needed. The auction barn’s professional-grade kitchen had the needed storage space, as did both schools, Peabody’s and The Daily Grind, and the town’s lone convenience store.

While the committee’s members had cleaned a portion of the corn that morning, just to make sure the vendors could keep up with early demand, the rest of it would be prepped by volunteers within the next two hours to make sure the ears were as fresh as possible.

“This corn looks wonderful,” Mae said as she peeled back the husks on her first ear. “We never know how far along the local crop will be when it’s festival weekend, but I think we hit it on the head this year.”

Kate looked around. “Where’s Jared?”

After much encouragement, her co-worker had agreed to represent the post office in the corn-shucking contest.

"He'll be here in a bit." Aaron laughed. "He's going to help us out after the competition, but only then. Said he didn't want to overwork his shucking arm before the big event."

The contest was incredibly simple. Competitors had five minutes to shuck as much sweet corn as fast as they could. To count, each ear had to be completely stripped of its husks, and have a majority of its silks removed. Other than the clean ears landing in the right bucket, those were the only rules.

"Jared's right to hold off on helping." Jack nodded with authority. "My wrist was sore the next day, after I competed. There's always the risk of repetitive-motion injury, you know. It's like tennis elbow."

"Did you win?" Bev's eyes twinkled, and Kate thought her friend knew the answer. But it was always fun to get Jack riled up. And it wasn't hard.

"I did not! Got beat at the end. I was faster with the shucking, but this other guy had a motion down where he could toss the clean ear with one hand, and pick up the next at the same time with the other. It was a travesty, I tell you."

"That doesn't sound fair." Bev couldn't hide her smile.

"All's fair when it comes to the contest," Jack intoned. "Everyone's out for themselves."

Kate wasn't sure how serious the competitors really were, as it was all done in good fun. But the winner did get to take home the traveling trophy, a piece of wood carved into a sort-of-realistic shape of an ear of corn. And claim bragging rights until next August, which was the best part of all.

A crowd of onlookers soon gathered around another, smaller tent, where the competition would start promptly at five. Kate wondered why the shelter was needed, as there was no threat of rain. During years when the weather didn't cooperate, both the general husking and the competition were held in the high school gymnasium.

"Oh, that was added last year," Mae explained when Kate asked about the tent. "The year before that, Edgar Doyle kicked up a fuss. After he came in last, he claimed his chair's position in the circle put the sun right into his eyes, which ensured he couldn't win."

"Sore loser," Jack muttered.

"There's Jared." Bev dropped another clean ear into her bucket and stood up. "Let's go find a good spot so we can cheer him on."

The contest might have seemed a little silly to outsiders, but Kate knew it carried historical relevance along with bringing some good-natured competition to the festival.

Several decades ago, before the arrival of modern agricultural machinery, farmers had gathered at the end of harvest to remove the husks from their field corn to get it ready for market.

Competitions sprouted up, and remained popular in rural parts of the United States for many years. Some of the old-time contests were more elaborate, as they tasked competitors to also pick the corn by hand and toss the ears into a wagon before they were husked.

Eagle River's modern-day event, which only required some plastic disposable gloves and a few buckets, was easy-peasy by comparison. Participants took a seat, and the sweet corn was brought to them. Cold beverages were part of the fun, before as well as after.

While traditional cornhusking had been considered a men's sport, the modern contest in Eagle River always had a female competitor or two. This year there was Cordelia, from The Daily Grind; and Betsy Carmichael, who worked at the auction barn. Betsy was Allison's sister-in-law, which meant she had to pick a side. Family won out in the end.

"It's about time the sale barn had someone in the contest again," Jack observed as they joined the throng around the competitors' tent. "I don't think they have for several years."

"Betsy's going to be tough to beat," Bev said. "She grew up on a farm. I'm sure she knows her way around an ear, with both the field stuff and the sweet stuff."

Marge pointed out Mitch Marshall, the high school's football coach. "Mitch is taking this very seriously." The coach was working a flexible stress-reduction ball in each hand. "He's warming up before the big event."

Reid MacDonald made his way through the crowd, microphone in hand, to enter the tent. While he owned an insurance office in Charles City, he spent his fall Friday nights announcing the Wildcats' home football games.

"OK, everyone, let's get started. I bet most of you know the rules, but I'll run through them quick for any out-of-towners, or hometown folks who've moved away." He gave Kate a smile before he started his rundown.

"See? It's simple. And now, let's meet our competitors."

Along with Coach Marshall, Jared, Cordelia and Betsy, there was Leo Deegan, the lead bartender at Eagle's Nest Bar and Grill. Reid then introduced Carl Friese, a retired farmer who was the reigning champion. His name elicited cheers and a few good-natured boos, along with lots of laughter.

"I keep telling Carl he needs to retire again," Reid told the crowd. "He's won three of the past seven years."

"It just shows us oldsters can still throw down with the rest," a guy shouted from the crowd.

"Who are you calling old?" Carl said. But he was laughing.

"OK, everyone, get ready," Reid told the contestants. "Beers down, gloves on." He turned to Grandpa Wayne, who held up his smartphone. "Burberry, you got the time?"

"Yep."

"Let's count it down," Reid shouted to the crowd. "Three, two, one ... go!"

The parking lot erupted in cheers of encouragement as well as laughter. When Kate was a little girl, the contestants shucked the corn with their bare hands. But several years ago, given health directives and whatnot, the plastic gloves were added. While they made the event more sanitary, they added a layer of absurdity to the contest.

The thin, oversized gloves were loose on everyone's hands, and quickly grew slippery from the corn's silks and juices. Adjusting them so they'd stay on was now part of the challenge, with comedic results.

Kate studied the crowd, and wondered if Alex was there. She decided he wasn't likely to come to something like this. It was silly and fun, so it didn't seem to be his speed. Besides, he had so little staff, he probably couldn't get away. The festival was the biggest summer weekend in Eagle River by far, which meant Paul's Place was sure to be busy.

She wondered if Alex liked those outliers crowding his little bar, or would have preferred the hangers-on stick to the festival's beer garden.

Betsy took a quick lead, her petite hands flying over the ears. "I don't think a woman's ever won," Bev whispered to Kate. "Maybe this is the year."

Reid kept up a running commentary as the minutes ticked by. "Carmichael's showing the guys she's a contender! But Coach Marshall is staying with the pack. Deegan, watch out! If you drop an ear, you're done for."

Jared was holding his own, and the other mail carriers cheered him on.

"You can do it!" Jack shouted and clapped. "Twist the end when you pull off the husk, it's faster. There you go!"

Bev and Kate exchanged bemused looks. Jack was certainly getting in the spirit of things.

"OK, folks, we're rounding the final bend. Just about a minute to go." Reid gestured at the crowd with his free hand, and the cheers grew louder. "Who will be this year's champion? We're about to find out."

"Jared's bucket is pretty full," Bev said. "Oh, maybe he's got a chance!"

"And we're done!" Reid announced. "Let's have a big round of applause for our competitors. That's hard work. Well, hard enough that you've all earned a free supper over there in the volunteers' tent."

Members of the steering committee came forward to count and inspect the cleaned corn. Two volunteers were assigned to each contestant, and the ears were transported into other sanitized buckets as they were tallied.

Jared came in third, with Carl narrowly besting him for second place. Leo was the winner. The crowd erupted in cheers when he jumped out of his chair and raised his arms in triumph, an ear of unshucked corn in one hand and a cup of beer in the other.

"Leo Deegan is our new champion!" Reid held out his microphone. "Any words for the crowd?"

"I just want to thank everyone for their support, as I've been training for several months." That brought a round of eye-rolling laughter. "But seriously, I want to remind you that The Eagle's Nest is open early tomorrow, starting at eight. Breakfast burritos will be $4, or two for $6, until we run out."

"There'd better be corn in there!" someone yelled.

"Absolutely. Right in the scrambled eggs, with the peppers and onions."

That sounded fabulous to Kate. Maybe she could swing by the bar in the morning and get one before she went to work. Because Saturday was a delivery day, and even Eagle River's biggest event of the year couldn't stop the carriers from making their rounds.

The carriers spent a few hours at the beer tent celebrating Jared's third-place honors, even though he didn't have anything to show for it. A band was set up on one end of the temporary site, which was in the city park, and the dance floor was soon packed with revelers.

Kate was content to remain at her picnic table with her colleagues. They worked together six days a week, but were always going in different directions. As they traded stories and shared laughs, Kate felt like she was, at last, part of a team again. She missed her Chicago coworkers, and kept up with several of them on social media, but wanted so badly to put down new roots in her hometown. That night, Kate realized, she had already succeeded.

Before they scattered for home, Bev pulled Kate aside. "Are we on the same page for tomorrow?"

Kate nodded. "I'll be walking around with my parents after work. Then I'm meeting up with Karen and her boyfriend at the street dance, if I have the energy. I don't think I'll approach anyone directly, just keep my ears open."

"We'll be at the parade." Bev stepped out of the way of a swarm of people leaving the tent. "I think Clyde wants to see the old-time farm machinery display up at the auction barn. Other than that, we'll just be wandering around, eating."

Bev smiled. But then, she shook her head.

"I don't know what we might pick up on tomorrow. It makes me sad. Because it seems like most everyone else has forgotten all about Milton."

She looked around. "See what I mean?" Several people were within easy earshot of Bev and Kate's conversation, but not one head had turned their way. "Clyde still thinks I'm sticking my nose in where it doesn't belong. Maybe that's true. But if I don't, who will?"

"I will." Kate gave Bev's arm a quick squeeze. "We need to stay vigilant, just in case. Who knows? People get a few beers in them, and stuff their faces with good food, and they might blab something useful."

* * *

Kate could barely get Bertha out of the post office's back lot the next morning. Eagle River's streets were jam-packed with parked cars and throngs of people, even at this early hour. One of the churches had kicked off the day with a community-wide waffle breakfast, and the food vendors opened early to accommodate the crowds. The parade started at ten, and Kate knew the congestion would get worse before it got better.

But this was Eagle River's chance to shine, so she didn't mind. Besides, she'd just chowed down on the best breakfast burrito she'd ever had, so her morning was off to a great start.

The lines were long at The Eagle's Nest, and she was glad she'd gotten up early to snag a burrito before they were gone. As Bertha crawled down a side street on the way out of town, Kate tried to pinpoint what made the burrito so tasty.

The corn and other veggies were mixed right into the scrambled eggs, but something else had made the flavors really stand out. And it wasn't just the sausage, provided by the local farmers' meat locker.

Kate suspected all the vegetables had been pan-roasted ahead of time with a blend of seasonings. If she could pinpoint what they were, she might be able to recreate the burritos at home.

Leo Deegan wasn't likely to spill the bar's secret spice recipe, any more than he would want to relinquish his new title. From what she'd heard last night, the wooden corncob would soon go on display at the bar. Inside a glass case, of course, to keep it pristine until next year.

And it might take until the following August for Kate to get out of town. She'd puttered her way toward the south end, but was now caught in the congestion near the high school's softball fields, where a tournament would start within the hour. Kate glanced at the dash clock, then had to laugh.

This was nothing like Chicago's traffic, which she'd battled for years during both her personal and professional hours. "I can see the cornfields from here," she reminded herself. "Five more minutes, and I'll be on my way."

With Jared being lucky enough to have the day off, Kate had been assigned to his southern route. All the in-town carriers were on duty, which at first had disappointed Kate. What fun it could have been to walk around during the festival! She might have felt like she was participating, just a little bit, through the throngs of people around her.

But last night at the beer garden, Randy and Marge had grumbled about the traffic, the crowded sidewalks in the business district, and the out-of-towners who would constantly flag them down for directions. In the end, Kate decided the gravel roads were the best place to be today. Besides, it was supposed to be terribly hot. Spending her working hours in Bertha's climate-controlled interior would be better than walking in town.

When her route was finished, Kate was glad to go home for a shower and a nap, and some playtime with Charlie. He didn't meet her at the door, but a few minutes of searching located him under her bed. Even with all the windows closed against the heat, the muffled buzz of the crowds below had wreaked havoc with Charlie's much-prized daily routine.

"Oh, I know how upset you are." Despite his scowl, Charlie was quick to leave his hiding space when Kate offered some of his favorite treats. Even so, his sonar-like hearing was still carefully calibrated toward the revelry outside, and his blue eyes kept straying to the front of the building. Kate found his favorite brush, and got to work.

"Today's the only day that'll be this upsetting, I promise. Everything will be back to normal tomorrow. Well, at least for you. Some of the rest of us will have to clean up the mess, first."

What Kate conveniently left out was that Charlie had a car ride scheduled for Wednesday. It was time for his annual checkup and, although there was a clinic in Eagle River, Kate had decided to take him to Prosper Veterinary Services instead. Her parents had patronized that practice for years, and now that Kate was friends with Karen, that was where she wanted Charlie to receive his care.

Karen had a few seven a.m. slots on weekdays, which meant Kate could squeeze in Charlie's exam before she had to report to the post office. Sure, they could have done this on Kate's weekday off, but Charlie hated to travel. This way, he could pout in private, and Kate would be mostly forgiven by the time she came home from work.

Only a few minutes after Charlie's grooming session was completed to his satisfaction, Kate got a text from her mom. *We're downstairs if you're ready to go.*

While there were some things Kate missed about Chicago, the fact she could now see her parents whenever she wanted made up for many of them. Charlotte and Curtis were outside the tenants' Main Street entrance, wide-brimmed hats on their heads and water bottles in their hands.

"Are you sure you don't need to come up for a bit?" Kate adjusted her ball cap against the bright sunshine. "It's beastly hot out here."

Charlotte smiled. "If we do, we may never want to leave. We just wandered through the drug store to bask in its air conditioning, so I think we're good for now. How is our grandkitty handling all this commotion?"

"He's sulking, of course. But he'll survive."

People were everywhere, wandering among Main Street's open businesses and the food vendors along the side streets. It was only five, which meant there were still many hours to enjoy the small carnival and other activities at the park.

Kate purchased a cherry slushie, and was content enough with her icy treat. In this heat, the idea of sweet corn probably wouldn't sound good to her until closer to suppertime. As she and her parents threaded their way through the crowd, Kate wondered who they might run into. But after a long day behind Bertha's wheel, she was willing to let her mind wander as much as her feet.

And then, right next to the pork-chop-on-a-stick stand, Kate saw a familiar face. One that, if she played her cards right, might be her best bet to get an update on Milton's case.

Auggie's half-eaten snack was precariously balanced on its wooden skewer, but he was too busy gabbing with two other men to notice. Just before Kate could alert him to the impending disaster, a woman about his age came to the rescue with a pile of napkins from the stand's dispenser. That had to be Auggie's wife, given his grateful smile. Kate scanned her memory bank. Was her name Jen? No, she was sure it was Jane.

Kate's parents were deep in conversation with some friends of theirs, so when the men around Auggie finally moved on, she moved in.

"Hey!" Auggie wiped his mouth with a fresh napkin and nodded in her direction, as he was unable to extend a free hand in greeting. "How's that fancy cat of yours? Does he like the grub you brought home?"

"Charlie loves it! He's mad right now, about all the commotion, but he'll get over it." She turned to Jane. "He's a Himalayan mix, with a brown face and a cream coat. We live over Sherwoods' furniture store, there on Main."

Jane gave Kate a friendly smile, then turned to her husband. "A 'fancy cat,' huh? Seems like we have one of those at home."

"Chaplin's not a purebred," Auggie pointed out. "He's a mutt, just like Pebbles and Mr. Checkers." But his warm smile told Kate that Chaplin was certainly adored. "He's really special," Auggie explained to Kate. "White with black patches, longhaired, has a cute little mustache mark on his face."

"Well, either way, he has more toys than any other cat I've known," Jane told Kate. "And a cat tree so huge, it takes up one whole corner of the living room. Auggie found him hiding in an old shed at the co-op, scared and hungry. But you'd never know it for how he's come around."

Kate had been looking for a way to steer the conversation in the direction she wanted it to go. "Speaking of cats, I have to tell you what happened to me the other day. Never seen anything like it."

She explained how Milton's cats jumped in the back of her mail car, and detailed her successful efforts to get them safe inside the barn before the storm rolled in.

Auggie howled with laughter, and Kate and Jane did, too. While the situation had been emotional for Kate at the time, she had to admit it was absurd to the point of being uproariously funny.

"That's a new one." Auggie polished off his pork chop and wiped his hands. "Wait until Dan and the other guys down at the co-op hear about this. Everyone's got an animal story, when they come in, and now I've got another one." He smiled at Kate. "I'll give you credit, of course."

"How nice of you." Jane rolled her eyes. "Since she's the one who saved the day."

Before Kate could mention Milton directly, Auggie was off in another, well-traveled direction: talking about himself.

"Did you make it to the recipe contest at the elementary school, earlier this afternoon?" He raised his chin with pride. "I entered a pie. Ever since Prosper started that competition during the Fourth of July celebration, I've been a bit, well ..."

"Obsessed?" his wife offered. "Now you have ten months to work on your crust before Prosper's event comes around again." She turned to Kate. "But really, he's turned into quite the baker. Saves me some time and effort."

"Wait." Kate frowned. "Our festival's food contest is focused on corn. Every entry has to have it. You brought a pie? You must mean a pot pie, like a main dish."

"Heavens, no! A dessert pie." Auggie grinned. "Corn custard. You know, whipped cream, a little lemon juice and, well, the rest is a secret. I mean, other than the sweet corn."

It sounded terrible. Jane had obviously experienced this confection first-hand and, from the look on Auggie's wife's face, Kate knew her hunch was accurate.

"So, how did it go?" Kate asked sweetly.

"It's an acquired taste, I guess." He sighed. "Maybe I should have blended the corn into mush first, not put the kernels in whole. Hey, look who's over there!"

Kate followed Auggie's finger as he pointed through the crowd and across the street. "Who is it?"

"It's Jasper Tindall, there under that light pole." Auggie gestured again. When Kate didn't respond, he blinked. "Oh, so you haven't met him yet?"

Kate never would have guessed the ponytailed man with the graying beard was Milton's neighbor. This was the chance she'd been waiting for ... if she could figure out a faux-casual way to make Jasper's acquaintance.

"Not everyone knows everyone," Jane reminded her husband. "And Kate hasn't been back that long."

"Well, then it's time. You need to tell him about those cats," Auggie told Kate. "He's looking after things at Milton's, he needs to know what happened."

Auggie's tone made it clear he suspected Jasper wasn't holding up his end of the bargain. Which made Kate wonder how much Auggie knew, or thought he knew, about Jasper and Milton's agreement.

"Please be nice," Jane warned her husband.

Kate smiled brightly. "I think I'll go say hello." Auggie was right, the cats were the perfect opener. "Thanks for pointing him out, Auggie. Jane, it was nice to meet you."

Before she even stepped off the curb, Kate knew she was going to have an escort. Auggie didn't even bother to explain why he felt the need to tag along, and Kate decided just to roll with it. Getting these two together, even in a sea of people, could prove very interesting.

As she followed in Auggie's wake through the throng of festivalgoers, Kate texted Bev. *Auggie's taking me to meet Jasper. I'll report back.*

Excellent work! Do you need backup?

Kate smiled as she typed. *Detective Duncan requesting assistance, corner of South First and Main.*

They hung back for a moment while Jasper finished his conversation with another guy, and Kate got her first good look at the other man at the center of this case. He seemed harmless enough, with his faded tee shirt and worn leather sandals. Jasper wore a National Wildlife Federation ball cap, and had some kind of medallion on a leather cord around his neck. If Kate had to guess, Jasper was what Auggie would refer to as a "tree hugger."

Once Jasper's friend moved on and he'd turned his attention back to his funnel cake, Auggie moved in. "Hey, Jasper. Nice day, huh? Looks like a record crowd."

"Auggie." Jasper barely offered a nod, his mouth set in a firm line. There was a wariness in his blue eyes that made Kate glad Bev was on her way. If Jasper's wife and kids were with him, they weren't close by. Jane hadn't followed Kate and Auggie through the crowd, and Kate saw her chatting with another woman across the street.

Despite the hot, humid afternoon, an icy silence settled between the two men.

"I'm Kate Duncan." She stepped forward but didn't offer her hand, as both of Jasper's were busy juggling his funnel cake. "I'm with the post office."

"I know who you are." Jasper was still wary, but his voice had turned kind. "Must have been quite the shock that day, once you realized Milton was gone."

We didn't know that for sure, she thought, but decided to keep that observation to herself. *But you obviously did. Or, at the very least, that's what you said.*

"Oh, a little." She tried to smile. "But I was pretty distracted helping Karen Porter deliver that calf. I'm glad I was driving by at the right time, and was able to help."

"That was quite the excitement, for sure." Auggie laughed, and Kate knew she wasn't the only one trying to smooth over the situation. "I can't imagine what it was like for Karen, either. She's just out on her rounds, and comes down the road, and look what she found."

Jasper glared at him. "I'd stopped by, not two hours before, to look in on that cow. She wasn't in distress when I checked on her last. And I'm still over there every day, sometimes twice, no matter what."

"I'm sorry," Kate said quickly, "I didn't mean to imply you were negligent."

But based on the look Auggie gave Jasper, he apparently did.

"It's good of you to keep an eye on things." Auggie's tone was less friendly now. "But all of this is a little hard to believe. Milton came to you for help, handed you a wad of cash, and just, what? Disappeared from the face of the earth? My cousin wouldn't take off on the spur of the moment."

Jasper swallowed hard, then dumped the rest of his dessert in the trash can under the light pole. Kate felt a wave of sudden interest ripple through the crowd around them. The conversations and laughter continued, but she was sure several pairs of ears were now listening.

At least most people tried to act like they weren't eavesdropping. But one guy openly gawked at Jasper and Auggie as he gnawed a foil-wrapped ear of grilled sweet corn.

"Your cousin?" Jasper's voice rose in pitch. "Barely! More like shirttail relation, I'd say. Since when have the two of you been so close? I'm not sure I've seen you around Milton's place much, these last few years, as he's had a harder time getting around."

"Oh, so you keep tabs on him?" Auggie's cheeks were aflame, and not from the heat. "Maybe you need to do a better job, then."

"No, more like he'd call me when he needed help, and I'd give it. That's what neighbors are for. Especially if you can't count on your family."

Kate exhaled when she saw Bev edge her way through the crowd. “Thank goodness you’re here. This isn’t going how I’d hoped.”

The people around Auggie and Jasper grew restless, with whispered observations about what they were witnessing. Suddenly, another man stepped forward and pointed at Auggie.

“Jasper’s been my friend for over twenty years. If you know something you’re not telling, then now’s the time to spill it.” He gestured toward the police officer directing traffic near the south side of the bridge. “There’s your chance. We don’t need you running around, spreading rumors. I spent two days out there in the heat, walking those fields and that ravine, hoping I wouldn’t stumble across Milton’s dead body.”

“You think I don’t care?” Auggie shouted. “Because I damn sure do. And I’ve talked to the authorities, more than once.” He gave Jasper another level stare. “Told them everything I know, which isn’t much.”

Jasper’s friend snickered. “Well, that’s a first for you, then.”

“What do you want from me?” Jasper was breathing hard now. “What are you implying? You better say it now, in front of everyone, and say it straight. I’ve cooperated with the sheriff, and will continue to do so. On top of that, we’re looking after the animals, picking up the mail, whatever needs to be done.”

Auggie turned to Kate and Bev, his eyes wide. “You’re letting him get the mail?” Kate could only shrug helplessly.

“And my family will keep it up,” Jasper insisted, “until Milton comes home. I don’t give a damn what people think I know, or don’t know. Milton’s gone. I don’t know where he is, but the least I can do is help out. Say, Auggie, what exactly are you doing to help? Because I don’t think running your mouth counts.”

Auggie raised his chin. “We’ll see about that.”

"See about what?" Jasper grimaced. "Now you're not even talking sense."

A woman grabbed his arm and, by the mix of rage and embarrassment on her face, Kate suspected this was Carrie Tindall. As they moved away, Jasper muttering to his wife under his breath, Bev swooped in on Auggie.

"What was that all about?" she hissed. "Are you crazy? Interrogating Jasper in public, right in the middle of the festival, where everyone can hear? You should leave that to the authorities."

Auggie raised an eyebrow at Kate, and then at Bev, and seemed about to say something smart. But he didn't.

With nothing left to see, the people around them lost interest. There were too many good things to eat, and too many friends to greet. Kate was glad the situation had been resolved, at least for now. And she knew most, if not all, of those who'd been so keen to watch Jasper and Auggie face off would forget about it within minutes. Unfortunately, it was likely to be the same for Milton.

"Hey," Auggie said suddenly. "We never got to tell Jasper about the cats." Then he sighed. "It's just as well. Like he cares, anyway."

Two men stopped to greet Auggie. He leaned in, eager to rehash his grievances with Jasper, and the three of them soon ambled down the sidewalk.

Kate looked at Bev, and shook her head. "The only thing I gleaned from that conversation is that Jasper might be as outspoken as Auggie. But I don't think that helps us any."

"From what I just heard, I don't think either of them is hiding anything. But they'd love to think the other one is." Bev rolled her eyes. "The only person who knows the truth, I'd say, is Milton. And I have a feeling he isn't coming home anytime soon."

* 18 *

Kate did her best to enjoy the rest of the festival, but the ugly scene between Auggie and Jasper was never far from her thoughts. And as she helped clean up the park Sunday morning, she replayed their confrontation from several angles. After all, wandering around with a grabber stick and a trash bag provided plenty of time for reflection.

She didn't know Auggie well, but he definitely matched his reputation as an outspoken, self-appointed community leader. Along with that, his ego was a bit bigger than what sometimes was in his best interests.

He relished his role as the local curmudgeon, and Kate suspected he was occasionally guilty of upping the theatrics just for fun.

Even so, his dressing-down of Jasper seemed a bit harsh. Especially since it was done in public. That made Kate think Auggie doubted Jasper's story.

Or, even worse, Auggie firmly believed Milton had already met a bad end. Because under all his bluster, Kate decided, Auggie had more empathy than he would ever admit to possessing.

For his part, Jasper's anger was probably just self-defense against Auggie's cutting comments. Or was it possible that, despite his reputation as an easy-going guy, Jasper had a hidden temper? Kate remembered what Grandpa Wayne's friends said about Jasper's father. She hoped it wasn't true, but maybe the apple hadn't fallen far from the tree.

And here came Grandpa now, behind the wheel of a large lawn tractor whose trailer was stacked with stuffed-full garbage bags. He throttled down the engine and stopped in front of the shelter house.

"Kate, my girl, I think we're almost done." He pointed over his shoulder. "Toss yours on the pile there, and I'll get those others on the trailer." Five more bags waited under the nearby light pole.

Grandpa Wayne got up slowly from his seat, and Kate gestured for him to sit back down. "I'll do it. You look tired. I hope you're going home soon to rest."

He didn't protest, just nodded his thanks while Kate loaded the trailer. "I've been at this for thirty years. Sometimes, it feels like longer than that."

"But you keep saying yes," she reminded him. "I know Austin can be pretty persuasive. But next year, maybe you should get up the gumption to tell him no when he begs you to be on the committee again. Let some younger people take over, for once."

"Oh, I don't know. Where's the fun in that?"

Kate wanted to ask Grandpa more about Jasper, and see if he'd overheard any useful information about Milton's case during the past few days. Because despite their efforts to keep their ears open, Kate and Bev hadn't picked up any gossip that could be useful to the case.

But she'd promised to not reveal she was helping Sheriff Preston collect information and, as the weeks dragged by, it was getting harder and harder to insert Milton into a conversation and not collect suspicious looks. Like Bev said Friday night, most people seemed to have moved on.

"Well, anyway, this year's party is about wrapped up." Grandpa shifted the lawn tractor into gear. "By next spring,

I'll probably be itching to get back into it again."

Then he laughed. "I know you're used to all kinds of excitement in Chicago, but you're going to be reminded quick that not much else happens in Eagle River. School starts tomorrow, of course, but beyond that? Expect things to be really quiet around here."

"Actually, that sounds good about now." Kate stifled a yawn as she waved her goodbyes. "I'll see you and Grandma for supper tonight. I'll come over around six."

Kate walked Marge's town route on Monday, and it was bittersweet to see the flood of children rushing out of the elementary school as she finished her deliveries that afternoon. It was still hot, of course, and August had over a week to go. But where had the summer gone?

Hers hadn't been easy. But Kate could see how she'd grown over the past few months. New friends, a new job, a new routine. And now, a new home on the horizon. Donna expected Kate would have the keys to the farmhouse later this week, even though the sale wouldn't close until mid-September.

There were so many possibilities in her future. And, for the first time in a long time, Kate could look forward with hope in her heart.

Roberta had taken some much-deserved time off, which meant Kate was in charge of the post office's counter the next two days. She barely had the front door unlocked Tuesday morning when Ward Benson rushed in, his forehead lined with worry.

The retired seed-corn salesman wasn't only the leader of the local veterans' organization, but currently served as Eagle River's mayor.

"Mayor Benson." Kate looked up in surprise as she tidied the counter. "What brings you in?"

"Where's Roberta?" His brown eyes darted about nervously as he stuffed his hands in the pockets of his cargo shorts.

"She's off today. Is there something ..."

To Kate's surprise, Ward pointed toward the bulletin board. "It's Milton." He tried to take a deep breath, and somewhat succeeded. "Or I mean, it's about Milton."

Kate gripped the counter for support. "What happened?"

"I don't know, and that's the problem." Ward was almost shouting now. "Sheriff Preston just called, told me he's having a press conference in a few hours and that I need to get over to the courthouse by ten-thirty." He glanced at the clock. It was just after nine. "They've found something, but he wouldn't tell me what."

Bev rushed up from the back. "Thank goodness I'm running late this morning," she told Kate, then went through the wooden gate to put a hand on the mayor's shoulder. "Ward, whatever it is, try to calm down. You look a fright."

"I know," he groaned. "I'm so upset, I don't know what's going on. And then, well, the sheriff told me I need to wear a shirt and tie, a jacket, the whole bit. Marie's off at her coffee group already and I have no idea what to do."

Bev gave Kate a wide-eyed stare that said, *is he serious?*

"Just put on whatever you might wear to church," Kate suggested. "White shirt, then dark, neutral colors. That way, you won't stand out too much to the cameras."

"Cameras?" Ward gasped. "Oh, no, you're right. The television stations will be there. And the newspapers."

"Now, what did you want to tell Roberta?" Bev tried to help the mayor focus. "You need to get a move on."

He blinked. "Oh. Just that there's a press release going out on this within minutes. Or it already has, I don't know." He looked at Kate, then back at Bev. "I wanted to warn her that everyone's going to be buzzing about it this morning. The press conference is at eleven-thirty."

"OK. Thanks for letting us know." Bev steered the mayor toward the door. "Go home and get changed. Everything is going to be fine."

Once Ward was gone, Bev turned toward Kate with tears shining in her eyes.

"Don't say it." Kate blinked back her own. "We don't know yet what they've found."

"It's been five weeks." Bev shook her head. "Actually, six weeks as of tomorrow. He's been gone too long." She tried to square her shoulders. "We have to be prepared for bad news."

The afternoon Kate helped Karen deliver that calf seemed like so long ago. When Kate turned up Milton's lane, her only motive a willingness to offer a helping hand, she'd had no idea what she was getting herself into.

The too-quiet yard. The empty house, and the package on the porch. Doc McFadden's insistence that something was wrong. And then she thought of those poor cats, and how they'd jumped in her car last week. And how Auggie and Jasper had shouted at each other on the sidewalk Saturday afternoon, tempers flaring and accusations flying.

Kate put her hands over her face and leaned her elbows on the counter.

"You going to be OK here, by yourself?" she heard Bev say. "Ward's right, everyone's going to be talking about it. And wanting to know what you think."

"I'll make it through." Kate took a deep breath and nodded. "On one hand, I wish I knew what this was all about. On the other, I don't have to fake it when I tell people I don't know a thing."

Bev gave Kate a hug before she started for the back room. "My load's pretty light today, so I'll be in for lunch before the press conference. You call if you need me before then."

The counter rarely saw a steady flow of traffic in a town this small, so Kate searched for something productive to do before the first rush arrived. She reached for the dust cloth and lemon-scented polish kept on one of the inside shelves and went to work, scrubbing out each handprint and rubbing the solid-oak surface until it shined. Next came the lobby windows, using the crumpled newspapers Roberta insisted made the glass gleam.

The pen caddy was swabbed, the stacks of forms and flyers squared and arranged. She couldn't control everything that was swirling around her, but she could bring order to the Eagle River post office.

It was going to be a lovely day; the late-summer sun streamed in and filled the small lobby with a warm glow. Maybe it was too soon to lose heart. Just because there was going to be a press conference, that didn't mean the news had to be bad. Right?

Even so, Kate was numb with exhaustion and worry just two hours later. Her customers had talked of little else, and Kate early on drafted a handful of noncommittal answers she rotated through the rest of the morning.

I haven't heard anything more, myself. We'll have to see what the sheriff says. We don't know if it's bad news.

"Well, you know it must be." One older woman dropped her purse on the counter. "If Milton's alive and kicking, why not just say so?"

"Bet they found a body." The man behind her shook his head. "Can't imagine where he'd go, and be gone that long."

"Oh, so you know him?" Kate tried for a smile. It was too hard to turn off her inquisitive mind after all these weeks.

"Not really." The man shrugged. "Just know the type, is all. Old bachelor farmer, keeps to himself. Doesn't get too far from home, is all I'm saying."

"Well, I want to know what's happened." The woman reached for her pocketbook, then frowned when Kate handed her a book of stamps. "What? They went up again? This is highway robbery! It's bad enough the feds keep raising our taxes."

Kate heard booted footsteps come up from the back, and then Jack appeared at her elbow.

"Well, Evelyn, how are you today? Cheerful as ever, I see." He smiled, and the woman handed over her money. Jack was in his fifties, but that still made him a handsome young man to the elderly ladies in town.

"You're right, inflation is terrible." Jack made change at the register. "It's the same for us here at the post office. Why, you should see our gas receipts! I swear, it's gone up a good five cents a gallon since last week."

That did the trick. The price of gas was one of the main topics of conversation around Eagle River, right along with the weather. With people driving miles in any direction to reach so many services and businesses, gas was a big-ticket item in everyone's budgets. Kate briefly thought of the gas pumps Auggie was installing at his co-op, and wondered where his prices would fit into the local mix.

His head had to be spinning right now as he waited to learn the latest about Milton. Jasper surely felt the same.

Unless one of them was the reason the sheriff had something new to reveal.

"Go take a break," Jack told Kate. "I'll watch the counter and switch over when it's time." There was a small television mounted on the lobby's side wall, and Roberta usually kept it tuned to a national news or weather station.

Bev soon came in the post office's back door. "Randy texted me, says he'll be ready for his break in about ten minutes. And I think we're going to have a lobby full of people, too."

She was right. Between the mail carriers and current customers, as well as several passersby who came inside just before the press conference began, it was a packed house. Most people could view the event on their phones, but they sought the support of their fellow residents as they braced for whatever news was about to be shared.

The Mason City television station soon interrupted its regular programming to show a live feed from a bustling conference room at the courthouse. The chairs closest to the podium were filled with representatives from the region's media outlets, with Sharon Myers, the Swanton newspaper's editor, right in the front row.

"Did you ever talk to Sharon?" Jack asked Kate as the lobby began to buzz.

"No, I didn't. And I won't now, either."

"If she wants reaction, she'll need to get it somewhere else," Bev said as she stared at the screen. "Oh, look, they're about to start. There's Jeff."

Jack shot Bev a strange look.

"Sheriff Preston," she said quickly. "And it looks like he has a whole team of people with him."

The sheriff introduced the county attorney and a man from the state's crime-investigation bureau, as well as a spiffed-up Mayor Benson. Kate wasn't sure why such a show of force was necessary, but based on how stressed Sheriff Preston looked, he wasn't comfortable being in front of the camera alone. And with only a handful of deputies spread across the county, he surely couldn't spare any of his own staff long enough to join him at the podium.

"I'll get right to the point." Sheriff Preston studied his notes carefully, then looked out over the audience. "We have an update in the Milton Benniger case, but I'm sorry to say it's not the outcome we've been hoping for."

Gasps and groans filled the post office's lobby. Bev grabbed Kate's hand.

"However, we are not ready to give up hope. Mr. Benniger's truck has been located, and our goal is to do the same for him."

A photo appeared on the monitor behind the podium, and the camera zoomed in on it while the sheriff continued to speak.

"This is the vehicle. It was discovered a few hours ago in a rural area of southern Minnesota, thirty miles northwest of Rochester. It is a 1981 Ford, registered to Mr. Benniger."

Jaws dropped around the post office. *Minnesota?*

"That's it!" one man shouted. "I'd know that jalopy anywhere."

Jeff's mouth settled in a firm line, and he seemed to choose his next words very carefully.

A deputy was on his early-morning rounds when he spotted the old truck parked at the edge of a pasture. No one was inside the vehicle at the time, or in the immediate vicinity. The deputy ran the truck's plate, matched the vehicle to Hartland County's continued request for assistance in locating Milton, and immediately notified Sheriff Preston.

"We are communicating with the owner of the property where the truck was found," the sheriff continued. "But as of right now, we don't have much to go on."

"What's that supposed to mean?" Jack's eyes narrowed. "Are they acting like they don't know anything about it?"

Kate stared at the screen, but found it hard to focus on what Sheriff Preston was saying. How did Milton's truck get so far from Eagle River? That location had to be over a hundred miles from here. And based on how his truck looked, she couldn't imagine how it got even halfway without breaking down on the side of the road.

The reporters wanted to know if the truck had been searched for evidence. Was there anything suspicious about the truck's condition? The state investigator spoke briefly regarding the examination of the truck, but revealed nothing about what had, or had not, been found.

Sharon raised her hand. "Sheriff Preston, I understand you can't share many details now, but there's something I think everyone wants to know: Does this discovery give you more hope, or less, that Milton is still alive?"

Everyone in the post office seemed to hold their breath.

Sheriff Preston stared at his notes. When he looked back up at the audience, discouragement and exhaustion were clearly written on his face.

"Oh, Jeff," Bev whispered, "you're doing all you can."

The sheriff's voice wavered at first. "When it comes to Milton's whereabouts, I wish I had some good news to share." But then he looked straight into the cameras. "I'm asking again ... no, I'm *insisting* ... that anyone with information that could help us, please come forward."

While authorities in Minnesota were now assisting with the case, he said, the residents of Hartland County needed to stay vigilant and report anything they knew, no matter how insignificant it might seem, to his office.

"As long as there's any hope Milton might be found, we're going to keep looking. I'm not ready to give up."

Sheriff Preston didn't answer Sharon's question. When it became clear he was struggling with his emotions, the county attorney stepped forward and took over the podium.

"We need everyone's help with this. Take another look around your property, especially those of you in the rural areas. Check your barns, sheds, ravines and fields. Mr. Benniger's truck is rather distinctive in appearance; when and where may you have seen it over the past six weeks or so?"

The county attorney checked his notes. "We do have one other bit of new information to share today. A five-thousand-dollar reward fund has been set up for information leading to the resolution of this case."

The reporters had a flurry of questions, but the county official held up a hand.

"The donor, or donors, wish to remain anonymous, so I won't discuss it further. But if you find anything, or hear anything, that might get things moving in the right direction, please contact the sheriff's office. Even the smallest bit of evidence might allow us to solve this case."

He turned toward the sheriff, who only gave a curt nod.

"I think we'll wrap up now," the attorney told the reporters. "As soon as we have anything more we can share, we'll get it out as quickly as possible."

As the officials filed out of the conference room, the camera feed cut to a television reporter out in the hallway.

"We're coming to you live from the Hartland County courthouse in Swanton, where Sheriff Jeff Preston has just informed the public that ..."

The post office had been silent for several minutes. But it didn't stay that way much longer.

"Wait!" one man shouted. "That's all they've got?"

"What do you expect them to do?" Another man tossed up his hands. "Wave a magic wand, pull Milton out of a hat?"

One woman burst into tears. "He's dead. You know he has to be."

"We don't know that." Another resident put her arm around the woman's shoulder. "The sheriff says he's not ready to give up. We can't, either."

Kate felt the same. But right now, the odds were stacked against a positive outcome in this case. If the lobby hadn't been so crowded, she would have marched over to the bulletin board, right then, and pulled down that flyer.

Not because she thought the situation was hopeless; at least, not yet. But because she couldn't bear to look at that photo any longer.

* 19 *

The discovery of Milton's truck put many of Eagle River's residents into a tailspin. Even for those who'd managed to set the case aside in their minds, the sheriff's press conference was a sobering reminder that one of their own was missing.

As expected, it was the talk of the post office the rest of the day, and Kate was drained by the time she closed the public portion of the shop at four.

We don't know if it's bad news. As much as she tried to hold out hope that Milton was alive and safe, one of the things she'd told anxious residents all morning seemed less and less likely to be true.

After all, Milton's old truck was mired down in a muddy farm field over a hundred miles from home, and there was no sign of him anywhere.

As she sold stamps and weighed packages and added a new box of tissues to the counter, one scary scenario after another played through her mind.

She grasped for something else she could offer the dozens of people who longed for a few words of comfort and support.

Maybe he'll turn up yet. Sheriff Preston is a good guy, he's doing all he can. I'm sure we'll hear more soon.

Kate was unable to put her worries to rest that night, much less fall asleep. Charlie kept vigil with her, curled up on the corner of the mattress next to her pillow. Her fluffy boy had his own worries as well, given the appearance of his carrier from the depths of the bedroom closet. Karen had to have him cornered, crated and in Prosper by seven in the morning, a deadline that compounded her stress.

As she tossed and turned, she wondered what, if anything, she could do to help at this late stage of the case. Staring at the ceiling with a heaviness in her chest wasn't doing her, or Milton, any good.

It was tempting to drop in at Paul's Place, to see if any useful information might come her way. Given how vocal the post-office crowd had been that day, the regulars at the bar had to be buzzing tonight.

It was just after eleven and, even on a Tuesday, she knew Alex kept the booze flowing until at least one. But she was too tired, and didn't feel comfortable going there alone. And then, there was Alex's warning for Kate to keep her nose out of things. No, that wasn't a good idea.

Alex was handsome and charming, but Kate couldn't shake the feeling he had something to hide. Maybe he did; but maybe it had nothing to do with Milton. Chris said Alex was a good guy, and Kate trusted Grandpa's friend. So why was Alex so adamant Kate stay out of it? If he wasn't somehow to blame, was he trying to protect her from something? And if so, what?

What exactly was going on here? She'd never thought her hometown's residents had many secrets. But now, she wasn't so sure.

Kate finally got up and padded to the tiny bedroom's lone window, which looked over the back parking lot and into the first block behind the business district. She stared into the shadows, at the homes crouched under the streetlights, and wondered about the people living in each one.

Because every house in Eagle River, every window, held someone's secret. It was the same in the country; inside every farmhouse, down every gravel road and around every bend. No one knew what went on behind closed doors, what other people were thinking, feeling.

In Chicago, it had been the same. No matter how well you knew someone, you never really knew what was going on inside them. She'd had plenty of surprising deliveries in her decade as a mail carrier, like court summons and collection notices for people she never would have guessed needed either.

But really, Kate was no different. When her marriage began to crumble, she'd projected an "all is well" attitude to her friends and coworkers, even her family. And sometimes, even to herself. When Ben admitted his infidelity and everything fell apart, everyone around them was shocked. Or at least, they'd claimed to be. She'd wondered, later, how many of the people in her life had suspected trouble but stayed silent.

"We're all hiding something," she told Charlie, who'd launched himself to the top of the nearby dresser. "We're so worried about what others will think. We want to seem fine, even when we're not." She rubbed his ears. "Well, maybe not you. You always make your needs clearly known."

So if everyone had secrets, hidden somewhere inside of themselves, then Milton did, too. Maybe his, like most people's, were relatively insignificant.

But what if they weren't? What if they were the root cause of whatever had happened to him?

Despite the warm night, Kate shivered. If only she knew Milton's secrets. If only there could be some closure.

She picked up her phone and stared at its silent, dark screen for a few minutes before finally putting it back on the nightstand. Sometime soon, she was sure, her phone would ring, or beep or chime. And there just might be an answer.

* * *

Charlie put up a fight about the carrier, as usual. Kate, who was groggy with lack of sleep, felt victorious to come away from the battle with only one small scratch on her right hand. With much howling and hissing from the back seat, they started out on their fifteen-minute drive to Prosper. Kate didn't think she'd ever been so glad to see its water tower appear on the horizon.

"We're here." Charlie answered with another long howl. Could cats make themselves hoarse from yowling? Kate decided she might find out before this vet visit was over.

"Karen promises to look at you right away, so we won't be hanging out in the waiting room. In and out. I promise."

Prosper's Main Street was nearly deserted at this early hour, although Kate saw a cluster of vehicles in front of Prosper Hardware. Morning coffee hour started at seven, from what Karen said, and wrapped up before the store opened at eight. John "Doc" Ogden, Karen's business partner, was always in the circle unless an early-morning farm call kept him away. Auggie was also a regular participant.

As Kate lifted Charlie's carrier out of the back seat and started up the sidewalk, she wondered if Auggie had told the coffee group about how she'd transported Milton's cats.

It was likely he'd spread the story around Monday morning, his very-first opportunity to do so. Had he also told his buddies about his run-in with Jasper?

Oh, to have been a fly on the wall for that. And after yesterday's press conference, the hardware store was sure to be filled with theories this morning.

Charlie's next howl of indignation brought Kate's musings up short. They were almost to the clinic's front door but, despite the one-story building's cozy, dark-green siding and fresh white trim, her boy had apparently decided it was a house of horrors.

"It's OK," she whispered as they went into the vestibule. "Karen is really nice. I know you're going to become friends."

The lobby was empty, so there were no other cats or dogs sulking about to ruffle Charlie's lush coat. Karen soon appeared through the swinging door by the front counter.

"You made it!" She leaned in to get a good look at her first patient of the day. "Oh, he's handsome! I've seen pictures, of course, but they don't do him justice."

"And he knows it. I'm glad you have this early slot so we can get this out of the way."

"We didn't use to do in-house clinical visits until eight, only drop-offs." Karen went around the counter and sat at the computer. "But they've proven to be popular. Oh, good, that new-patient paperwork you filled out yesterday came through fine. Let me print this out, and we'll get started."

Karen ushered them down the hall, and took a right into the first exam room.

"This is so homey and cozy." Kate looked around with admiration. "Charlie's vet in Chicago had a nice office. But it was, I don't know, a little too modern. A bit cold."

"I'm guessing they didn't have a barn out back," Karen said as she washed up at the sink and readied her supplies. "This clinic's been here for several decades. Before that, we think it was the site of a livery stable."

"Really?" Kate was intrigued. "So, where's Thomas McFadden? Is he still helping out?"

Karen laughed. "No, thank goodness. We were in desperate need, and he was willing to fill the gaps. But John and I are glad to be back to a duo." She raised an eyebrow. "In our case, three really was a crowd. John went back to a full schedule last week, and I hope things settle down around here. But then, this line of work is never dull."

"I can imagine." Then Kate laughed. "Actually, I know that to be true, firsthand."

Charlie hissed and pouted when Karen opened his carrier door, then braced his fluffy paws against the inside of his safe space when she tried to lift him out.

"Sometimes, this is a show for Mom or Dad," Karen explained to Kate. "Classic guilt trip. 'Look what you've done! I'm terrified!'"

"Do you think I should leave the room? I mean, if he doesn't have an audience, he might behave."

"Let's do that. Across the hall is the boarding room, we have one dog and two cats in there right now. They might like a little company."

Kate let herself out into the hallway, and closed the door as quietly as she could. She put an ear to the door for just a moment. All she could hear was Karen's gentle voice; Charlie had suddenly decided to cooperate.

"He's quite the actor." Kate rolled her eyes and went into the boarding area. One of the cats was open to the idea of socializing, but the other was too busy hiding under its blanket to do more than throw a glare in Kate's direction. The dog, however, wagged its tail the moment Kate appeared.

"Well, hello." She checked the tag on the oversized kennel. "You must be Hazel." The German Shepherd mix let out a whimper of happiness when she heard her name. Kate had just inched open the kennel door to give the dog a pet when she heard Charlie's exam-room door open and close.

"Hey, I see you met Hazel," Karen said. "If you're willing, I have a favor to ask. I haven't had time to take her for a walk yet this morning. We went out to potty, of course, but never made it out of the yard. But I'll warn you, she's energetic."

Hazel gave another whimper and pushed her plush neck further into Kate's outstretched hand. "Sure, I can do that."

"She's from a special facility, out past the far side of Swanton. They take in certain breed mixes from shelters and rescue groups, train them to be working dogs. Veterans' companions, K-9 officers for law enforcement, that sort of thing."

Kate was impressed. "I don't think I've heard of them before. Is it new?"

"Oh, they started maybe two years ago. Hazel here is about three years old, they think. Maybe part sheepdog, or Lab; they're not sure. She hasn't been at the facility for very long, so she's not the best at following all the commands yet." Karen pointed out the paperwork on top of the kennel.

"Or impulse control. Which is why she stayed with us last night. Someone left a bag of treats within easy reach, and Hazel decided she needed to sample every single one. Too much of a good thing brings on a tummy ache."

Josh Vogel's Swanton veterinary clinic was closest to the rescue program's home base, but his recuperation kennels were full right now. Through Doc and Karen's work-sharing agreement with Josh, Hazel had ended up in Prosper for her exam yesterday.

"I think she'll be good to go back this afternoon." Karen selected a lead and handed it to Kate. "In the meantime, a little exercise will do her good. By the time you get back, I think Charlie will be ready to go home, too."

Hazel knew what the leash meant, and obeyed Karen's command to remain still while Kate hooked it to her collar.

"She sits well, at least." Kate might have been sleep-deprived, but she was suddenly excited to spend more time with this special girl. "Where do you usually walk the dogs? I know Prosper's tiny, but are some streets better than others?

"Oh, she'll let you know where she wants to go." Karen laughed. "Just hold on tight, and you'll be fine."

"Are you ready?" Kate asked Hazel as she opened the clinic's back door. The dog's bright brown eyes said she was eager to explore. "OK, let's go right."

Hazel wanted to go left, so they did. Down the path that passed the little barn, whose outer door was latched open to reveal a screen door and, beyond that, a recuperating horse in one of the two stalls. Hazel went into a sit and barked as the horse, which answered with only a disdainful shake of its mane.

"No, no, we don't need to go there." Kate's right arm was already tight with tension. Karen was right; Hazel was strong and full of energy. "Leave the horse alone." Kate jangled the lead. "We need to move on."

The dog finally obliged, and they started down the side street behind the clinic, headed south. Hazel trotted on, and alternated between straining at the leash and stopping to point out any squirrels she spotted up in the trees.

The houses on Cherry Street were around a century old, and many were in immaculate condition. Kate even spotted a "for sale" sign in front of one of the Victorian beauties, but she could only shake her head in admiration. First of all, she'd found a wonderful home of her own; and second, such a grand place would cost a fortune to maintain.

A car approached the next corner, and Hazel turned her laser-like focus toward it with a sharp bark. Waylon was mellow compared to this pooch and, given his farm-dog lifestyle, wasn't too clear on commands. Kate wondered what to say to Hazel to keep her from rushing toward the car. Did working dogs follow the same directives as regular pups? Or did they learn military-type orders instead?

As Hazel jerked on the lead, Kate braced her sneakers on the sidewalk and decided to toss out whatever came into her fatigued mind.

"Stop! Hazel, stay!" That one made the dog turn to look at her, at least, but it wasn't enough. "Halt!" Kate tried again. "At ease!"

Either that one did the trick, or Hazel simply lost interest as the car passed through the intersection and continued toward Main Street.

Kate was panting now, too, from exertion of a different kind. Her right wrist throbbed, and she switched the lead to her left.

"Hazel, you need to listen when I tell you something." The dog was now busy sniffing a light-colored patch of grass near the curb. “How are you ever going to serve and protect the community if you don’t pay attention to what anyone says?”

That elicited a happy whimper and a tail-butt wiggle that Kate couldn’t help but love. Hazel was a cute dog, and obviously very smart. If she would just settle down a bit, she’d be the perfect companion for anyone in need of the program’s specialized services.

They were off again. Two more blocks of steady strolling, and Kate thought the dog had calmed down a bit. They reached the southwest corner of Prosper and, between the houses, Kate caught a glimpse of the pasture that rolled on behind the railroad tracks.

But then, Kate’s left shoulder jerked suddenly as Hazel did the same. Frantic barks, a firm stance, and then a flat-out run. “What?” Kate gasped. “What now?”

A cat. A shorthair orange tabby, sunning on a front stoop.

“Hazel, leave him be.” The dog whimpered softly, and Kate thought she’d finally gotten the upper hand. “He’s a nice kitty, and he doesn’t need you to bother him.”

More barks now. And Kate quickly saw why: more cats.

Three of them appeared around the corner of a house. There was another over by a flagpole. An elderly woman popped out one garage’s side door, a plastic bucket in one weathered hand. Hazel went into overdrive when a fluffy black cat suddenly burst out of the bushes at the edge of the driveway, not two feet away.

At least a dozen more cats clambered up and over the train tracks. Four slid out from the hidey hole under another neighbor’s porch. From the woman’s muffled greetings as she walked around the side of her house, Kate could tell even more cats waited out back for their breakfast.

Hazel was beside herself with glee. There was so much to see, so much activity. She didn’t act as if she wanted to attack the cats; rather, it was like she wanted to run among them and play.

Kate tried to pull Hazel on, and only succeeded when the show was over. With their tails held high, all the cats had hurried after the woman and disappeared around the back of the house. At last, Hazel settled into a brisk walk. "That's better." Kate tried to catch her breath. "Let's go back up Main, it's the shortest way."

They passed several empty storefronts, but Kate also got a good look at the new barbershop in town. One block down, they strolled into the heart of the tiny business district. The historic city hall was just across the street, with the library tucked against it. Meadow Lane, the gift shop, had cottage-style windows that highlighted a fascinating mix of antique finds, ceramic collectibles and seasonal housewares.

Kate was intrigued by the shop's displays, so much so that she didn't notice right away when Hazel came to a stop. But then, she smelled why.

"Oh, no! Right here on Main Street? I didn't think to grab a baggie. Karen said you already went potty this morning." She wrinkled her nose. "I guess that's what happens when you eat too many treats, huh?"

Kate shuddered to think of Meadow Lane's proprietor strolling up the walk in an hour or two to find a disgusting pile right by the shop's charming entrance. She looked around. There was just one car parked across the street at city hall. Prosper Hardware was next to Meadow Lane, and Kate really hoped Melinda was working today. She'd have a plastic bag, or paper towels, or something else to clean up this mess.

Before Kate and Hazel made it to one of the benches in front of the hardware store, Melinda ran out to greet them. And so did Auggie. And four other men Kate didn't know. In a town of two hundred, any unexpected visitor was worth a look. Especially at this early hour.

"Well, now!" Auggie let out a hearty laugh as he patted Hazel on the head. "Who do we have here? Kate, does your cat know you're sneaking around with someone else?"

Kate explained her errand, as well as her doggie-doo emergency. Melinda soon returned with supplies, and Hazel's potential disgrace was eradicated from public view.

The man with the wiry frame and the suntanned crinkles at the corners of his eyes introduced himself as John Ogden. "I see Karen's put you to work." He laughed. "Miss Hazel's a handful, but what a personality! Once she calms down a little, gets more training, she'll make a wonderful service dog."

"We've seen all the sights. At least, on the south side of town. Including the house with all the cats."

"That's Gertrude's place. She looks after the strays. Karen and Melinda are working with her to get all those cats spayed and neutered, it's been quite a project."

The other coffee-club regulars, including Auggie, had already drifted back inside. Despite Doc's easygoing banter, Kate sensed something was troubling him. It wasn't too hard to guess what it was.

"I suppose everyone's talking about Milton, huh?"

"Yep. Number-one topic this morning, but I expected that." He rubbed his chin. "And everyone has a theory. None of them are very positive, I'm afraid."

"It's to be expected, I guess." Kate shifted the leash from one hand to the other. Hazel had enjoyed a bathroom break and some attention, and now seemed content to rest on the sidewalk for a moment. "That press conference gave people more questions than answers. I hope we hear more soon."

Doc sighed. "Me, too. Because the rumor mill churns awfully fast around here, and it often spits out stuff that's not even remotely true."

Jerry Simmons, Prosper's mayor, wondered if Milton had been carjacked. But Doc couldn't figure that one out. They would have taken the truck, then; and it was so old, who would want it? George Freitag insisted there must have been a medical emergency. Heart attack or some such thing. But then, where's Milton? Someone would have come along and found him, or he would have called for help. No way he could walk very far. And Melinda's uncle, Frank Lange, was working a theory that Milton left on his own accord. The truck broke down, he hitched a ride. But to where?

None of those theories seemed plausible to Doc, and they were all compounded by the fact Milton's truck was found so far from home.

"What's Auggie say?" Kate wanted to know. "He always has an opinion."

"Or five." Doc grinned. But then he frowned. "Actually, now that you mention it, he's been rather quiet this morning. Hasn't said one word about Milton."

The store's screen door squeaked open again, and Melinda was back. "Treats for our friend here." She handed the first pouch to Kate. "We don't carry much of this stuff, not like the co-op, but Hobo's a big fan. And these are for Charlie. Crunchy and fish-flavored; all my cats love them."

Kate expressed her thanks, but handed back the dog snacks. "Hazel's had enough to last her for some time, from what Karen says. We should get going. Charlie's probably wondering when I'm going to spring him from prison." She waved, Hazel barked, and they set off down the sidewalk as Doc and Melinda went back inside Prosper Hardware.

The post office was on the corner, and Kate's memories of the years when Grandpa Wayne managed that shop made her smile. But as they crossed into the next block, her mood dimmed. The coffee group's morning chatter was disturbing, to say the least. And not only for the grim theories offered by its attendees.

Because one member in particular, the one Kate suspected couldn't keep his mouth shut to save his life, apparently had nothing to say. What did that mean?

Kate knew after she got Charlie home, and hurried over to the post office, she'd still be giving that one some serious thought.

* 20 *

The keys were heavy in Kate's hand. She gave them a squeeze for good luck, then lifted the front-door key away from its ring and slid it into the lock.

"This is the big moment!" Donna gestured around them at the farmhouse's open front porch, where a sultry summer breeze drifted in from the field across the road. "This place has so much potential. I can't wait to see what you do with it."

"Well, first, I have to get the door open." Kate jiggled the key a bit, and it started to turn. "A little oil should do it. Can you add that to the list, please?"

"Sure thing." Donna had her notepad ready. "Well, five things so far, and we're just getting in the door. But you have all the time in the world to fix things right. Or you will, once you move in."

Kate wouldn't close on her little farm for two more weeks, but she now had possession of the property. This was her day off, so she'd met Donna at The Daily Grind for a celebratory lunch before they drove out to the acreage to give it a good look.

No work would be done until the papers were signed, but forming a game plan was a way for Kate to refine her ideas and dream about the future. It was also a welcome distraction from waiting for word about Milton. It was Thursday, two days since his truck was found, and the continued silence from the sheriff's office was deafening.

Kate wasn't sure what would happen next in her own life, either. After all, she'd bought this house after touring it only once, and was nervous about more than the sticky lock on the front door.

It had felt like the right decision at the time, but she'd had several breathless moments since then when she wondered if it had been the best choice. But she'd fallen in love with the property right away, and it would have been off the market quickly if she hadn't jumped on it.

Even so, visions of leaky shingles and rusted pipes sometimes crowded her thoughts. The windows would probably need to be replaced. How good were the hardwood floors under all that carpet? Did she really want to spend days up on a ladder, stripping wallpaper? And those kitchen cabinets, they were so ugly! What had she done?

But just as Donna promised, the old house was solid and sound. The property passed all of its inspections with only minor issues being noted. Several times over, Kate studied the photos that were posted online when the property hit the market. They reassured her that what she saw during her rushed tour had been reality, and not a mirage. And it was a good thing she'd saved those snaps, because Kate had been in too much of a hurry to take her own.

What she saw now, right in front of her and all around the house, thankfully matched her expectations. Granted, they were low, but Kate had decided that was the best way to approach this house. It would be a work in progress, just like herself. And she vowed to give both of them the time they needed to bloom.

Of course, it was almost September. And some things couldn't wait.

"I'll need to get a furnace guy out here as soon as possible," she told Donna, who nodded over her notepad. "It might have another winter or two in it, but maybe I should replace it now."

"Some of them cut you a deal if you do the air conditioner at the same time. A few calls, and you'll know what's what."

"Snow removal." Kate peered out the front room's picture window, past the porch to the expanse of lawn. "That line of evergreens on the north side of the driveway will be a big help, but there's no way I can tackle all of that on my own."

"Get a lawn tractor." Donna grinned. "Stick a blade on the front, and you're good to go."

Kate shook her head. "You overestimate my farm-girl skills. And Mom and Dad are out west of town, the opposite way, so he can't just buzz over. No, I'll need to find someone."

The house had been nearly empty when it went on the market, but a quick tour of its rooms showed every closet, every nook was now totally bare.

But the old pinch-pleated draperies still stood sentry over the windows, and Kate was happy to leave them up until she could find something better.

It was going to be like living in a time warp until she could make this place her own. But she loved old things, and the welcoming feel of this house. If you squinted a bit as you looked around, and leaned into the avocado green-mauve-rust color scheme, you might almost find it retro-cool.

Well, not quite.

"The kitchen," Kate announced with a sigh as they passed through the doorway from the dining room.

"What are you going to do in here?"

"Everything. Someday." She rubbed the faux-tile linoleum with the toe of her tennis shoe. "First, though, I'll need some strong tape so I don't trip over this peeled-up edge before I can replace it." She looked around, thinking. "I wish there was a bathroom on the first floor, but where?" She opened the pantry door, and sized up the space. "I hate to lose this, it's such a nice feature."

"Just big enough for a toilet and a tiny sink. That's all you need." Donna pulled a tape measure from her purse and handed it to Kate. "Water and sewer are all in this corner of the house, up and down, which is in your favor. But the pipes will still have to be redone to work it in."

"So, a powder room's going to be pricey." Kate sighed again.

The upstairs was just as vacant as the downstairs, with one notable exception: the can't-miss aroma of mothballs still wafted out of its closets. "It's a good thing winter is a few months off yet," Kate told Donna. "I'll need to have the windows open for some time to get that stench out of here."

Despite the odor, the large front room made her smile. It had three windows, two looking west toward Eagle River and one looking south. Beyond the cabbage-rose wallpaper and the shag carpet, Kate saw a roomy master bedroom that would be flooded with light in the afternoons.

"This is going to be fabulous," Donna proclaimed. "Let me guess: paint, flooring, window treatments, light fixture?"

"Yes, and that's just about everything."

They ducked into the next room, which was as charming as it was small. "This will be Charlie's space, as well as for guests," Kate decided. "Just look at that window seat! He's going to love it." The view was just as wonderful, as it looked out over the south lawn's garden plot and the pasture beyond. A dark squiggle of trees showed where the creek passed through the far corner of the property.

The third room would be an office and sewing room. To save money, Kate was already plotting how she could turn lengths of fabric into curtains that would rival anything she could order from an online housewares store. And with so many windows, this house would require some serious yardage.

She was resigned to keeping the pink-and-cream tile in the bathroom, as that renovation would be a big job. Donna, however, wasn't so sure. "You're not in a hurry to move out of your apartment, right? Since it's currently the only bathroom in this house, maybe you should get it done first."

"You're right. I'll get some estimates and see what they say." Kate unlocked an exterior door at the other end of the tiny hallway. "And now, one of my favorite features: the sleeping porch."

Its east and south walls looked over the yard, and were currently cloaked in window screens. They swapped out for storm windows when cold weather came, and the whole series waited down in the basement. But Kate wasn't so sure about its door's ability to keep out drafts. "This has to go." She rattled the loose knob. "I need something insulated. I'll have to replace this in the next few months."

With the house examined, the ladies went out the enclosed back porch and into the yard. The former owner had long ago arranged for a neighbor to mow the lawn until frost, and he'd been by with his rider just yesterday. Late-season perennials bloomed in beds along the house's foundation, and a series of mature trees gave the ladies shade as they wandered toward the outbuildings.

"What about the sheds?" Donna gave them an appraising look.

"I have no idea." Kate looked back at the house. This was all hers! Or it would be, officially, in a few weeks. But she needed to keep her dreams in check. She had a little war chest, but it would only go so far. "The outbuildings are in decent shape. And as of now, no one needs to live in them, anyway."

Donna raised an eyebrow.

"Don't start down that road," Kate said. "One thing at a time. I'm just glad I have movers lined up."

She'd told Roland yesterday that she planned to be out of her apartment by the end of September. Which had been a fun conversation, as he'd already heard of her impending purchase. She asked why he hadn't said anything, and he'd laughed.

"Dad always says, it's best to stay out of people's business. If someone's buying new furniture, or dumping the old, big changes are usually ahead. Often it's related to 'for better or worse,' if you know what I mean. I knew you'd let me know, eventually."

There'd been another surprise, but this one made Kate's day. Roland already owned a small fleet of trucks, as his crew hauled furniture all around the region. Who was better equipped to expand into the moving business, which had little competition in such a rural area?

He'd only been offering the service for a few weeks, but Kate was relieved to put her possessions in the hands of someone she trusted. Besides, that was one less lead she had to track down in the coming days.

Donna and Kate strolled over to the garden, which was still lush thanks to recent rains. The weeds almost outnumbered the vegetables, but several tomatoes clung to their vines yet, and a few peppers still peeked out from under their canopy of leaves. Kate had told the seller's family to help themselves to whatever was still thriving until frost. Her mom's garden bounty already strained the basement shelves of Kate's childhood home, and she wouldn't have time to can or preserve anything here before winter. Next year, however, would be a different story.

"It's all going to come together," Donna promised as she closed the notebook's cover and presented it to Kate. "Get the big stuff out of the way before winter, and move on from there."

With their tour complete, the ladies started back across the yard. Just before they reached the back steps, Kate's phone rang.

"Hey, Bev! Yeah, I'm out at the farm. I'm happy to report it's the way I remembered it. Which is really good, since ..."

Kate's jaw dropped, and she lowered herself to the steps. "What?" She leaned forward. "Are you sure?"

"Jeff called a few minutes ago." Bev's voice carried such a mix of emotions that Kate wasn't sure which one to focus on first. "It's Milton. They know where he is! A press release is coming out yet this afternoon."

Bev gave a little laugh. "Jeff wanted me to tell you, right away. He said all his regular staff knows already, so we're next on the list."

Kate gasped with joy. "You're saying Milton's alive? After all these weeks?"

Donna reached for Kate's free hand and gave it a squeeze. Her smile said it all.

But when Bev didn't answer right away, Kate took a deep breath. "He's OK, right? Oh, Bev, if he's not, just say it."

"Milton is alive." Even so, Kate could hear the waver of tears in her friend's voice. "But oh, honey, it's not that simple. I just can't believe it! This might take a while to explain. Are you sitting down?"

"I am. Tell me everything you know."

* * *

Kate didn't solve the mystery of what happened to Milton, but she'd been right about one thing: He certainly had secrets.

Two big ones, in fact.

One from his past that had been a mixed blessing, and a more-recent one that no one hoped to have.

The sheriff's press release, however, didn't mention either of them. Between following privacy laws and showing respect for Milton's personal life, the sheriff wasn't officially able to say much beyond the fact that Milton had been found and was alive. He was "staying with friends" who were "adequately meeting his needs," and was "being evaluated by health-care professionals."

Off the record, however, Jeff had a green light to share the details with Bev, Auggie, and some other local residents. Milton and his "friends" had given consent for word to be unofficially spread to members of the Eagle River community.

Because they knew that in a town that small, it was better to step forward and set the record straight before more rumors took hold.

When Milton was twenty, he had a brief affair with a young married woman from over by Meadville. They met at a wedding dance for a mutual friend. She became pregnant, and the woman concealed her daughter's possible paternity for obvious reasons. When her husband's employer offered a transfer to a town in Minnesota, the woman was relieved to put some distance between her past and her future.

Milton didn't know about his daughter until just a few years ago, after the woman's husband passed away. She decided it was finally time to come clean with her family and, following some DNA tests and much soul-searching, Milton's old love reached out to him with the shocking news.

Camille, the daughter who was now a grandmother, drove down with her husband for a visit one spring afternoon. The meeting went better than any of them expected.

Milton wanted to stay in contact with his daughter, but fretted about the steep fees for long-distance calls made through the landline at his farm. Camille suggested he pick up a cheap, basic cell phone for their talks, the kind with no contract, and only purchase minutes as he needed them.

Like so many other parts of his life, Milton kept this discovery to himself. For his own privacy, of course, but also out of respect for his former love and her family.

He and Camille grew close, and talked at least once a week. So when Milton wasn't feeling well in the spring, and finally went to the doctor, Camille was the only person he felt comfortable telling his new secret: It was pancreatic cancer. And already advanced.

Milton didn't want to take treatments, and they argued about it. He'd known people who struggled their way through chemotherapy only to succumb to their diseases. And he'd seen how fast his parents went downhill after they landed at the nursing home.

Besides, someone would have to look after his animals, keep an eye on things, if he wasn't at the farm.

He didn't want live-in help, either. Milton had been on his own for many years, and he refused to be a burden to anyone. No, he'd stay home, the only place he'd ever lived, and make the most of whatever time he had left. His doctors tried, too, but Milton was stubborn. They provided some medications to ease his symptoms, but his mind was sound and they had to respect his wishes.

Milton did surprisingly well for many weeks, surrounded by the comforts of home. But last month, his health rapidly started to decline.

After talking it over with her husband, Camille made her father an offer. "Come stay with us, until the end. Spend time with your grandchildren; there's another great-grandchild on the way. Let us look after you, and we'll bring in specialized care when the time comes."

He finally agreed. Milton would leave; but for now, his animals would stay.

Jasper Tindall had always been a good neighbor, despite the grudge his father held against the Bennigers years ago. And he was of a practical sort, he'd understand a man's need for privacy.

Even so, Milton decided not to tell Jasper very much. If he didn't know the secrets, he wouldn't have to wrestle with how much to share with people when they started to pry. Which Milton knew they would.

And someday, sooner than Milton liked to think about, his story would come to an end. Camille promised to call Jasper after that happened. Of course, that would tell everyone that she existed. But with her mother's blessing, Camille decided it was time to step out of the shadows.

So one day, Milton hopped in his old truck, drove down to Jasper's place, and knocked on the door.

"I'm going to be gone, for a few weeks, at least. It's a lot to ask, but would you be willing to look after things? You're responsible, take such good care of your own animals."

Milton wasn't yet sure when he'd leave, but promised to give a day's notice. Jasper was fine with that, and made his own promise not to tell folks Milton was gone.

That's when Milton reached for his wallet and pulled out a crisp stack of hundred-dollar bills.

"I've stocked up on food for the cows and the cats, but you never know what might be needed. Here's some money, don't spare any expense. Please keep the rest for yourself."

Jasper's support lifted some of the weight off Milton's shoulders. With his animals' needs cared for, he was able to focus on resting up for his journey and tidying up loose ends. His doctor's office and pharmacy were over in Charles City, and he picked up refills on his medications. The monthly bills were paid, and the invoices added to the stack inside the cover of his father's rolltop desk.

It took him a while, given how tired he was these days, but Milton changed the old truck's oil and gave everything a good look-over. That Tuesday, he drove into town, filled up with gas, and passed through Eagle River one last time.

He almost stopped at Paul's Place, thought about buying a round for everyone, but wasn't sure he could make it through even one hour without spilling both his secrets. In the end, he decided, silence was the safest way to go. His last stop was Jasper's farm, to say he was leaving in the morning, before it got too hot. And thanks again for agreeing to do chores.

That evening, Milton packed the essentials into an old suitcase he found in the spare-bedroom closet, cooked supper and cleaned up the kitchen, then made sure the rest of the house was tidy. He turned off the air conditioner and opened several windows, then fell asleep as a muggy, midsummer breeze drifted across his bed, just as he had as a boy.

In the morning he did chores, bid his animals goodbye and, mustering all the courage he could find, fired up the old Ford and started down the lane. Camille said it would take him a good two hours to reach her farm. This trip was going to be the biggest adventure of his life, as well as his last.

Busy with his last-minute tasks and mixed emotions, Milton overlooked the dining room's open window when he closed up the house for the last time. He also forgot about the work boots he ordered several weeks ago.

He'd worn that brand for years, but they'd become hard to find locally and Milton didn't like to take his old truck very far. So he'd selected a pair from a catalog, mailed off his order form and a check. But he wasn't the only one who preferred those mud-kickers, and his size was temporarily out of stock.

They arrived at Eagle River's post office the day after he left home. And then Kate, still unaware of how her life's path would intersect with Milton's, dropped the box on his porch.

In her defense, Camille wasn't really comfortable with her father's plan. It wasn't enough for him to stock up on his medications before he left home. Shouldn't someone know where he'd gone? But Milton made it clear that if he couldn't do this his way, he'd live out his last days at the farm, alone.

And honestly, all of them, Milton included, didn't think he had much time left. Two weeks, maybe three.

But being surrounded by his late-found family raised his spirits and eased some of his pain. Letting them love him, and showing them love in return? Well, that was a journey all in its own. The outcome would be the same, unfortunately, but maybe it wouldn't come as soon as everyone expected.

As the weeks slipped by, Camille and her husband were torn between continuing to honor Milton's wishes and doing what they thought was right. They were still considering their options when the other day, out of the blue, Milton insisted they take his old truck for a spin. It had been sitting in a shed at Camille's farm for too long. If someone didn't drive it once in a while, it might not start at all.

So Monday evening, Camille's husband and oldest son took the keys from the kitchen drawer, and started out for a friend's acreage ten miles away. Halfway there, the truck began to sputter and cough. Her husband hoped to get it off the gravel road before it rolled to a stop, and turned down the next field drive.

The guys called Camille to give them a ride, then looked up the property's owner. As soon as the wet field dried out, and they could arrange for a tow, they promised to have someone haul the truck away.

The next morning, that farmer got the shock of his life when Hartland County Sheriff Jeff Preston called the house before his family had even sat down to breakfast. The old Ford was connected to a missing person's case in Iowa. How did it end up in his field?

The first time the sheriff called Camille's husband's cell phone, he didn't answer because he didn't recognize the out-of-state number.

The second call came while he was on the line with an attorney, still reeling from Sheriff Preston's voicemail and trying to figure out the best way to explain the situation yet honor Milton's continued requests for privacy.

It was still early on Tuesday morning, but Sheriff Preston needed answers. And he wasn't sure how, or when, he'd be able to get them. He decided to roll the dice and call a press conference. Letting Hartland County residents know the truck had been found, and making another plea for information, might motivate someone around Eagle River to finally share whatever they'd been hiding for several weeks.

As it turned out, the only people who knew the truth lived far over the state line.

With shaking hands, Camille called Sheriff Preston back that afternoon.

"We need to talk," the sheriff told Camille. "I've lived in Hartland County most of my life, and I have no idea who you are, who your family is. Tell me what's going on."

Flooded with relief, Camille did. And then, she put her father on the phone.

"I have to bring this case to a close, one way or another," the sheriff told Milton. "It's up to you. How would you like this to go down?"

The cancer diagnosis wasn't a secret to Sheriff Preston. He'd finally been granted access to Milton's medical files under the premise they might hold clues to his disappearance. The records didn't tell where Milton had gone, but they did offer a possible explanation for why he'd left. Sheriff Preston wasn't able to share that information with anyone, including Bev, so her requests for details had started to go unanswered.

Tuesday afternoon, however, the sheriff and Milton discussed everything in great detail. When they finished, the sheriff had one more question.

"Would you be OK with me sharing your situation with some folks? Milton, you say you've always kept to yourself, but that's not really true. People are worried about you. They care. They want to know what happened, that you are safe. And now, at the end, wouldn't it be nice to hear from some of them?"

It took a few days, but Milton finally agreed.

So Thursday afternoon, with a knot in his stomach and a fresh cup of coffee within reach, Sheriff Preston sat down at his computer and tried to figure out how he was going to explain this one.

* 21 *

“I just can’t believe it.” Grandpa Wayne passed the syrup to Max, then tucked into his own pancakes. “Milton, you sly dog! A secret girlfriend, a love child? He’s the last one I would have suspected of something like that.”

“Why?” Lena asked gently. “Everyone needs love. We’re all human, and life’s complicated. Besides, that was sixty years ago. What matters now is, we rally around him if we can.”

“I completely agree,” Grandpa Wayne said. “It’s a sad thing, how sick he is. What a shame he didn’t say something to someone. I’m glad he’s with family now, at the end. But I can’t help but think how much easier this would have been for him if he’d just confided in people.”

“Oh, so we could have more of this?” Max pointed around Peabody’s, where every table was packed. And every conversation, if you listened in, was about Milton. “I’m sure this is exactly what he wanted to avoid.”

Like everyone else, Kate was still reeling from all those revelations about a man people said lived a simple, ordinary life.

So when Grandpa Wayne called last night and said the gang was getting together a little earlier than usual to review and discuss, she’d jumped at the chance to come along.

So did Chris. The pharmacy opened at eight on Fridays; but like Kate, he wasn't about to miss out.

"Well, count us guilty, too," Chris said as he refreshed his coffee. "We're chewing it over, along with our eggs and toast. I'm glad people care now, but I have to wonder: Where were some of them once the initial excitement dwindled? At the pharmacy, Milton was all anyone talked about for maybe three days. And then, it's like some people started to lose interest until his truck showed up this week."

"I'm one of them, I'll admit it." Harvey reached for the ketchup and splashed it over his hashbrowns. "We're all that way these days, seems like. Short attention spans, always looking for the next shiny object. It just goes to show, we all need to be more mindful of those around us."

Grandpa Wayne grunted. "Too many distractions. Social media, email. I blame the internet."

"Spoken like a retired mail carrier," Harvey retorted. "But you know, that's an interesting thought. If Milton had a computer, he would have been emailing his daughter. The sheriff would have been able to get those and track him down that way. But Milton was too old-school for that."

Joan shook her head. "Let's not talk about him like he's already passed on. That'll come soon enough."

Being with his family helped Milton rally at first, but word was he'd declined quickly in the last day or so. Kate suspected once he'd made peace with his past and torn down his emotional walls, he was getting ready to let go.

Hospice care would start this weekend at Camille's house, and Milton's journey was expected to end in the next week or two.

Talk around the table soon turned to Camille's role in the situation. Why didn't she call someone, especially as the weeks went by?

But then, she and her biological father had missed out on so many decades together; one could understand why she wanted his last weeks to meet his wishes. Grandpa's friends decided that, in the end, that was the deciding factor.

This was how Milton wanted things to be. While he was physically failing, his mind was sound. He could still make his own decisions. And really, wasn't that what everyone wanted, to pass away among those who loved you? To go peacefully, if you could?

"I feel terrible for Milton, of course." Joan took a sip of her tea. "But this must have been so hard for Jasper and his family, too. He helped out a neighbor, no questions asked. And then all these people were judging him, whispering about him behind his back."

"I wouldn't do things the way Milton did," Max said, "but when it came to Jasper, that was the right way to go. Jasper didn't have to fake it around everybody. He was as much at loose ends as everyone else. Imagine if he'd known! What was he supposed to do, lie to the sheriff?"

Grandpa Wayne smiled. "Milton knew it, too. He needed Jasper's help, but he didn't want him caught in the middle any more than what was absolutely necessary."

Max was surprised that old truck made it that far, and guessed Milton had avoided the interstate and kept to the county highways. "Just think of it! He probably white-knuckled it all that way. He's lucky he didn't break down somewhere."

Harvey laughed. "Funny how the next time anyone turned the key, it went only a few miles before it bit the dust. Well, at least Milton had a cell phone on him when he left. No one knew about that, either."

"You just wonder, how much did he use it?" Kate mused as she leaned over the table. "But since it's one of those that's not on a regular plan, it wouldn't have mattered. You'd need the number and have to know the carrier to attempt to get the records. Maybe he didn't even carry it with him, away from home."

Chris shrugged. "He probably didn't. We're all so tied to our screens, but people didn't use to be that way. Wayne, I think you're right. Technology isn't always our friend."

"I agree, to a point," Lena said. "But I don't know if I'd want to go back in time. Sure, life was easier before we all got so high tech, but people weren't open about things the way they are now. There's always been children born out of not-so-perfect situations, but much of the stigma and shame's been removed. I think that's a good thing."

While the kaleidoscope of facts related to this case fascinated Kate, it was the emotional ramifications that meant the most to her now.

"Can you imagine what that would be like, for Camille? All your life, you think things are a certain way. This is your mom, this is your dad. And then, when you're sixty years old, you find out differently."

"And here Milton thought he was so alone." Grandpa Wayne patted his granddaughter on the arm. "I can't imagine how that must have felt, all those years. His sister moved out west right after she married, so he's not close to her kids. His parents passed on. But then, he learns he has this whole family he never knew about. Daughter, grandkids, great-grandkids ... wow."

Eloise came around with the checks for their table. Kate had to get to the post office, but she took a moment to study the lined faces of her grandpa and his friends. These people had lived long, full lives, and hopefully had many more good years to come.

Sometimes, thirty-two seemed old to Kate. But today, she felt like a child by comparison. Certain parts of her life were over, but others were about to begin. The best she could do, that anyone could do, was live life to the fullest, every day.

That's what Milton had always done. He didn't have a high-profile job, or drive a flashy car. Instead, he'd enjoyed fresh tomatoes from his garden, maybe a quiet stroll around his little farm just before sunset. And, every once in a while, a round of beers at a local bar.

A simple life. Some might say it was a boring life. But no matter what, it was still very much worth living.

Max appeared to be thinking the same thing.

"Before we adjourn, I think we should have a toast." He picked up his coffee cup, and the others did the same. "To Milton. I wish I'd known him better. He made it all that way, on his own. And we can take comfort in that his last days will be filled with peace."

Jack was off that day, so Kate and Bertha had his route northeast of town. As they rolled from the end of one farm lane to the next, Kate's mind stayed mostly on Milton.

So many of the puzzle pieces had come together since yesterday afternoon, but there was one outstanding item that still needed closure. What about the attorney's office in Des Moines, the one that sent Milton that letter? Maybe it wasn't a factor in this situation. Or maybe, something would come out about it once Milton passed on.

Tears formed in Kate's eyes, and she blinked them away. Her life had intersected with his for so many weeks. But now, it seemed she'd never get the chance to meet him, to say ... well, what would she say, if she could?

She wasn't even sure. Her heart waffled between hoping Milton didn't linger in discomfort, and wanting him to have as many days with his family as possible.

Either way, she wasn't sorry she'd handed off that letter's information to the sheriff.

"Eyes and ears. That's what we do." She slowed for the next crossroads. The corn was higher now, with harvest only a month or so away, and many of the rural intersections had to be approached with great caution. "We serve the community. We help out when, and where, we can."

Two miles and seven deliveries later, Kate's phone started to sing from its tucked-in spot behind the mail case. She frowned, wondered who it could be. But given the events of the last twenty-four hours, maybe she'd better pick up this call. She reached for it with one hand and guided Bertha to the gravel's shoulder with the other.

The number looked local, but she didn't recognize it. "Hello?"

"Detective Kate Duncan!" a man said with a laugh. The voice was familiar for some reason, yet she couldn't quite place it. "I bet your head is spinning from all the news, huh?"

"Who is this?"

Was that a groan on the other end? "It's Alex."

"OK. I got you now." She hated herself for it, but a little thrill made her sit up straighter in her seat. "Wait. How did you get my number? I don't give it out to too many people."

"You mean, lowlifes like myself? Look, it doesn't matter. I know how you like to be involved in what's going on around here." Kate overlooked the hint of sarcasm. "I have an idea, but I can't execute it myself. You got a minute?"

"I guess so, as I'm on the side of a gravel road in the middle of nowhere. I'm making good time this afternoon, so tell you what: you can have about three before I have to get back to work."

If Kate wanted to do some good, Alex said, how about she set up a care-package box in the post office's lobby? Some of the bar's regulars wanted to send cards to Milton, but this would give other residents a few days to drop off greetings, too. Early next week, Alex promised to stop in and pay the parcel's postage himself. He could start spreading the word around town this afternoon, and call the Swanton newspaper's office and ask the staff to post something to their social media pages and website.

Kate's grin stretched from ear to ear. "I'd love to help. That's a wonderful idea."

"Of course it is. People can show Milton some support and ease their own guilt, all at the same time."

Ouch. But Kate had to admit, his assessment of the situation was spot-on. "Since you called, I have a question of my own."

"Sure."

"Did you know about all this? I mean, where Milton was?"

"Nope."

"Should I believe you?"

"Do you have any reason not to?"

Kate wasn't quite sure how to answer that. "OK, so you're taking the fifth on that one. What about the reward money, then?"

"That's two questions. I don't recall agreeing to those terms." But there was a hint of humor in his voice. "Look, if you're wondering, I don't have that kind of cash, myself. And before you can ask again, I'll just say this: Smart bartenders know to listen far more than they talk. It's the safest way to go."

She wouldn't get any more information out of Alex, that was obvious. And, based on the parameters she'd given him, they had maybe sixty seconds left.

"I'll call Roberta right now and make sure. But if I don't call you back, consider it done. I have errands to run after work, but I should have just enough time to get a box prepped and out on the counter before I leave."

"Where are you going?"

It was Kate's turn to laugh. "I'm not sure that's any of your business."

* * *

The Prosper co-op was busy, as usual. Auggie was at the end of the first aisle, deep in debate with some farmer about soybean futures. Which was in Kate's favor, since the guy wasn't very happy and Auggie looked eager to be rescued.

"Well, hello Kate!" he boomed out as soon as he saw her approach. Just in case the farmer didn't catch the hint, Auggie deliberately turned his back. "What brings you in today?"

"I need cat food." She gave an exaggerated shrug, as they were obviously being watched. "But there's so much to pick from, I'm not sure what I should get. Maybe you can help?"

For a second, Auggie was confused. Charlie was particular, but Auggie already knew that. Kate cut her eyes toward his open office door, and he quickly took the hint.

"I'm sure I can, if you tell me what the situation is." He patted his right-hand jeans pocket. "Oh, must have left my phone in my office again. Never want to be without it. Why don't you tell me what's going on while I hunt it down."

It wasn't a question. Kate followed him through the door, then shut it behind her.

"I always enjoyed being in our high school plays." Auggie reached into his left pocket and smirked as he held up his phone. "Now, tell me why you're really here. But I think I can guess."

Kate dropped into the battered chair on the other side of the desk. "Did you know about Camille? I have to know, it's been driving me crazy."

"You don't have to know. But you want to know." He shrugged. "Honestly, I didn't. Not at first. But when Milton didn't turn up after a few days, I really started to get worried. The sheriff kept calling, asking again and again about any and every possible family connection. Anyone Milton might have talked to, gone to visit."

He peeked past Kate's shoulder and made sure the door was firmly closed.

"A long time ago, and I'm talking like forty years back, I overheard two old aunts talking at a family reunion. I wasn't trying to listen," he added. "I just happened to be getting another slice of cake. Teenage boys are always hungry."

Kate nodded solemnly. Of course.

"Anyway, they were whispering about Milton and some girl. A woman, I mean. It had been twenty years at that point, so water under the bridge and all. I didn't hear everything, but enough that it caught my attention."

He shook his head. "And I never again heard a word from anyone. Not once. I'd forgotten about it, until all this came up."

It was a long shot, but Auggie decided he had to try. Decades had passed, and these things weren't as scandalous as they'd been back in the day. There weren't many cousins and in-laws and such to ask, and no one that lived close by, but he started working the phone.

On one hand, he hated to drag up Milton's supposed past. On the other, a man's life might be at stake. It was a risk worth taking.

"As you might guess, the old folks whose minds are still sharp, they clammed up right away," he said. "Shame on the family, and whatever. But that told me there was some truth in there, somewhere. So I kept on, reaching out to people my age and younger. About three weeks ago, I found one person who seemed to know something. It wasn't much. But it was a lead. And that's when I called the sheriff."

Kate nodded. No wonder Jeff had stopped talking to Bev about the case. He'd had more than confidential medical records in his possession. There was also a tip from Auggie that would blow the doors off Milton's personal life.

"I was so close." Auggie pinched together his thumb and index finger.

"One more week of nosing around, and I would've had it. I was given a surname; as it turns out, it was the right one. The mom's married name."

Kate marveled at Auggie's tenacity and discretion. All those weeks, while she and Bev were doing everything they could to help solve the case?

Someone else was doing their own detective work. And had unearthed something very valuable.

And then, for not the first time that day, Kate wiped away a few tears.

"It's so sad that Milton's sick, and he's not going to recover. I'm sure you've heard about the care package, the card drive and such. I'm sure he'll like that. But still, I keep thinking about it, about everything that's happened."

Auggie studied her face for a moment. Then he pulled a box of facial tissues out of a drawer and dropped it on his desk.

"It's the end of the road for Milton, I'm afraid. But Kate, this is closure for you, if you're willing to accept it."

She stared at him.

"What I mean is," Auggie said gently, "not one more day should go by where you feel guilty about that package you left on his porch, or how much mail was piling up in his box. Sure, Milton went missing. But it was his choice. He spent weeks on this, figuring it all out."

Then Auggie smiled. "Milton wanted to make himself disappear, and he succeeded. And not one bit of what happened was your fault."

"You're right." She took a tissue. "He made only one real misstep, and it was that box. Well, and the open window."

Auggie shrugged. "A pair of back-ordered work boots isn't exactly top-of-mind when someone's plotting their escape."

Kate wondered who had passed her phone number to Alex. At first, she'd assumed it was Chris. But now, she wasn't so sure. And if anyone around here had the cash flow to put up a reward, it was likely to be the successful businessman sitting on the other side of this desk.

But given the knowing twinkle in his brown eyes, Kate figured Auggie would never admit to either.

"What about Jasper?" she asked instead. "That was quite the showdown at the festival. Are you still mad at him?"

"I was never mad. Just frustrated. Jasper's too quiet. A man like that, he makes you think he's hiding something, even when he's not. I guess he wasn't holding out on us, after all."

Auggie called Jasper last night to make amends. Both guys apologized for their behavior, and they even made plans to go up to Camille's with their wives on Sunday afternoon to say their goodbyes to Milton.

"You and Jasper, stuck in a car together?" Kate grimaced. "Isn't it a two-hour drive?"

"Oh, we'll behave. There's lots to discuss, for sure."

Then Auggie smiled.

"You know, while we were talking last night, I got an idea. You were so eager to help find Milton. Do you feel like doing one more thing? Because if you do, I think there's something that would put his mind at ease."

* 22 *

Kate pointed right as they approached the next crossroads. “Turn here,” she told Karen. “This is the shortest way.”

They passed the Tindalls’ farm, then traveled the last half mile to Milton’s lane. “I can’t believe it’s the middle of September already,” Karen said as they approached the drive. “The fields and pastures are turning brown, just a little. And every day, when I’m on my rounds, I’m seeing more red and orange in the trees. They’re supposed to be especially pretty this year.”

“I can’t wait.” Kate smiled. “Fall in Chicago is lovely, but it’s nothing like it is out here.”

“Your new place has all those big oaks and maples. Lots of color, but lots of raking, too.” Karen let out a laugh and slapped the steering wheel with one hand. “Kate, you own a farm! I can hardly believe it.”

“I still have to pinch myself sometimes. But like you said, all those leaves; it’ll seem real enough when I have to mulch them all.” Kate’s first big purchase for her little acreage had been a lawn tractor; it was delivered just yesterday. “You know what else I still can’t believe?”

“What?”

“That Milton really was a millionaire. Those crazy stories turned out to be true.”

Milton's family was behind a generic-named trust that owned farmland in several locations near Eagle River and around Hartland County as a whole. The way-back Bennigers may have sold off the cattle herds that first made them wealthy, but they'd rolled the cash into small purchases here and there that, over several decades, added up to quite an impressive estate.

And as the oldest surviving direct descendant, Milton had overseen it all.

At arm's length, however. Business wheeling and dealing wasn't his thing.

Many years ago, Milton's grandpa turned management of the trust over to that attorney's office in Des Moines. Its holdings had grown to the point that Grandpa Benniger didn't think anyone around Eagle River could continue to oversee it properly, and he apparently shared Milton's appreciation for discretion. What better way to ensure the continued privacy of the trust's beneficiaries than to have it managed by a firm more than a hundred miles away?

It was a good thing Auggie and Jasper visited Milton that last Sunday in August, as he passed away the following Saturday. He'd hung on just long enough to meet his latest great-grandchild, and to enjoy the stuffed-full box of cards and letters from Eagle River residents.

Camille reported that while her father was too weak by then to read the messages himself, small smiles had spread across his face as she sat by his bedside and shared the warm wishes contained in each envelope.

After Milton passed away, word began to spread about the details of his estate plan. He'd insisted on being cremated, and his ashes interred in the family's plot at Eagle River's only cemetery.

And the few relations Milton knew of around the country would each receive a nice little stipend. Nothing unusual there.

The real news was that several organizations in the Eagle River area were about to become recipients of Milton's unexpected generosity.

A sizeable chunk of cash had been set aside for Eagle River's school system, and another hefty bonus was dedicated to the public library. The county nature preserve, just a few miles from Milton's farm, received a generous award that would ensure its upkeep for decades to come. Even Eagle River's little historical society would get a financial pat on the back for its efforts to preserve the town's past.

Milton had long ago made sure his community would benefit from his forefathers' frugal ways. But in the weeks before he passed away, he made a few updates to the trust.

Despite insisting they weren't entitled to any of the Bennigers' cash, an allotment was carved out for Camille and her family. And Milton left the home place, five acres with the house and the outbuildings, to Jasper Tindall.

For being a good neighbor, Milton directed in his amendment. *The best anyone could hope to have.*

Milton's farmhouse remained empty, but his yard had visitors on this cool, sunny Sunday afternoon.

"Looks like we're the last ones to get here," Karen said as she pulled her SUV up by the barn, where Jasper's truck was already parked. Auggie was there, too, but Kate wasn't surprised. He was too nosy to stay away and, after all, this had been his idea.

"Everyone's inside." Auggie ambled their way, a grin on his face. "Want to hand me one of those carriers?"

"Thanks." Kate already had the back hatch open, and slid one crate in his direction. "They're going to have a tough transition, but I'm ready for that. We just have to catch them, first."

Kate's machine shed was now fortified and secure, thanks to Karen and Melinda's help. Inside, the three women had built a generous enclosure from scrap lumber, plywood and old window screens that would be the cats' home for at least a few weeks. Until they adjusted to their new place, Kate didn't even want them running loose in the shed. It was sturdy enough, with no escape routes, but there was always the possibility a kitty could slip out when she opened one of the exterior doors.

"Jasper and his daughter brought a mix of tuna and raw hamburger." Auggie wrinkled his nose. "Nasty stuff, but the cats are sniffing that bucket like its filled with caviar."

"When's the place go on the market?" Karen asked as the three of them started for the barn, carriers in hand.

"Maybe not until spring," Auggie said. "It's already fall, and there's all that estate paperwork to be sorted out. I think the cows are going to the sale barn next week, though."

Jasper and his family already owned their home, so they didn't need a place to live. But Milton knew times had been hard for the Tindalls, and his well-maintained acreage would bring top dollar. Camille had promised to fulfill her father's wishes, and she and Jasper were in close contact about the situation with the farm and the cows.

That left only the cats. As it turned out, there were three. And at Auggie's suggestion, and with a few days to think it over, Kate had agreed to take them in.

"I'm so glad you're willing to do this," Jasper told her when she entered the barn. "We've been worried about them. Winter's coming, no one's living here. We could continue to look after them until the sale, but we don't know who will buy the place, if they'd even care about the cats."

He smiled at his teenage daughter, who cradled an oversized orange tabby in her arms. If Kate had to guess, this guy was the tuxedo cat's brother.

"I wish we could take them, but it won't work," Jasper said. "That black cat, he likes to come to our place, but only to tussle with our boys. And it's too close to home; they'd just come back here."

"I'm going to lock them in kitty jail for a few weeks," Kate promised. "That, along with a lot of good food, love and patience, will help them adapt to their new home."

Karen pulled on a pair of thick gloves. "Well, let's get this rodeo started."

All three cats were very tame, as they were accustomed to Milton showering them with affection and offering hearty meals. Karen checked the community cat clinic's records, and Milton had brought the gray cat, a female, in last year to be spayed. She was skeptical of the carrier at first, but the smelly treats inside enticed her to hop in before she'd realized her mistake.

Karen didn't think the two males had been crated before, which actually made them easier to catch. They were too busy sniffing and studying the carriers to realize the nice people visiting their barn had a secret plan in mind.

"This was all meant to be," Karen told Kate as they walked the carriers out to her vehicle. "They chose you. Not Mae, or even Jasper, but you. That day those two jumped in your mail car, they didn't know where they were going. But I believe they knew exactly what they were doing."

Kate had expected the black cat, the farm's guardian, to put up a fight this afternoon. But it had taken only one gentle nudge to get him in the crate, and he'd settled in so quickly that Kate could hardly believe what she was seeing.

Even so, as they rounded the back bumper and his barn disappeared from his view, he let out a plaintive yowl that brought tears to Kate's eyes.

"I know, it's so hard to say goodbye," she whispered to him. "But I have a wonderful farm for you and your friends. You all get to stay together. And once you've settled in, you and your buddy are going to get your surgeries scheduled."

Kate settled him inside the hatch, then put one hand on the metal grate of the carrier's door. The black cat sniffed her palm and looked at her with wide, knowing eyes.

"I don't know about the others yet, but I think I'm going to call you Scout." Word from Camille was that Milton had never given his cats official names. "All those weeks, you kept watch here after Milton left. And you did a good job. But you can let your guard down; you don't have to worry now."

It was a beautiful day. The maple tree by the side porch was about to burst into a blaze of orange. The lawn was still green, but Jasper had already cut back and raked the garden plot. Kate studied Milton's house, which was quiet and dark in the waning afternoon light of autumn, and offered up a promise.

I'll take good care of them, she said in her heart. *I can't take your place, but I'm going to love them. You don't have to worry about that.*

Karen arranged the other two carriers in the back of the SUV, and she and Kate covered all of them with a bedsheet so the cats would feel more secure.

"Well, that's it," Karen said. "Looks like we're ready to go."

Jasper and his daughter had stayed behind in the barn to feed the cows. And also, Kate suspected, so they wouldn't have to watch the cats being driven away. Auggie was still there, leaning against the side of his truck, taking in the beauty of the farm in fall. And then, Kate saw him wipe his face with one hand. Was he crying?

She walked over and slouched next to him, unsure of what else to do.

"There's not many of us left," he finally said. "Not around here, anyway. Things certainly aren't the way they used to be, everyone's scattered to the four winds. We haven't had a reunion for several years now. "

"Well, maybe it's time to start them up again." Then Kate laughed. "You know, take some of that cash Milton left you, and throw the biggest Benniger party the world has ever seen." She gave him a look. "Did you know about that?"

"About what?" He played dumb, but didn't try very hard.

"The trust. The money."

"Hmm." He crossed his arms against the breeze. Even with a warm jacket, it was a bit brisk up on this hill.

"Let's say that, when it comes to what goes on in this part of the county, it's safe to assume I know just about everyone, and everything. Even so, family always comes first."

"I agree." Kate straightened up, as Karen was waving her on. It was time to go.

"Come by the co-op when you get a chance." Auggie pulled out his keys. "I carry a good-quality cat food that comes in large bags. It's on the house, and always will be. It's the least I can do."

Kate was touched. "Oh, thank you! I'll get over there soon, maybe tomorrow."

As they started down the lane, Karen kept the radio at a low volume to ease the cats' jangled nerves. Kate refused to look back, but she blinked away more tears when they reached the road.

Because there was Milton's mailbox, a bit rusty with a tiny dent in the door. The adhesive letters on the east side had long ago been bleached by the sun and dulled by the wind, but "Benniger" was still visible if you bothered to look close enough. Camille had arranged for Milton's mail to be forwarded to her, and Mae knew to not leave advertising circulars in the box.

There was an official form for that, too, a "vacant" card that could be taped inside to remind carriers a mailbox wasn't currently in service.

But for a shop as small as the Eagle River post office, it wasn't needed. And after all that had happened in the past two months, how could any of them forget?

Kate certainly couldn't. Not anytime soon, and not ever.

And someday, when spring was in full bloom over the countryside and about to give way to another summer, another family would arrive. The mailbox would be cleaned up, the name on the side would change. Or maybe a shiny-new box would appear on the side of this road.

Nothing stayed the same forever. Kate's life had definitely taken off in directions she never could have anticipated.

The ladies rode in comfortable silence until they reached the first corner. Karen took a left, then gave her friend a knowing smile.

"You know, the guy in charge of the canine training facility called Josh yesterday. Everyone there loves Hazel, but they're starting to think she's not cut out for community service. She's super-smart, to the point she seems to get bored when they revisit the same commands over and over."

"Oh, that's too bad." Kate frowned. "She's such a sweet dog."

"So, there's maybe going to be a change in plans," Karen said casually as she stared straight ahead. "They won't send her back to the shelter. The program coordinator is asking around, he'll find a good home for her. There's no rush, of course, it has to be the right fit."

Kate gave her friend the side-eye. "And what did you say?" she asked slowly. "Let me guess: You might know someone?"

Karen shrugged. "Maybe."

Kate rolled her eyes, but she was smiling. "Oh, boy," she sighed. "So much for Charlie being an only child. Three more cats, already. And I have been thinking about getting a dog." She sat up straighter and turned toward Karen. "You don't have any orphan chickens squirreled away somewhere, I hope? Or some stray goats?"

"Really?" Karen was excited. "I could ask around."

"Uh, no. One thing at a time, OK?"

"One thing at a time."

The trip wasn't a long one, maybe fifteen minutes or so. Since they'd already turned the first corner, it was just two more miles down to the county blacktop. Then three miles to the outskirts of Eagle River, and eight blocks to the intersection with Main Street.

When the stoplight went from red to green, Karen stepped on the gas and they rolled through the east end of town. At the first crossroads, she turned south. Up the little hill, then down again. And there, on the left, one last turn.

As they started up the driveway, Kate powered down her window and leaned into the still-warm sunshine, welcomed the cool breeze that brushed her face.

She'd moved just yesterday, and the farmhouse was still a maze of unopened boxes, but that didn't matter. She was home. And the cats were, too.

Milton's story may have come to an end, but the next chapter in Kate's life was just getting started. And she couldn't wait to turn the page.

Read on for an exclusive excerpt from the second book in this series!

What's Next

More to come: Kate's adventures back in Eagle River are just getting started! Read on for an exclusive excerpt from "The Path to Golden Days," Book 2 in this series. Kate's settling into her farmhouse, and looking forward to all the fall fun that's headed her way. But when a neighbor's barn is destroyed by fire, she begins to wonder which of her hometown's residents can, and can't, be trusted. Look for this title in January or February 2023.

Get on the list: If you haven't already, sign up under the "connect" tab at fremontcreekpress.com to find out when future titles will be released. Because ...

Home for the holidays: Book 3, "The Lane That Leads to Christmas," will be full of seasonal spirit! I don't have all the details worked out yet, but it's safe to say the Eagle River community is upended when an heirloom Nativity display goes missing from a local church. Can Kate help track down the sentimental set before the holiday bells ring? This festive book will be out sometime in fall 2023.

Want more heartwarming rural fiction? Explore Melinda's return to Hartland County through the "Growing Season" series! And don't miss the hearty, tasty recipes from those books ... they're available on the website.

Thanks for reading!
Melanie

SNEAK PEEK: THE PATH TO GOLDEN DAYS

Early October
Union Township

The iron handle on the machine shed's side door was cold to the touch, and Kate almost wished she'd worn gloves. It was an unseasonably cold evening for early fall, a reminder of all that was to come.

The cats dashed toward the entrance when they heard Kate enter the building. Their tails were held high, and their eyes glowed with excitement and, Kate was proud to see, at least a bit of trust. Milton's kitties had settled in better than she'd expected, and she'd given them free run of the shed just two days ago.

Of course, they were focused on the food bucket in her hand. But Kate hoped that someday soon, the affection she showed them would elicit the same response.

The cats ran ahead to their bowls, and meowed their impatience as she knelt down to dump out the mix of warmed canned food and cooked-chicken scraps. The free dry food from Auggie was enjoyed around the clock, but these evening snacks were the highlight of the cats' day.

"Scout, back up for a second! I'm trying to fill your dish." In a motion that was apparently his favorite way to show disgust, the big black cat gave a quick flick of one front paw. But he finally moved over, and Kate was once again glad she'd agreed to be the cats' new caretaker.

Because being Scout's "owner," Kate had learned early on, wasn't what he had in mind.

After she fed the cats, Kate made sure the machine shed's door was securely latched. It was a damp, raw night, and she shivered as she hurried behind the shed to start her nightly security walk.

This routine might be excessive and unnecessary, and Kate suspected she'd give it up once the weather turned for good. But it was reassuring to check all her outbuildings, walk the fence that separated the yard from the overgrown pasture, and make sure everything was as it should be before she headed in for the evening.

"I can't help it," she muttered as she double-checked the garage's side door. "Living in the country again has been a big adjustment. At least I can see the lights of Eagle River from the front of the house. If this place was even one more mile out, I don't know if I'd feel safe here yet."

Charlie had taken to the farmhouse faster than she'd expected, so much so that he barely looked up from his plush bed when she came into the living room. The fireplace was his favorite feature of his new home, even more than that window seat upstairs. He loved the hearth so much, in fact, that he wanted to be next to it even when it wasn't in use.

"After dinner," Kate promised Charlie as she patted him on the head. "Let's eat, then I'll get us a cozy fire going. That's going to feel really good tonight."

While the television murmured in the corner and Charlie dozed before the dancing flames in the fireplace, Kate settled in with a book. It wasn't long before she thought she heard something outside.

"What was that? It sounded like a siren."

Charlie only yawned and stretched out his front paws in bliss, but Kate hurried to the picture window and parted the old pinch-pleated draperies. They were ugly, of course, but came in handy as the temperatures dropped at sundown.

Kate heard it again, and her jaw dropped when flashing emergency lights flew past the end of her lane. It was too hard to make out the vehicle in the gloom, but the lights' height made Kate suspect a fire truck.

She'd had little time to meet her new neighbors, but that didn't matter. The thought of anyone's home engulfed in flames was a terrifying one. And the moan of the wind as it slipped around the corners of her farmhouse added to her worries. Where exactly was the fire?

Kate didn't even reach for a coat, just unlocked the front door and hurried out to the open porch. The cold air nipped at her hands and her face, and she wrapped her arms around herself as she ran down the steps.

She didn't smell smoke. Or see flames anywhere near her farm. That helped her breathe a little easier.

Back inside, she rubbed her hands together and locked the door. "I don't know what to do," she told Charlie. "There's nothing to call in, since I can't see anything. And the fire department's already responded, so they know about, well, whatever is going on."

Seconds later, her phone rang.

"Kate!" Auggie shouted. "I heard everything on the scanner. What's going on out there?"

Kate had no idea, so Auggie told her what he knew.

About two miles south of her acreage, a barn had caught fire. From what Auggie picked up on the regional emergency departments' dispatch channel, the flames had a good start before the incident was called in. Now, he said, it sounded like the structure was likely to be a total loss. Their main objective going forward was to keep the flames from spreading into the nearby fields.

"You should head down there." Auggie was insistent.

Kate shook her head. "Seriously? Shouldn't I stay out of the way?"

"You can do both." Auggie rattled off the address. "Don't you want to know what the deal is?"

Kate hated to admit it, but she did. It wouldn't be right to stay long, she didn't want to be in the way. But if she could just verify what Auggie told her, see for herself that the authorities had everything under control, she'd be able to come home, pick up her novel, and carry on with her evening with more peace of mind.

"Charlie, I'm so sorry." Kate doused the fire, and made sure it was out. One out-of-control blaze in the neighborhood was certainly enough. "I'll be back in a little bit."

She grabbed her purse and a coat, then a stocking hat and gloves. The darkness pressed in around her as she hurried out to the garage and started down the lane.

Kate gripped the steering wheel tight as she carefully made her way south on the gravel road, and hoped her headlights' beams would show her any roaming deer before they could jump in front of her car.

One crossroads, then another. And soon, Kate saw a wall of flames soaring into the night sky.

She slowed the car to a crawl, and sought out the next field drive. She'd pull in, study the scene for a few minutes, and head home. Because given the cluster of vehicles, both emergency and otherwise, that she spotted down the road, she wouldn't get any closer to the fire.

Kate cut the engine, reached for the flashlight kept under the seat, and opened her door. The blaze was both terrifying and awe-inspiring and, even from a quarter-mile away, she could smell the smoke.

She'd been leaning against her car for only a few minutes when she spotted another flashlight bobbing toward her in the gloom. Kate cringed. Exchanging greetings while someone else's barn turned to toast wasn't exactly the best way to introduce yourself to your new neighbors. But as the man came closer, Kate realized he looked familiar.

"Deputy Collins!" she gasped. "How are you? I mean, I'm sorry, I shouldn't be out here." She reached for her keys. "I'll head home now, I just had to see ..."

"You and half of the neighborhood." But even in the dark, Kate sensed his wry smile. "We expected it, actually."

Then he looked over his shoulder. "It's an impressive fire, to be honest. We don't see many of these around here, thank goodness."

"Fire's always a danger on a farm." Kate thought of her dad's constant warnings about sparks from overheated machinery, sheds with outdated electrical outlets, and barns packed with straw and hay. "I know it's early, but do you have any idea what happened?"

"That place is abandoned, has been for a long time." Deputy Collins sounded weary and worried. Especially for so early in a night that was certain to be a long one. "The house was torn down years ago. No one's living there."

"Well, that's good, I guess." Kate zipped her coat higher against the chill. "So no one was hurt, and no animals were caught in the fire."

"Yes, and we're glad for that." Then he sighed. "But that's sort of the problem, too. No one should have been on the property. There's not even a yard light, anymore. And no electrical service coming up from the road."

Kate shivered in the rising wind. "You don't mean ..."

"I wish I didn't. It'll be daybreak before we can start an investigation. But if I had to guess? It has to be arson."

Look for "The Path to Golden Days" in early 2023.
The book will be available in Kindle, paperback,
hardcover and large-print paperback editions.

ABOUT THE BOOKS

Don't miss any of the titles in these heartwarming rural fiction series

THE GROWING SEASON SERIES

Melinda is at a crossroads when the "for rent" sign beckons her down a dusty gravel lane. Facing forty, single and downsized from her stellar career at a big-city ad agency, she's struggling to start over when a phone call brings her home to Iowa.

She moves to the country, takes on a rundown farm and its headstrong animals, and lands behind the counter of her family's hardware store in the community of Prosper, whose motto is "The Great Little Town That Didn't." And just like the sprawling garden she tends under the summer sun, Melinda begins to thrive. But when storm clouds arrive on her horizon, can she hold on to the new life she's worked so hard to create?

Filled with memorable characters, from a big-hearted farm dog to the weather-obsessed owner of the local co-op, "Growing Season" celebrates the twists and turns of small-town life. Discover the heartwarming series that's filled with new friends, fresh starts and second chances.

FOR DETAILS ON ALL THE TITLES VISIT FREMONTCREEKPRESS.COM

THE MAILBOX MYSTERIES SERIES

It's been a rough year for Kate Duncan, both on and off the job. Being a mail carrier puts her in close proximity to her customers, with consequences that can't always be foreseen. So when a position opens at her hometown post office, she decides to leave Chicago in her rearview mirror.

Kate and her cat settle into a charming apartment above Eagle River's historic Main Street, but she dreams of a different home to call her own. And as she drives the back roads around Eagle River, Kate begins to take a personal interest in the people on her route.

So when an elderly resident goes missing, she feels compelled to help track him down. It's a quest marked not by miles of gravel, but matters of the heart: friendship, family, and the small connections that add up to a well-lived life.

A TIN TRAIN CHRISTMAS

The toy train was everything two boys could want: colorful, shiny, and the perfect vehicle for their imaginations. But was it meant to be theirs? Revisit Horace's childhood for this special holiday short story inspired by the "Growing Season" series!